When Cloughie Managed England

Rick Crowe

Norm Wilson Publishing

Published in 2012

Copyright © Rick Crowe 2012

rick.crowe@ymail.com

Dover, New Hampshire

Printed in USA

ISBN-13: 978-1475172645

ISBN-10:1475172648

This book is sold subject to the condition that it shall not, by way of trade or otherwise, be lent, re-sold, hired out or otherwise circulated without the publisher's prior consent in any form of binding or cover other than that in which it is published and without a similar condition including this condition being imposed upon the subsequent publisher.

Acknowledgements

When Cloughie Managed England is a football fan's account of what might have been. Therefore, although it is based on facts, a lot of it is fiction!

Rick Crowe has been an ardent Nottingham Forest fan since 1963. He also had the privilege of playing for the Derby County Youth Team in 1968 when Brian Clough and Peter Taylor were in charge at the Baseball Ground. He has always been a great admirer of Brian Clough and Peter Taylor.

The author hopes that no offence will be taken where none was intended.

For

Dave Crowe

When Cloughie Managed England

Early August, 1977. England.

Peter Taylor walked into Brian Clough's office at Nottingham Forest Football Club. He was reading ***The Sporting Life*** and didn't notice that Clough was sitting, hunched over, with his head in his hands. Clough knew it was Taylor who came in because Taylor was the only one who was allowed to come into Clough's office unannounced.
"It's terrible. Terrible. What is the world coming to?" said Clough without looking up.
Taylor stopped reading. "What, you mean that Admiral who's taken over the CIA, and everybody's either resigning or being sacked? It's like a Pentagon revolt. They've given one man too much power, if you ask me. That never works."
"No."
"Then it must be that chap in Jimmy Carter's government who won't sell his shares in the National Bank of Georgia because he'll lose a million dollars. That's wrong because he was in charge of the bank himself, so he must have known he was buying shares on the cheap to begin with."
"No, for Christ's sake."
"Then it's that abortion thing."
Clough raised up. "What abortion thing?"
"Some women who were in the White House sauna were apparently shocked when Carter said he wouldn't allow federal government money to be used for abortions. Think about it. He must have been in the sauna with them."
"It's not about a sauna or a fucking abortion. I'm talking about football. This last month has been a nightmare."

"What do you mean? Our pre-season was spectacular."
"What? We pissed on Neuburg, a team called Wacker Innsbruck and Skegness Town."
"That was the idea. Score plenty of goals. Gives the lads confidence."
"Fuck that. The whole football world is going crazy."
"You mean Docherty getting the sack for having an affair with the physio's wife?"
"No, but he should have kept his flies done up all the same."
"Revie then, lining up the Arabs. And lining his pockets too before leaving England in the shit."
"No. I don't blame him for that. We're safe here because I dropped a bollock at Leeds."
Taylor took a few more moments to ponder the question. "It can't be Man City paying three hundred grand for Mick Channon. He's a good lad. Knows his horses. Wouldn't have paid that money though. Southampton did well there. Now, that Scots lad, Dalglish to Liverpool. Worth every penny."
"For Christ's sake," screamed Clough. "Don't you keep up with events? Derby's done a sponsorship deal with Saab. All the players are getting a Saab each."
"I've looked at a Saab. They're all right.'
"They're Swedish!"
"Nowt wrong with Swedes. Britt Ekland's a Swede. Fancy being Swedish but having the name Britt. And think about it. Ekland is very nearly England."
"They make Rolls-Royces in Derby for Christ's sake. If I'd have thought of that, I'd have had at least McGovern swanning round in a Roller. And you and me, of course."
Clough paused and eyed Taylor with curiosity. "I didn't know you knew so much about American politics."

"I don't. I was talking to this bloke at the racecourse yesterday. Over from Kentucky. Got some good tips off him. Three hundred notes in my pocket, that's how good." Taylor drew long and hard on a cigarette. "He knew fuck all about football though. We got Birmingham's centre forward to come and play centre half alongside Larry Lloyd. Nobody else would have thought of that. Kenny Burns, great defender. Now that's football."

***

Nottingham Forest Football Club, historically a mediocre provincial club at best, was riding high. The team had been elevated to the First Division by virtue of clinching the third promotion place at the end of the 1976-77 season. With Brian Clough in charge, anything could happen. And it usually did. What Clough was about to do, with the considerable help of his assistant and mentor, Peter Taylor, was to take a group of ragbags and might-have-beens and turn them into an unbeatable unit.

The genius of Clough and Taylor rested in their choice of players and their ability to motivate those players. They constructed a Forest team by very simple methods - in fact, in exactly the same way as they had done with Derby County, a team that went on to win the First Division title a few years before. Their secret lay in man management. Each player was told, and if necessary taught, his job on the field of play. Each player knew what to do with the ball wherever it was on the pitch. Discipline was essential. Do what you were told to do, without question, and everything would be fine.

***

John McGovern, the captain of the promoted team, knocked on the open office door of Peter Taylor. He had thought things through carefully and, at breakfast that morning, his wife had agreed with him.

Players had to go through Taylor first to get to Clough, unless of course it was a fine for some paltry breach of discipline. In those instances it was straight into Clough's office. The letter containing the amount of the fine and the reason for the fine was placed on Clough's desk in front of him. Clough never spoke during these ceremonies and the letter on the desk was often the first indication to a player that he had committed an indiscretion.

However, McGovern had instigated this meeting so, surely, there could be no fine.

McGovern suggested to Taylor that, because he had captained the team to promotion, he felt he was entitled to a wage increase. Taylor pushed his tongue into the side of his cheek, like he often did when he was about to thoughtfully answer a journalist's probing question. But he said nothing.

After a moment, Taylor rose and accompanied McGovern into Clough's office, next door down the corridor.

McGovern sat down on a single chair facing Clough's large desk on which a squash racquet trapped a squash ball. Clough stared at McGovern all the time as Taylor carried a chair alongside Clough's, so that McGovern would have to turn his head from side to side to see each of them individually, in case either of them happened to say something. He felt like he was about to watch an imaginary tennis match.

"Who told you to sit down?" barked Clough.

McGovern sprang from his chair, both feet leaving the carpet. When McGovern had landed, Clough snarled, "What do you want?" in an even more pronounced nasal whine than usual, a whine that spewed contempt into the atmosphere.

"I just thought," started McGovern, "that as I've just captained the team into the First Division, you might just think that I deserve just a wee bit of a pay rise."

"You've just used the word 'just' four times," snapped Clough.
"How many games did you play last season?" asked Taylor. McGovern's head swivelled to the left.
"Thirty eight out of forty two."
"So you're not even a regular in the team."
"That's right," exclaimed Clough triumphantly as McGovern's head oscillated right. "Now, clear off. And just for that you'll get a fine, young man."
McGovern left the room quickly, pleased that he had got off lightly, and made a mental note never to allow such an absurd thought enter his head ever again. Wage rise! What was his wife thinking of?

Brian Howard Clough was charismatic, brilliant, outspoken, eccentric, arrogant, ferocious, controversial, big-headed, idiosyncratic, confident, always right, and generous at times. But rarely to his players.
Peter Thomas Taylor was quiet, thoughtful, confident, clever, funny, always right, and often underestimated. But not by his players.

Clough sidled up to Peter Taylor as the Nottingham Forest first team squad played a practice game on a pitch alongside the River Trent. The tempo of the game increased, as usual, when the players became aware of Clough's presence. Clough fired off a few rounds of abuse at the players before addressing, to his long time friend, the state of play of life in the United Kingdom at the time. "Isn't it great that The Queen is visiting Northern Ireland as part of her Jubilee celebrations?"
"You don't like the Irish."
"Yes I do. Whatever makes you say that?"
"You don't like Martin O'Neill. He's Irish."

"It's not that he's Irish. He's too clever for his own good."
"You mean he's too clever for you."
"Bollocks. Anyway, I'm getting excited."
"You mean you think we'll do well this season."
"Not a chance. No, I mean my mate Geoffrey Boycott's on for his hundredth hundred for England up at Headingley. Wish I could be there. Cricket. Now there's a proper game."
Taylor puffed on a cigar.
"Bloody rubbish. You are a bloody disgrace," Clough shouted at no one in particular.
Clough's prognosis for the season ahead was based on the talent kicking a football about on the pitch in front of him. Forest had squeaked into the First Division on the last day of the season and largely by dint of other teams' failings as much as their own efforts. The squad mainly comprised those who seemed past it and those who had never got there and never would.

However, the opening day of the season saw Forest at Goodison Park to take on an Everton team that was highly fancied to win the league. Forest won comfortably, three goals to one, with critics pointing out that the Merseysiders were without free scoring centre forward Bob Latchford.
Clough and Taylor insisted that it didn't matter how many crosses the immensely skilful Everton left winger, Dave Thomas, making his debut, put into the box. Burns and Lloyd would have dealt with them even if there had been three Bob Latchfords.
What was of more concern to the management was that Thomas had given Forest right back, Viv Anderson, a royal blue roasting.
Taylor put his arm round Anderson after the game and pointed out that Thomas was bound to be excited, and galvanised by his first performance in front of his home crowd, and that it was no wonder that he had played exceptionally well. Clough

gave Anderson a massive bollocking in front of the rest of the team.

On Forest's left wing, John Robertson had torn the Everton right back, Dave Jones, to shreds, and had a hand in all three Forest goals, including scoring one himself.

Clough praised the left winger for causing havoc, and heaped even more praise on captain John McGovern and fellow midfielder Ian Bowyer for having the wit to get the ball to the mesmerising left winger in the first place.

Taylor bollocked Robertson for being overweight. Nobody mentioned the goalscorers.

The blueprint for the season ahead had been established. Hard work, unyielding central defence and get the ball to Robertson. However, on the coach home from Liverpool, Clough turned to Taylor and said that he thought the team had a chance that season. "Not without a better goalkeeper," responded Taylor, himself a more than adequate exponent of that art in his playing days.

"There's nowt wrong with Middleton," was Clough's robust reply about Forest's incumbent keeper.

"You look after the attack and I'll deal with the defence," said Taylor. "I'll get Shilton from Stoke. He's the best and I'll get him for a song."

"You're right," said Clough, "and maybe we can strengthen midfield."

So, it was clear to the management, even after the first game, changes needed to be made.

The next game, at the City Ground in Nottingham, was a 1-0 win against Bristol City that left Forest on top of the league and preceded a derby against Derby at home. It turned out to be a thumping three nil win against their bitter rivals. Clough described it as a breathless, end to end affair, and Taylor commented, "Aren't affairs supposed to be like that?"

The win, and the two points, cemented Forest's position at the top of the table. But that was of no consequence to Clough when he realised that a few of the Derby players had travelled the fifteen miles from Derby to Nottingham in their new Saabs.

A few days later, Forest entertained West Ham at the City Ground in Round Two of the League Cup. The Londoners were thrashed 5-0 with two goals from stalwart Ian Bowyer, and one each from Martin O'Neill, Peter Withe and Tony Woodcock.

Afterwards Clough said that he thought it was an adequate display against a poor side and that he had 'a funny feeling' about the League Cup competition.

Forest travelled to London for the next game to be confronted by an Arsenal side that boasted two out-and-out centre forwards in Malcolm Macdonald and Frank Stapleton. Forest lost 3-0 and prompted the following observation from Clough. "Burns, you and Lloyd are the ugliest bastards on this planet. I pay you to frighten the death out of their forwards. You should be doing that in the tunnel before the game. Today you played like a pair of girls."

Burns had been spotted by the television cameras nutting an Arsenal player, Richie Powling, on the back of the head as they lined up to take a free kick just outside the Forest penalty area.

"You didn't need to give away that free kick in the first place," ranted Clough. "Then you gave away a penalty by decking Stapleton. What a pair of wankers. I wish I'd played against you two. I'd have scored half a dozen every game."

Lloyd protested, "Excuse me. I didn't do anything wrong."

"You play as a pair,' screamed Clough. "You are equally to blame."

"He's got a point," said Taylor.

So, having plummeted to fourth spot in the league because of that catastrophe, Peter Shilton joined from Stoke City. There was only one other player that would prevent a spiralling into the relegation zone predicted by the newspaper columnists. A human dynamo was needed to complement the already tireless McGovern and Bowyer, and the clever person on the right wing of Irish descent, Martin O'Neill.

The fact that the incoming recruit was a virtual midget was of no consequence to Clough and Taylor because they knew him well - he had helped them win the First Division with Derby a few years before. It was Archie Gemmill.

Football was really simple, according to the Clough and Taylor philosophy: get the ball and give it to the wingers.

The idea was that if the wingers had half a brain between them, they would get the ball into the box where there would be a couple of forwards, who might have half a brain between them. One of them, with luck, would stick the ball into the back of the net.

Clough would rationally point out, on more than one occasion, that 'two heads are better than one', though most people thought he was talking about himself and Taylor.

The press highlighted the battering the Forest team had taken at Highbury by a good Arsenal side, but what they had overlooked was that Forest had had several chances themselves to score. Tony Woodcock, in particular, felt the rough edge of Clough's tongue. "Woodcock, you're crap," was the least rough description Clough bestowed on him.

But the defeat proved to be a blip. After seven games, Forest had amassed twelve points out of a possible fourteen and sat in second place behind current League and European Champions, Liverpool. It was a position that wouldn't last long.

Clough and Taylor had decided that there was no point in being in second place and it only took a couple of weeks before they reached the top again.

It didn't stop the doubters though. Clough even had to explain to John Motson in a post match interview on BBC television that, "We play with discipline, we don't play with any problems with referees, we try to entertain, and you never know, John, you and your profession just might recognise that we are a good side."

In every pub around England, opposing football supporters waited for Forest's bubble to burst. Of course, pub goers in Nottingham didn't waste any of their time on that nonsense.

Forest's team bus, driven by Albert, turned into the players' and officials' car park at West Ham's Boleyn Ground. Brian Clough stood up and faced his players.
" West Ham. Known for their quality football. They have a tradition, and quite right too, that the ball is played on the floor. You, Burns and Lloyd, it's a pity that Bobby Moore isn't playing. He was the best defender I have ever seen. You could have learnt something from him. Best defender in the history of the game. He was their captain, a leader, the heart and soul of the team. A cool, calculating footballer. You could trust him with your life."
Peter Taylor stood up and joined in as Albert eased the bus into the space reserved for the visiting team's coach.
"Jock Stein, who knew a bit about football, said, 'There should be a law against Bobby Moore. He knows what's happening 20 minutes before everyone else.'"
Martin O'Neill piped up, "I saw him on ***This is Your Life*** several years ago when he was still playing for West Ham."
"Well, there you go," continued Clough. "You don't normally get that accolade while you're still playing. The supreme professional."

"Yes, but quite coincidentally a couple of day s later, he and some of his team mates were sent home after they were caught drinking in a night club in Blackpool in the early hours before a cup tie. They lost four nil."

"By the way," snapped Clough, "you're not playing today." Clough and Taylor sat down. After several minutes, Clough suggested to Taylor. "Can't we tell the police we suspect he's the Yorkshire Ripper?"

"I don't think we'll have to," countered Taylor. "We'll just kill him and leave him outside a mortuary. There's an undertakers' strike on down here and there's about 800 corpses lying around unburied. They won't spot an extra one."

"Who'll play on the right wing?"

"He's the best we've got."

"Bastard." Clough stood up again. "O'Neill. You've got to thank Mr. Taylor for getting you back in the team. He has just put forward a very persuasive argument for your inclusion today. Go on, stand up and thank him."

O'Neill stood up. "Thank you Mr. Taylor," he said, and sat down.

The game ended 0-0 and the return journey to Nottingham saw O'Neill take the brunt of Clough's tongue for the first half hour until Albert lit up a cigarette. This, effectively, forced Clough to take the seat behind the driver so that he could share the benefit of Albert's nicotine habit. O'Neill was relieved that the verbal abuse had subsided and pointed out to goalkeeper Peter Shilton that he was glad he'd not let any goals in that afternoon. If he had have done, O"Neill surmised, he would have been blamed for them too.

Not much happened for the next couple of weeks, apart from Forest winning in the league, but they had been drawn at home to their rivals from across the River Trent, Notts County, in the next round of the League Cup. Clough spoke to his players in the changing room before the game.

"Some old bloke told me County haven't lost here for 20-odd years. You'd better knock that on the head tonight. It's a good job you're cup-tied Shilton because I was going to drop you anyway. Woods, you're playing."

A few of the players looked surprised and some of them didn't even recognise the new recruit from the youth team.

"This young lad will be better than you one day," Taylor said to Shilton. "So you'd better watch out."

Goalkeeper Chris Woods, who was a 17-year-old England youth international, made his debut for Forest in place of their new signing Peter Shilton and he kept a clean sheet in a 4-0 home win. Bowyer, with two, Woodcock and Robertson were the goalscorers.

***

The 1970s were a terrible time for English football, not least because of violent, indiscriminate hooliganism, but most of all due to woeful performances by the national side. Even so, surely England, the country that gave the game to the world, should still have been a major influence. It was not. In fact, it was a laughing stock.

Unfortunately, one of the most powerful malignancies affecting the English game skulked within the Football Association itself, in the person of Professor Sir Harold Thompson. He was an Oxford chemistry don. He was a bullying autocrat. 'He was a bastard. He treated the staff like shit,' one former FA official had said.

As a senior member of the Football Association, Thompson was the instigator behind the sacking of Sir Alf Ramsey in 1974. England's failure to qualify for the World Cup that year might have justified Ramsey's dismissal but the whole episode was handled with brutal insensitivity. Despite having won the World Cup for England in 1966, Ramsey was kicked out after eleven years of unstinting, patriotic service and, in terms of winning the World Cup, unprecedented success. His salary at the time was less than some Division Three managers were earning. He was given a pitiful payout and a meagre pension. Don Revie, Alf's successor, was paid a salary nearly four times as much.

The Football Association's disgraceful behaviour was largely down to Thompson, who had developed an intense animosity towards Ramsey, a lot of it due to nothing more than snobbery. Thompson was obsessed with public school and university backgrounds. Ramsey had neither.

At the England team's hotel, one morning on a trip to eastern Europe in 1972, Thompson was smoking a large cigar at breakfast. Alf approached him on the behalf of the players who found the smoke unpleasant.

"Ah, Ramsey, what do you want?" asked Sir Harold upon Alf's intrusion. He always called him by his surname as, indeed, he did most people.

Ramsey said in his best, clipped Dagenham accent, "I believe it would be in the best interests of the players if you put out that cigar or at least went somewhere else to smoke it."

Thompson nearly choked at Ramsey's effrontery. Stubbing out the cigar in the ashtray was the symbolic stubbing out of Ramsey's England career. From that moment on, Thompson waged a campaign within the Football Association to have the World Cup winning manager sacked. Failure to qualify for the 1974 World Cup was the final nail that Thompson hammered into Ramsey's coffin.

In July of 1974, following Alf's dismissal, Revie accepted the England Manager's job. He had won two First Division Championships with Leeds United and was widely regarded as one of the most successful managers in the country. The

Football Association hierarchy was impressed with Revie's personality and ideas.

However, Revie's personality was basically cemented in an abruptness that proved ill-suited to international team management.

His ideas, particularly in terms of how to qualify for tournament football, were conspicuously absent. Under Revie's watchful eye, England failed to qualify for the 1976 European Championships and had messed up qualification for 1978 World Cup Finals.

His personality and ideas made him one of the least successful managers of the England national team.

In 1977, Revie did actually do what no other England manager had done before. He resigned.

While still under contract to the English FA, he accepted a lucrative offer to become coach to the United Arab Emirates. And Revie sold the news of his departure to the ***Daily Mail*** where the story broke before the FA had actually received his letter of resignation.

The FA, now under the chairmanship of the malevolent Sir Harold Thompson, and against the advice of the FA's lawyers, suspended Revie from football for ten years on a charge of bringing the game into disrepute.

Thompson had arrogantly dismissed the Right To Work Act. Revie contested his suspension in a lawsuit against the FA, and the court, obliged by legal precedent, overturned the suspension.

The challenge in the court had been one of Revie's better ideas, and a poke in the eye for Thompson. However, Revie was refused damages after Justice Cantley described him as 'a very prickly man' who had committed a 'glaring and flagrant breach of contract.'

After Revie's departure in the summer, Sir Harold Thompson had appointed his old friend, Ron Greenwood, the General Manager at West Ham United, as the caretaker manager of the England national team.

***

Now, it was the night of November 16, 1977. England had just beaten Italy 2-0 at Wembley.

England football fans streamed hurriedly out of the giant stadium. A boy, about ten years old, pulled his England scarf around his neck to keep out the increasingly cold night air. The lad turned to his father and asked a question that only his father could answer. "But, Dad, if Luxembourg draw against Italy, England will qualify for the World Cup Finals, won't they," he said.

His father answered the question as best as he could. "Son, we're out," he said. "There's more chance of me walking to the moon."

A hundred and thirty miles to the north, in the village of Quarndon, Derbyshire, Brian Clough and Peter Taylor had watched the game on the television in the lounge of Clough's palatial home. His mother's mangle sat alongside the television, a reminder, as he liked to tell people, of his humble beginnings.

It might also be unintentionally significant that Clough had moved his family to Quarndon from the neighbouring Allestree, itself a pleasant suburb of Derby, the city where Clough and Taylor had had so much success a few years earlier.

What Quarndon had that Allestree hadn't was, in Daniel Defoe's words, 'a famous chalybeate spring, to which an abundance of people go in the season to drink the water and have a cold bath'.

'Famous', 'Spring', 'abundance of people' (crowd), 'season', 'drink' and 'bath'. These were all football terms to Clough so there seemed to be a magnetic attraction to the village. Maybe Clough heard about this watery allure and thought he might, somehow, be able to incorporate it into his management techniques. After all, he had had bizarre ideas before.

Maybe, too, he had read Defoe's ***Robinson Crusoe,*** credited with being the first novel not dependent on historical figures or legends.

Clough obviously knew that Defoe was presenting an artistic philosophy that emphasises instructional and informative qualities in literature and other art forms.

Yet the intention of didactic art is to present a profound lesson, not merely to entertain. Indeed, exactly how Clough and Taylor marshalled their teams: taught to play the game how it should be played, on the ground, but entertainingly too.

It was the original, inspiring, inventive, revolutionary Clough, just like Defoe. Clough, shipwrecked at Leeds United, was Robinson Crusoe, and Taylor, his trusted sidekick, was Man Friday.

The two football men, returned to the screen.

Robinson Crusoe spoke first. "Load of bollocks. They're a bloody disgrace. What you got was a two nil win against a team that wasn't bothered."

Man Friday followed with, "Shush, here comes Greenwood." The game against Italy had not long been over when the caretaker England team manager entered the Press Briefing Room for the after match conference.

Greenwood spoke eloquently about his team's performance. "It's always very satisfying when you take a gamble in choosing a side and the players respond. The gamble paid off because everyone went forward as I had urged them to do. The players said that it was nice to be cheered off the Wembley pitch. We set out to restore pride and respect in our football and we got the verdict from the crowd at the end."

"Gamble, my arse," said Crusoe.

"We played with a lot of emotion and freedom for the first time in a long while. I am proud of English football and proud we showed millions of people up and down the country we are not down and out as people think we are."

"You're right," said Man Friday. "It is bollocks."

"We were able to pull apart Italy's man for man marking system and create space. We found this difficult against Luxembourg as their defenders just stood around like lamp posts. I hope they do the same when Italy play them. The qualifying position is out of our hands now."

"We're not going to the World Cup. Just say it," urged Man Friday.

A journalist asked a question. "Luxembourg haven't won a game in this group and have only scored two goals. Do you think they can go to Italy next week and come away with a draw to take us through?"

"This is the last of my three games as caretaker manager and I'd like to be remembered for having an unbeaten record and no goals scored against my team. We must not get carried away with this result but whoever takes over has young players available who are obviously ready for internationals. We mixed good continental football with the best in English football and this gives us a platform to show we can compete with the rest of the world if we are prepared to go forward and be positive.

"Some of those lads won't get in our team," said Man Friday. Crusoe scoffed. "And you really think the Football Association will give us the job?"

"It's a certainty. Trust me. Certainty. Have I ever let you down?"

"Ron Greenwood's a nice bloke but he's out of the Walter Winterbottom mould. Winterbottom didn't know football. And he didn't know footballers from …. that picture on the wall."

"He only picked you twice for England, didn't he Brian?"

"Fuck off. I had a better scoring rate than Greavsie. And he was the best."

The boy and his father boarded the tube train at Wembley station, the boy having thought about his father's appraisal of the situation. Being a bright young lad, keen on science at school, he had a naturally probing mind. He spluttered another suggestion. "But, Dad, why don't they get Brian Clough?" The father replied, brusquely, not annoyed by his son's questioning nature but by the plight of his national football team, "Mr. Clough to you, son. His name is Mr. Clough."

All this brouhaha, and Forest's brilliant play in the First Division so far that season, led football fans across the length and breadth of England to cry out for Brian Clough to be appointed England Football Manager. There was no other man for the job. He had to be interviewed for the job. The Football Association had no option. There was only one problem – Sir Harold Thompson.

Brian Clough versus Sir Harold Thompson. The bell rang for the first round of the Heavyweight Big Head Championship of England.

Sir Harold Warris Thompson was an English physical chemist. He was educated at King Edward VII school in Sheffield, then at Trinity College, Oxford. He graduated in 1929 and worked with Fritz Haber and Max Planck in Berlin before returning to Oxford in 1930 after receiving a Ph. D from the Friedrich Wilhelm University of Berlin.

His research interests included chemical reactions in gases, photochemistry and spectroscopy.

During the Second World War he worked on infra-red spectroscopy for the Ministry of Aircraft Production, and afterwards continued research in this field.

He was elected a Fellow of the Royal Society in 1946 and knighted in 1968.

When he was invited to deliver a scientific lecture in Moscow he learnt fluent Russian in three months.

In 1971, he was made a chevalier of the Légion d'honneur, the highest decoration in France.

As an Oxford chemistry don, Professor Sir Harold Thompson had taught Margaret Thatcher, the future first female Prime Minister of the United kingdom, when she was a chemistry student.

Brian Clough was a footballer. It was no contest.

Inside a vast lounge at the Football Association headquarters, several newspapers lay haphazardly on a coffee table. The back page headlines screamed 'Cloughie for England', 'It's Clough's', 'Cloughie at last!'.

Several men in suits were sitting round the table. All except one, FA Chairman Sir Harold Thompson, were studying the newspapers.

"Look at them. It'll have to be Clough," said a committee member.

"I can't stand him," said Sir Harold Thompson.

"We'll get lynched if we don't appoint him," said a second committee member.

"He hasn't been interviewed yet," Sir Harold Thompson reminded them. "He's got to get through that without shouting his mouth off."

A third committee member ventured the opinion that Clough might actually do a good job.

A fourth committee member pointed out, "He'll be here in a minute."

Still Sir Harold Thompson complained. "He's too risky. You never know what he might do next. I forbid a vote to go in his favour."

At precisely the same time in Nottingham, several players sat around the Forest changing room, muddy and dishevelled, after a morning training session. Jimmy Gordon, Forest's trainer, complimented several of the players individually as dressing room banter filled the room. Archie Gemmill teased Peter Shilton about nutmegging him twice that morning. Shilton looked annoyed and slapped Gemmill's bald patch playfully. Peter Taylor entered.

"Well done lads," he said, "Good workout. Do you good. Some of you are fat. Robertson."

"I've lost weight," said Robertson.

"Not enough. Lose some more. You might turn into a half decent player."

Martin O'Neill said, "So if he loses weight he becomes a half decent player. Does that mean he's a decent player right now? Isn't it better to be a decent player than a half decent player?" Peter Taylor ignored him.

"He's our best player," said Larry Lloyd.

"How would you know anything about that? And you're fat too," said Taylor.

Kenny Burns laughed, adding, "Heard from the gaffer yet?"

"Don't need to. He'll get it," said Taylor confidently.

"Let's just suppose, for one miraculous moment, that Mr. Clough gets the England job. What will happen to us?" asked Martin O'Neill.

Peter Taylor was incredulous. "What do you mean what will happen to you? You'll carry on playing the way we've shown you. You know what to do now, and how to win. They could put a monkey in charge and you'll be all right. And if they do, ignore the monkey and do what we've taught you anyway."

"Won't you stay?" asked Larry Lloyd.

Peter Taylor continued. "Look, we created a winning team at Derby, we've created a winning team here. What's wrong with us wanting to make England win? Don't worry, plenty of you will be playing for Brian and me again. For England. You Scots and Irish, you'll have to keep this ship afloat. This is a winning team. Make no mistake about that."

"I don't think in a million years the FA will give Mr. Clough the manager's job," suggested Martin O'Neill.

"That's what you know about football," advised Taylor.

O'Neill continued, "Well, I think ..."

Taylor interrupted. "That's your problem. Pack it in. Or think about something you know about."

Clough had arrived at Lancaster Gate, the headquarters of the English Football Association wearing a tan, double-breasted leather coat and briefly spoke to expectant reporters on the steps outside.
"It's a bit cold isn't it?" he said.
A reporter, with a reputation for asking insightful questions, asked him whether he thought he would get the job and Clough replied, "I believe that the Football Association should have the best manager ..... and please don't ask me who I think that is."
Clough skipped up the steps and entered number sixteen.
Lancaster Gate is a mid-19th century development in the Bayswater district of west central London, immediately to the north of Kensington Gardens. It consists of two long terraces of houses overlooking the park, with a wide gap between them opening onto a square containing a church. The development takes its name from Lancaster Gate, a nearby entrance to Kensington Gardens, itself named in honour of Queen Victoria, as Duke of Lancaster.
The terraces are stuccoed and are in an eclectic classical style featuring English Baroque details and French touches. Clough immediately felt comfortable in the surroundings.

Clough entered the ornate Committee Room where the Football Association interviewing panel was sat behind a long Brazilian mahogany table. A lone chair faced the panel.
"Shall I sit here?" asked Clough as he took off his coat and sat down. "Stinks of cigars in here. If it wasn't so bloody cold outside I'd open a window."

Sir Harold Thompson began the proceedings. "Clough, we're here to interview you, for the position of Manager of the senior England football team."

"Yes, Thompson, I know that," said Clough. "Now, I'm not one for wasting time. What's on your minds, gentlemen?"

Dick Wragg, the Chairman of the International Committee began. "Mr. Clough, what do you think you could bring to the position of England Manager that predecessors haven't?"

Clough responded instantly, "The World Cup for a start. Wouldn't you like to be associated with the best team in the world? Aye, I bet you would. Sir Alf gave you it, bless him. Mind you, look what you did to him. Shafted the poor old bugger."

Matt Busby of Manchester United, also an International Committee member, despite being Scottish, entered into the discussion. "But, Brian, you can't guarantee the World Cup."

"I don't know as much about football as you, Matt, but I do agree that nothing is guaranteed in football. Especially if you get a referee who's a bent bastard like we had at Derby when we played Juventus. Cheating bastards. Anyway, that's gone. What you need is the best management to get the players to do what you tell them."

"And you think you can get England players to do what you tell them?" asked Bert Millichip, the Chairman of West Bromwich Albion.

"My bloody record speaks for itself. I'm not saying I'm the best manager in the business .. but I'm in the top one. All I want is for that ball to brush the grass. Just pass it around among friends. For the best players, the ball *is* their friend. We don't want smart-arses. We want players who will do things simply and quickly, and when they're told. The things that are

hard work to other managers are not hard work to me. The discipline side, the judging of players, the training and coaching. These are not problems as far as I'm concerned."
"Would you curb your language please, Clough?" suggested Sir Harold Thompson.
"No I bloody won't, Thompson. I'm a football man. That's how we speak. What's your background? Oh, I know, you're a chemist, aren't you? Bloody good one I understand. Got a Ph.D. Well, that's good. I'm pleased for you. It wouldn't do for you to be running round your laboratory effin' and blindin'. Something unstable might blow up. I can understand that. And if I was in your laboratory I would behave myself. I'd keep my big gob shut because I don't know anything about chemistry – except with my missus Barbara. But then, I wouldn't advise you to come anywhere near my football dressing room. That's my laboratory."
Matt Busby chipped in, "I know there is no way you could guarantee the World Cup, but I'm with you on this Brian. I know you know your football." Dick Wragg nodded in agreement.
"You appoint me as manager and you will be able to tell your grandchildren you had a hand in bringing the World Cup back to England. Not this next one. You already cocked that up by giving Revie the job. Enjoying the sun and the sand, is he?"
Bert Millichip and Dick Wragg now nodded together. Peter Swales, the chairman of Manchester City and another International Committee member couldn't control his enthusiasm.
"Mr. Clough has given by far the best interview of all the candidates – confident, passionate, full of common sense and above all patriotic. I think we have the new England manager. He's clinched it for me."

Sir Harold Thompson looked pained. "Wait a minute. I'm the Chairman of the Football Association. Surely I have some say in all this," he bleated.

"Looks like you've been outvoted Thompson. Now, let's get on with the job. I'd like to tell Peter our good news as soon as possible," advised Clough.

Thompson was astonished. "But we are only interviewing you. We can't afford two of you."

"We come as a package. Peter can smell if a player can play or not. And don't worry about the cost. I'll cut enough costs round here to give ourselves a hefty pay rise by the time we qualify for the European Championships in two years. And, incidentally, as those qualifiers don't start till next season, I'll be staying with Forest till the end of this one. We're top of the league, going great guns. I don't think anyone will catch us now, so we've a championship to win. And I still want to win that bloody European Cup that the bastard Italians cheated us out of at Derby. Now, gentlemen, if you just nip down and tell the press I'll be there in a minute. I need a slash."

Clough stood up and left the room.

The selection committee members, with the exception of Professor Sir Harold Thompson, looked pleased.

Bert Millichip, who had felt the lash of Clough's acerbic tongue before, because of bad treatment to his own club manager, had not wanted Clough, but now had a change of mind.

"Sir Harold, you didn't want to give him an interview in the first place. You promised to sort him out. You didn't do that, did you?" chided Millichip. "McMenemy, Charlton, Sexton ... not a patch on Clough."

"I'm adamant he's far too risky. The man's unbalanced. You just never know what he might do next," countered Thompson.
"You're right," said Peter Swales. "He might go and win us the World Cup."
Sir Harold Thompson looked bewildered.

Along the corridor, Brian Clough poked his head round a door where four people were working at desks
"Get me Peter Taylor on the phone would you, please? Here's his number," he said, writing on a piece of paper. "Back in a minute." Clough left the room but as he did so he began to sing, "There may be trouble ahead ... but let's face the music and dance."
As he closed the door, he paused and looked back. His new staff looked startled.

A minute later Clough returned, took the telephone and spoke into it. "Pete, yes, went like a dream. The job's ours. I didn't so much walk out of the room as float. I was absolutely brilliant. I told them what I'd do and how I'd do it. I was so passionate about the job I'm sure the three lions appeared on my chest as I was chuntering on. I was utterly charming too. I walked in, introduced myself individually and I saw Thompson look so startled I thought his glasses were going to slide off his nose. At the end I thanked them all very much and said, 'Hey, you're not a bad bunch.' Just going in to see the press now. This is going to be fun. And tell our lads we'll stay till the end of the season. But get them in for extra training this afternoon. One or two look like they're overweight to me."

In the Football Association Press Briefing Room, the International Committee members were sat with a forlorn Sir Harold Thompson and several members of the press who had been invited to join them.

Sir Harold stood up and approached a podium, behind which, on the wall, was a large example of England's three lions insignia, incongruously hanging against a wide-striped wall paper.

Sir Harold Thompson spoke in a less than enthusiastic tone. "I would like you to meet the new England manager. Brian Clough." A spontaneous round of applause greeted this announcement.

"Good afternoon gentlemen," said Clough.

The first reporter opened with, "Great news, Brian."

Clough said, "You can call me Mr. Clough."

"Sorry, Mr. Clough. What will be your first task as England manager?"

"Get rid of this bloody wallpaper. It's a disgrace. Crap. Those three lions should stand out on a pure white background. It's like talking to you from inside a circus tent. Mind you, it's been a bit like a circus here. Up to now, that is."

A second reporter chimed up, "Are you serious Mr. Clough?"

"Please, you can call me Brian. I've never been more serious in my life. And we'll be getting rid of those bloody shirts that Revie brought in. Three Lions, white background. Unless we have to play in red, of course, in case we need to beat the Germans. They shot me Dad, you know."

Sir Harold Thompson whispered to Bert Millichip that he was disgusted at Clough's rudeness but Millichip pointed out that the reporters seemed very enthusiastic.

After the press conference Clough returned to the outer office where the four people were still working at their desks. Brian Clough joined them and looked out of the out the window.
"I think I'm going to work from home," he said, "I'm not saying London's a shithole, it's just a pain in the arse to get in and out of. Even if you come on the train, it's always a hassle. Mind you, I've never paid a taxi fare yet."
Linda, a young office assistant, stood up and approached Clough.
"Mr. Clough," she said, "I want to get an idea of the details for the trip in February for the friendly against Germany."
"Young lady, what's your name?" asked Clough.
"Linda, sir."
"Linda, that's the name of me favourite Auntie. Lovely woman. Now, Linda, I don't want you ever call to me sir again. I'm Brian to you. Now, what can I do for you, Linda?"
"It's about the Munich trip..um, Brian," she hesitated. "I normally book a private charter flight for the committee members and their families, usually about thirty or so, to arrive the day before the game and return the day after. Will you and Mr. Taylor…"
"Peter. Call him Peter." Clough took Linda aside, as if to keep the conversation private. "Step into my office."
"Will you and Peter want seats for your family members?" she whispered.
"No we won't. Peter and I will be working. We'll be travelling with the team before the game. Have you got a passport?"
"Yes," Linda confirmed. "My Mum and Dad took me and my sister to Majorca last year."

"Champion. Now, you book that charter flight for thirty or forty people, whatever you normally do, but book it to leave two days before the match. Two days before. Got it?"
"Yes Brian," Linda said.
"And another thing. You can keep a secret, can't you, Linda?"
"Yes, of course, Brian."
"Good. You tell your Mam and Dad, that they, and you and your sister, are coming with me to Germany, but you'll be coming with the England team. If your Mam and Dad work, just tell them to politely inform their bosses that Brian Clough has requested their presence to represent England. There won't be a problem."
Linda was delighted at this unexpected turn of events. "Fantastic!" she exclaimed.
Clough continued. "Now, that's our secret, isn't it, Linda? Don't tell anybody here. In fact, let them believe everything's arranged as normal."
"Yes, Brian," she confirmed.
Clough picked up the phone on his desk and dialled a number. "Hello, Shack. How's it going?" he said. After a few pleasantries Clough continued. "I want you to do me a favour. Get fourteen Forest fans and fourteen Derby fans. And you and your missus, of course. I want you all to accompany me to Munich for England's friendly in February against Germany." On the other end of the telephone Len Shackleton pointed out that the rival fans would start fighting
"No they won't," said Clough. "Tell them they are not only representing England, they are representing me." Clough rang off, satisfied with his work. "Do you know who Len Shackleton is?" asked Clough.

Linda confirmed that she didn't know. "He's known as the Clown Prince of Football," said Clough, "and he's about to pull off one of his pranks."

In his playing days, Shackleton often performed deliberately in a way to entertain the fans, though this upset some of the dullard establishment figures at the Football Association, who thought some of his antics were lacking in sportsmanship. He had been known to waste time by dribbling into the opposition penalty area, stopping the ball and pretending to comb his hair or look at an imaginary wrist watch.

Shackleton would play one-twos with the corner flag, sit on the ball during the game to taunt defenders, and once dribbled round a goalkeeper before stopping the ball on the line to maximise the drama before scoring the goal.

Clough explained. "His ball control was immaculate, instant, like it was attached to his foot by a short piece of string. He could drop his shoulder as if to go one way and then take off in the other direction. What a body swerve! His passing was exquisite but, you know, he did all that because he made himself space on the pitch. Gave himself time. All great players do that. It's called positioning."

Linda had long since lost interest but Clough continued, his eyes cast skyward to a dream world that only he was in at that time.

"And you know, even though his legs were a bit spindly, he couldn't half belt the ball. Now that's timing. Some players, professionals, can't even kick the ball properly. Do you know that? Some can only kick with one foot. It's almost scandalous. Look at Norman Hunter. Great left foot but his right foot was only for standing on. He's still playing but when he was in his heyday at Leeds he was regarded as one of the best around. England international and all that. In fact, when the Professional Footballers Association started that award thing a couple of years ago he was the first ever winner of the PFA Footballer of the Year. Professional footballers themselves voted a player the Footballer of the Year who could only kick with one foot. That's how much most footballers know about football.

Shackleton, different class. Had everything. Do you know, when he packed in playing because he'd knackered his ankle, he decided to become a journalist? To announce his retirement to the press, he threw a penny in the air, caught it on his instep, flicked it back into the air and caught it in the top pocket of his jacket.

These clowns here at the FA didn't like him because he took the piss. Out of some of them too, really, because of their connections with clubs. He wrote his autobiography, it was called The Clown Prince of Football, and it had a chapter called The Average Director's Knowledge of Football. That chapter was just a blank page. Funny that, isn't it?"

Clough transferred his gaze to Linda who, clearly, was still unimpressed.

Len Shackleton was the man who had started Clough and Taylor's managerial careers by suggesting Clough to Hartlepools' chairman Ernie Ord. The first thing that Clough did was to go to Burton Albion, then managed by his old mate Peter Taylor, and persuade Taylor to join him at Hartlepools. There were two important reasons why Taylor joined Clough at Hartlepools. First of all, Burton Albion was not in the Football League and that's where Taylor was desperate to test his talents. At least the Hartlepools team was in the Football League, even if it was bottom and clinging on by its fingertips as usual. The other important reason was the two hundred quid that Clough pressed into his palm.

So Shackleton had always been a friend to Clough and Taylor, even though Taylor's first words to Clough after he arrived at Hartlepools and had a look around were, "Something's got to be done about this lot – and quick. We're in the shit, good and proper. We'll be asking for re-election at the end of the season with this team. They're bound to finish bottom unless there's a place even lower in the bloody table."

As far as Derby County and Nottingham Forest were concerned, Clough and Taylor's links with the two East Midlands rivals were inextricable. They had led Derby to the League Championship six years previous and were now on target to do the same with Forest. The two cities, only fifteen miles apart were divided by the A50 and years of neighbourly rivalry, a rivalry that bordered on hatred.
"They're bound to start kicking shit out of each other," Shackleton pointed out in a telephone call to Peter Taylor, but Taylor was of the same mind as Clough. "No they won't. Tell them they are not only representing England, they are representing Brian Clough and me."
Apart from the usual pleasantries at the end of a telephone conversation, those were the final words on the subject and Taylor knew that Shackleton would come up with the goods, especially after he realised that he would be pulling the wool over those arrogant, self-aggrandising arseholes at Lancaster Gate.

Clough and Taylor sat on top of the First Division with Nottingham Forest and sat on top of England with England.

The phone rang in Clough's office at the City Ground in Nottingham. A young receptionist advised Clough that Sir Harold Thompson was on the other end of the line wanting to speak to him.

"Thank you very much, Mary," said Clough. "By the way, did your Mum and Dad enjoy themselves when they came to the game last week? They did. Good. Well, you tell them if they want to come to Manchester with us this coming Saturday they'll be very welcome. And if you want to come too, and bring a friend, just let me know by Friday. Now, perhaps you'd be good enough to put Mr. Thompson through."

Clough listened for several seconds to Thompson then broke in.

"You don't get it, do you? Me and Peter aren't coming down there just to hold press conferences or waste our time hanging around the FA offices. There are plenty of people doing that as it is. I'm quite prepared to have a press conference when I think it is necessary but I've looked on a map and Doncaster seems about right. On the A1 so it's quite accessible to newspaper people and, more important, it's easy enough to get to from here. Incidentally, I bet you're a bit pissed off."

Clough picked up a newspaper and began to read out loud. "Nevill Francis Mott, Philip Warren Anderson and John Hasbrouck van Vleck have won the Nobel Prize in Physics for their fundamental theoretical investigations of the electronic structure of magnetic and disordered systems."

At the other end of the telephone line Thompson mumbled something before Clough continued, "I know you are a physical chemist. I was talking about the disordered systems …. meaning you lot at the Football Association. Anyway, I'll get Mary to let you know if and when I arrange something. I'll have to dash. We've got a big game at United on Saturday to prepare for."

Clough put the phone down as Taylor entered the office. "What are you doing here? I thought you were going racing."

"I'm just off. The lads are well pissed off we lost to Chelsea. They don't like losing at all. Hate it."

"Call in the changing rooms on your way out and drop a hint that if they do well at Old Trafford I might take them to Spain for a few days. And I'm going for a game of squash. Send that young lad Birtles up. He gives me a good game. He keeps letting me win though. The day he gets fed up of doing that, and beats me like he should, I'll put him in the first team. I've high hopes for him."

The game at Old Trafford proved to be the point where the media finally realised that Forest were actually a class act. It was a game where the young Woodcock would get most of the plaudits but in which the brilliant Gemmill would show counter attacking at its very best. Manchester United were not just run ragged at their fortress, they were humiliated. Woodcock, chasing pretty much a lost cause, forced an own goal from desperate defender, Brian Greenhoff, on the near post. He then scored one himself before Robertson added a third. And it was Gemmill again who threaded a pass through for Woodcock to slide in a fourth without reply.

Clough relentlessly praised the midfield after the game, particularly Gemmill, but never said a word to Woodcock apart from telling him that he'd seen his sock round his ankle after his second goal and that he hadn't been quick enough to pull it up. If it hadn't been such a good away win, orchestrated by a magnificent midfield display, he would be looking at a fine for slovenly behavior.

***

The back room at the Blue Boar, just off the A1 near Doncaster, was hardly big enough to house the finest football hacks of the English press. But they did a good fry up, so Clough had arranged for traditional English breakfasts for those who had ordered in advance. Clough paid. Those who hadn't ordered in advance would have to fend for themselves. Breakfast over, the press conference was due to start at ten o'clock and did precisely that.

"Why have you dragged us up here?" asked a disgruntled representative from the Daily Telegraph.

"Next question," responded Clough.

"I think what my colleague meant, Mr. Clough," suggested a seasoned journalist from The Times, "is that we normally meet for briefings at Lancaster Gate."

" Well, the thing is, gentlemen," Clough explained, "we're off on holiday this afternoon, and we want to be near the airport. We're going to Cala Millor. It's lovely there and we can get direct from East Midlands. We have airports up here you know, that have planes that go where we want to go. There's more airports than Heathrow and Gatwick, you know. All that bloody aggravation to get through London to get there. Might as well go from here. Spend more time on the beach instead of hanging about in one of those big bloody airports. Makes more sense to go from here."

"But this is a press conference about the England team."

"That's all right. We're in England. Ask me any question you like about the England team."

"What's happening with it?"

"That's none of your business." "It is, really. We've come all the way up here for a press conference about the England team and you tell us you're going on holiday with your Forest team."

"That's right, young man. I will always tell you the truth. You might not like it sometimes, but it will be the truth."

"But we've heard nothing about your plans for the England team."

"Nor will you. That's between me and Peter Taylor. Peter has been watching certain players, keeping an eye on them to see whether they're up to scratch for the national team. The national team is very important, you know."

"Mr. Clough," said another reporter, "I travel to all the Forest games and Peter Taylor is at every game with you. How can he be watching players for the national team when he is always with the Forest team?"

"Young man, is this the best league there is?"

"Well, yes."

"Is Forest the best team in that league?"

"So far this season, yes."

"Then it makes sense that if we are in the best league and we are top of the best league then we are the best team. If we are the best team, then the teams we beat are worse than us. Now, I grant you that we have a few in our team who are not English. There's even an Irishman who thinks he is better than he is.

But, Peter Taylor is so good at his job that he can watch our players, and the opposition players, at the same time, during the same game. I'd be lost without him. I've said it before, I am the shop window but he's the goods in the back."

"But that doesn't give us much to go on regarding the England set up and the prospects for the national team."

"For crying out loud, the next England game isn't for a couple of months and we at Nottingham Forest need a short holiday.

And anyway, we've already chosen the team to play Germany in February. Barring injuries, that is."

"Would you give us an idea?"

"Don't be silly young man. Go away and make something up. You will do anyway. And now, you'll excuse us because we have a plane to catch." Clough walked out briskly.

The representative from the Daily Telegraph turned to the seasoned hack from The Times and said, "For fuck's sake."

One hundred and fifty miles to the south, at the Football Association headquarters in Lancaster Gate, Sir Harold Thompson leaned forward in his chair and, in a conspiratorial tone, said to his guest.

"Look, you want to get on in your trade, you want to rise up the ladder. I'm giving you the opportunity to make a name for yourself. What do you say?"

The guest was Tim Cox, a freelance journalist from a tabloid newspaper who was desperate to get a full-time job with the paper. He worked the night shift on the news desk and was quietly making an impression with the newspaper's editorial staff. But he desperately needed a full-time job because his girlfriend was pregnant and the reassurance of a regular salary would provide his relationship the stability he thought it would need to keep it together. "What's in it for me?" he asked.

Professor Thompson continued. "Look, just poke around and see what you can get on him. There must be something."

"You mean some shit?"

"If you need to put it like that, yes. You find it and bring the information to me. If I think it's worth it we'll get it into your sports editorial staff. If it gets in print, I'll reward you.. And, depending on how it goes, I'll see you get a full-time job reporting First Division matches or whatever."

Thompson leaned over and poured a sizable dose of Armagnac into two glasses.

"What have we got on him so far?" asked the young journalist.

"Nothing yet. But there must be something. Womaniser, gambler, you find it."

The two conspirators chinked their glasses and gulped their drinks to seal the deal. The subject of this conversation was Brian Clough, manager of the Nottingham Forest and England football teams.

Thompson continued, "Now, I know that the bastard is flying off to Spain for a holiday today with his Forest team. Right in the middle of the season. The man's clearly mad. Here's some money. You find out where he's going, get yourself over there and do some poking around. By the time you get back you should have found something I can use."

Clough stood up on the coach that was transferring the Nottingham Forest team from the airport to their hotel in Cala Millor and began to read aloud from a brochure.

"Cala Millor is a tourist destination on the Spanish Balearic island of Mallorca. It is the largest tourist development on the east coast of the island. Nearly all shopkeepers and receptionists speak some degree of English, with many also speaking a limited amount of German. Well, we're not bothered about the German bit. They shot me Dad. We'll just deal with the English but some of you even have a problem with that. Cala Millor, which means 'Better Bay, is also situated close to the tourist resort of Cala Bona which means 'Good Bay' but you don't need to know that because you won't be going there.

The nearby beach is popular. Ah, there we go. The beach is 1.8 kilometres long, whatever that is, but it sounds plenty long enough for our purposes.

Please note the hotel will not accept bookings of minors aged 17 years old or younger unless they are travelling with someone 18 years of age or older. That doesn't bother us. There's a restaurant, cafe, pool bar, two lounge bars and Piano bar with live music and dancing. Now you're talking.

There's various outdoor swimming pools surrounded by gardens with sun beds and sunshades, indoor heated pool, and two tennis courts.

Guests can enjoy other activities for rental or hire including sailing, cycling, horse riding, scuba diving and snorkelling. We're doing none of that shit. There's a souvenir shop, if you want it, a newsagent, supermarket, currency exchange, tour desk, sauna, hairdresser and car park.

I bet some of you will want to ponce around at the hairdresser's. But you won't need the currency exchange because I've got your spending money.

All guest rooms are well appointed and are fully equipped with bathroom, ceiling fan, safety deposit box, for which there is an extra charge so you won't need that, a fridge to keep your beers cold in and a balcony to each room. You're sharing by the way. I'm not. I'll give out your roommate's name in a minute.

But none of that other shit has anything to do with you. As soon as you've got your bags dropped into your rooms, I want you in your shorts down in the foyer. We're going off to the beach to play cricket. I've brought a bat and ball. Cricket. Now, that's a proper game."

The players disembarked the coach, some excited, some not. Those that weren't excited tried not to show it because they knew the consequences of not doing whatever Clough had in his plans.

"Oh, and by the way, Gemmill, don't come any of that 'I feel tired from travelling' shit. You're on my side. I'm opening the batting . Lloyd, you are captain of the other side.

"I can't stand cricket, you know that," protested Lloyd.

"I don't give a shit what you like and don't like," said Clough.

Clough operated a dictatorship, a form of government that has the power to govern without the consent of those being governed and describes a state that regulates nearly every aspect of public and private behaviour of the people, that is to say, in this case, Nottingham Forest Football Club. But as Clough would suggest on more than one occasion, there was nothing wrong with a dictator as long as it was a good one.

At an appropriate point on the 1.8 kilometres long beach, Clough organised his team against a team captained by Larry Lloyd. Clough had provided the bat, a tennis ball and one cricket stump.

Clough opened the batting against Lloyd's fast bowling, taken off a shortened run up of three steps, and seemed to be aimed at Clough's head.

The ball was smacked for four, the runs being amassed in singles because the only boundary noted thus far was the water's edge and that was a long way off.

Lloyd bowled again, and again Clough dispatched the ball towards the Mediterranean.

Clough ran four runs but had spotted that the fielder hadn't made the greatest of efforts to retrieve the ball. Clough called him over.

"O'Neill, you are not the fastest player we have at this club," said Clough, "but you are not the slowest either. You sauntered over to get that ball. I ran four runs and if you'd tried harder, and run faster, you could have restricted me to two runs. What were you doing?"

"But I'm on your side," said O'Neill. "Surely you'd want me to take my time so that you could score more runs for our team."

"You are a bloody disgrace. If I catch any of you not trying your hardest, whether you are on my side or not, you'll get a fine."

"You haven't allowed us to bring much money with us," said O'Neill, "so how can you impose a fine?"

"Because I'll take it out of your allowance, you idiot. And you're fined."

"So, if I continue to run less fast when I am fielding for the other side, then I will incur more fines, up until the point where I have no money left for you to take from me. And it is purely your whim as to whether you judge that I am running as fast as I can, for the benefit of the opposition, or whomsoever. So what happens when my fund is depleted?"

"You'll find some of your wages missing when we get back, that's what," said Clough.

"Fuck this," said Lloyd in an aside to his roommate Kenny Burns. "I'll twat him right between the eyes."

Clough hit the next ball violently and, despite O'Neill scampering after it at a blistering pace, he was able to chalk up his third consecutive four.

Clough smiled to himself. He could see this match dragging on into the evening, with his innings taking on a significant obstinacy, as if it was Geoffrey Boycott opening against the might of the West Indian bowlers.

Another four, a single and a six, because the ball went straight into the sea, and Clough had seen off Malcolm Marshall in the guise of Larry Lloyd.

Michael Holding pitched up looking remarkably like Viv Anderson. "At least you're the right colour," barked Clough. "Now, give it your best, young man. And it doesn't matter if you try to knock my head off like that ugly bastard Lloyd was trying to do in the last over. That doesn't intimidate me. I'm a Yorkshiremen. Have you heard of Brian Close?"

"No," said Anderson.

"Well, Brian Close was a Yorkshiremen. He opened the batting for England when he was forty five years old against the West Indies when the West Indies had the most formidable line up of fast bowlers in the history of the game.

The most graceful was Michael Holding. But he was also vicious. Lethal. And he kept trying to hit Close with bouncers. And he did hit him, several times. Ended up black and blue. But did Close flinch? Not a bit. Yorkshireman, see.

In a different game he was fielding near to the wicket at short leg when the batsman hit a full-blooded pull shot. The ball smacked Close hard on the side of his face. The ball flew up in the air and the batsman was caught at slip. Somebody asked Close what would have happened if he'd been hit right between the eyes. Do you know what Close said? He said, 'in that case, the bugger would have been caught at cover'. Now give it your best, young man."

Anderson bowled a dolly that looped up into the air. Clough judged the flight of the ball calmly but, as it descended, took an almighty swing, missed completely, and the ball dropped onto the single stump.

"Well played, young man. Good ball," said Clough. "Gemmill, you're in."

"Don't you want somebody who can play bloody cricket?" asked Gemmill.

"I want you," said Clough. "You're the best batsman we've got. Apart from me of course."

"Big headed bastard," muttered Lloyd.

"I heard that," said Clough. "I might be big headed but I'm entitled to be. When you've won a league championship medal you can talk to me on equal terms. Anyway, I might be big headed but you're ugly. I can change if I want to."

The game continued until all players had had a bat and a bowl and, as it started to get dark, Clough declared his team had scraped a victory. Narrow though the victory was, it was still a win and Clough instructed his players to shower quickly and get down to the dining room in half an hour.

McGovern, as team captain, suggested to Clough that they might have a little longer because that was only fifteen minutes each in the shower since they were sharing a room, and it was his knowledge that several of the players took longer than that to dry their hair.

"Thirty minutes, prompt," said Clough. "If you are not in the dining room before me you won't be getting any dinner tonight. And, anyway, some of you aren't old enough to have hairstyles," he snarled as he stomped off.

The team sat at a long dining table that had been arranged especially for them when Clough entered wearing a pair of shorts and a sweatshirt top. The team had assembled in their club blazers and ties. "Ah, gentlemen, I see you haven't ordered any drinks yet."

McGovern pointed out that the manager hadn't actually given them their spending money yet.

"That's no problem." He beckoned to a waitress who arrived instantly. "Get these lads what they want," said Clough and the young girl began to write down orders. "Oh, and by the way," he continued, pointing at Archie Gemmill, "that balding one there drinks Scotch with a teeny bit of water. Bottled water, mind. None of that crap out of your taps."

A man and a boy approached Clough and the man said in a guttural accent, "My son would like your autographs please."

"What's your name?" Clough asked the boy. The father answered, "Karl with a K."

"Where are you from?" continued Clough, as he began to sign a piece of paper the boy had proffered.

"We are on holiday from Dusseldorf," Karl's Dad explained.

"Dusseldorf. That's bloody Germany. Your lot shot me Dad. Here you are lad."

He handed Karl his piece of paper and instructed the players to sign the paper for the boy.

"What he wants your autographs for, I don't bloody know. You've only won the Anglo-Scottish Cup. Mind you, it was worth winning. Gives you a taste of what winning's like. Now we want the league. We're top of it, you're not playing too badly and I personally can't see any team catching us. As long as you keep doing as you're told. Think about it. Do you want to win the league?"

It was a rhetorical question and, as Clough moved off towards the bar, he added, "Now, enjoy your meal, get what drinks you want, and then join me in the bar when you've finished. Now, Hans, or whatever your name is, tell your lad to meet us in the bar when he's got their autographs. You can come and buy me a drink for shooting me Dad."

As the Yorkshireman and the German walked off to the bar, Gemmill pushed his whisky to Peter Shilton who downed it in one, just in case Clough turned round unexpectedly.

Peter Taylor got out of a taxi in Lancaster Gate and skipped up the steps of Number 16. He entered the revolving door where he got stuck. Inside the reception of the Football Association, a woman of indeterminate age, but nearer sixty than forty, was sat behind a wood-panelled desk, reading a book. Taylor tried to push the revolving door open, quite violently, but it didn't budge. He banged on the glass of his prison. The woman at the desk didn't budge.

'Fuck me, nothing moves round here,' thought Taylor. He banged again on the glass of the revolving door, this time very violently. The woman looked up. Taylor motioned to her that he was stuck. The woman picked up a phone and spoke into it, then continued reading.

After a minute, a man in overalls appeared, fiddled with something at the bottom of the door, and freed Peter Taylor.

"It often does that," said the man in the overalls.

"Are you in charge of these things?" asked Taylor.

"Yes."

"What's your name?"

"Sam Crabtree."

"Well, I'll tell you what, Sam. I'm going to be leaving here in a couple of hours, less if I'm lucky. Get this fixed now because I don't want to get stuck in there again."

"Yes."

Taylor approached the wood-panelled desk. The woman looked up and said, "Are you expected?"

"I doubt it," said Taylor.

"Who do you want to see?" she asked.

"I don't want to see anybody. I want to see the phone in my office because I want to use it."

"Your office?"

"I'm Peter Taylor. Assistant Manager of the England Team."

"Oh, crumbs," said the lady. "I'm sorry. Just a minute." She picked up the phone. "Hello, Linda, Peter Taylor's in reception." She put the phone down and advised Taylor that help was on its way and asked him to sign the visitors' book. Soon a young lady appeared and introduced herself as Linda.

"Hello, Mr. Taylor, Brian said you might turn up."

"Ah, Linda, Brian spoke highly of you. Can you show me to a phone? And did you get those decorators Brian wanted?"

"They've already started in the Briefing Room as instructed," she said. Linda took Peter Taylor to a small office. "We put you in here, right next to Mr. Clough because there is a connecting door."

"Very good. And call me Peter. I just want to have a look round and make a few phone calls."

"Do you want me to get you anything?"

"No thanks, I'll find my way around."

"Well, I'm in here if you need me," said Linda, pointing to an office opposite. "I'm in admin."

Peter Taylor looked around his office which contained a chair and a desk with a telephone on it. There was a filing cabinet against one wall. He opened it. It was empty. He sat down at his desk and leaned back on his chair, deep in thought. He picked up the telephone and called his wife, Lillian, and told her the place was as desperate as he had expected. After a while, he left the room and wandered around the building. He opened the door that had a sign Post Room on it. Inside, a lady was opening letters and placing them on different piles. "What are you doing?" asked Taylor.

"I'm sorting the post," she said.

"But you are opening the letters," said Taylor.

"Yes," she said, "I open them and put them in the right pile for whoever they're addressed to."

"Who told you to do that?"

"It's always been done this way."

"What if there are letters to me?"

"I'm very sorry, I don't know who you are."

"I'm Peter Taylor."

"There's nothing for you. I'm good with names. There's no Taylor here."

"There is now. You don't open any letter addressed to Brian Clough or Peter Taylor. You just take the post, unopened, to Brian Clough's office and leave the letters on the desk. You know who Brian Clough is?"

"Yes, he's the new England Manager. I haven't met him yet though."

"You won't want to if you open his letters."

"I'm sorry. If there is confidential information …"

"It's not that there might be something you shouldn't see. It's the principle."
"I'll have to get permission to take his post straight to Mr. Clough's office."
"I've just given you permission."
"I mean from the Head of Admin."
"Where do I find the Head of Admin?"
The woman redirected Taylor back down the corridor towards the room that Linda had returned to, opposite Taylor's office. Taylor entered.
"Hello, Peter," said Linda.
"Who's in charge here?" he snapped.
"Mr. Tibbs is Head of Admin," said Linda. "He's in his office through there."
Taylor walked straight into Tibbs's office.
"Hello, I'm Peter Taylor. Just to let you know that Linda will be in charge of any post that is addressed to Brian Clough or me from now on and when Brian or I are in London, which won't be often, Linda will be on duty with us."
"I can certainly put it to the committee," said Mr. Tibbs. He looked at a wall calendar. The next meeting is next Thursday afternoon."
"That's not necessary," said Taylor. "What's your first name?"
"David."
"Okay, David. Consider those arrangements in place. You can inform your committee next Thursday that it's all sorted. I'll tell Linda."
Taylor left Tibbs's office and returned to Linda.
"Now Linda," he said, "you come with me." He led Linda to his office. "You can sit there. When Brian or I are in London at this office we will need you to be on hand here in case we need you. When you get our mail in the morning, you can open

it. If it's a waste of time, bin it. If it looks like it's something we need to know about, you can call our office at Forest and tell us over the phone. I'll tell that woman in reception to pass any phone calls for us through to you. Then you can pass any messages through to Nottingham. Now, I'm going to have a look round this place. If you can be back here with a cup of coffee in ten minutes, that would be good. Milk no sugar." Taylor wandered off.

Sam Crabtree came along the corridor. "Did you fix that door, Sam?" asked Taylor.
"Yes," said Sam. "It's funny, it's been sticking like that for years. I undid the guts of the latch at the bottom and tightened it up. Shouldn't be any problem now."
"Good lad. By the way, get some white paint and paint our offices. Brighten the place up a bit. Thanks."

Taylor came to some stairs and climbed them where he found a long corridor. At the end, he came to large double doors and opened them onto a room where six men sat round a dark mahogany table. They all turned and looked at Taylor.
"Excuse me, we've booked this room. We're having a committee meeting," said one of the men.
"I can see that," said Taylor. "Carry on. Enjoy your tea and biscuits." He closed the door.
Taylor poked his head round every door he came to, some rooms empty, some with people in sat at desks, some talking into telephones, before returning to his office where Linda had arrived with a cup of coffee.

"I was in Lincoln prison once," Taylor said. Linda looked shocked. "As a visitor, not an inmate. And the thing that struck me straight away was that nobody was smiling. Well, you can't expect them to be rolling around laughing, it's a prison for Christ's sake, and a proper prison at that, Victorian, five floors of cells. Nasty! Horrible! But, you'd think they'd try to find something to smile about, just to lighten the passage of time. Well, it's like that here. Look in these offices and most people's desks face the wall. What's all that about? Don't people like to talk to each other? By the way, I've asked Sam to paint our offices white but if you fancy a different colour you'd better tell him since you'll be in here too. Keep it bright though. Last thing, me and Brian prefer our coffee in mugs, so get a couple for us. Now, where do I find the chairman?"

Taylor walked down the corridor, as directed by Linda, and knocked on the door that was designated 'Professor Sir Harold Thompson, Chairman'.
A voice from inside called out, "Come." Taylor entered.
"Oh, Taylor, it's you," said a surprised Sir Harold.
"It is, Thompson," said Taylor.
"Sir Harold," to you.
"Bollocks. You call me Taylor, I'll call you Thompson. You can stop that shit from now on. I haven't got time to hang about. Brian and I will drop in here from time to time so I've just been poking my nose around the place. Barrel of laughs here, it ain't. Just so you know, Linda in admin will be our point of contact but don't expect us down here too often."
"I understand Clough has gone on holiday to Spain."
"You're doing it again, Thompson. Brian has taken the Forest lads abroad for a break. It's not a holiday. It might look like a holiday to people who don't understand footballers, but it most

certainly isn't a holiday. How did you know he'd gone to Spain?"

"Obviously, as chairman of the Football Association I make it my business to know what's going on."

"Well, that's Forest business, and has nothing to do with you. Brian knows what he's doing. You just leave him to it. If you poke your nose in, it'll get him rattled, and you don't want to be doing that. Anyway, I'm not hanging about."

Taylor left and went back to his office where Linda was waiting. "I'll be off soon, but I need you to do me a favour. But it's between you and me."

"Of course," said Linda.

"When I arrived here, that woman on the reception desk asked me to sign a visitor's book."

"That's normal. She'll enter the name, who they've come to see, and at what time. And she'll write down when they leave."

"Right. Can you sneak me a list of people who have visited Sir Harold over the last couple of weeks?"

"I expect so. First of all, she leaves at half past five on the dot so I can hang around a bit to get a peek at it. Everybody's gone by quarter to six anyway."

"Everybody's gone by quarter to six? Who locks up?'

"Well, Sam stays until night security arrives."

"What about midweek matches. And weekends?"

"No different."

"What do you mean, no different? There must be people here for England's midweek matches. And the league matches at the weekends."

"No, not at all. These offices close at five thirty. The security people are usually here about six o'clock and they stay on the premises overnight. There's nobody here at weekends."

"Not when there's a full league fixture list? Not if England has a game?"

"No. Some of the FA officials and councillors go to Wembley but mostly they've left early afternoon to go for a meal before a game."

"So, you are saying that the headquarters of the Football Association is shut when England play. So nobody is manning the post in case something crops up. And at weekends when there is a league programme on, nobody is here either."

"That's right."

"Bloody hell. This place is more of a shambles than I thought." Taylor thought for a moment. "Do me another favour please. Come in early tomorrow and turn round anybody's desks that are facing the wall. When you walk into a room you should see people's faces not the back of their heads. And don't forget, if you want to choose the paint for our offices you'd better have a word with Sam as soon as possible. He fixed the door straight away when I asked him to so he might be a bit sharp off the mark."

"Sam's fixed the door? It's been like that ever since I've been here."

"Right, thanks for the coffee. I'm off. Get that information for me and I'll call you tomorrow."

Taylor went to leave but Sir Harold Thompson burst in.

"Taylor, what's all this about the wallpaper?" he screamed.

"Get out of my office now, you ignorant bastard," shouted Taylor. "You want to come in here, you knock first."

Thompson left the room, embarrassed and a little shaken, then knocked abruptly on the door. There was a long pause.

Taylor called out calmly, "Come." Thompson entered.
"Ah, Sir Harold, what can I do for you?" asked Taylor.
"What are those men doing to the wallpaper in the Briefing Room?" asked Thompson.
"They should be stripping it off," explained Taylor.
"But I chose it. It cost thousands," bleated Thompson.
"Sir Harold, what do you do round here?" asked Taylor.
"I'm the chairman, of course," he responded.
"Well, you be a good chap and go off and do what chairmen do. And don't go choosing wallpaper. You're crap at it. Now bugger off." Thompson withdrew indignantly.
"Um, Peter," said Linda. "I think I'll choose the paint for your offices. I've nothing against white but it's a bit boring."
"Just as long as it's bright and cheerful, Linda. Bright and cheerful. Just like me."

Taylor went out first time through the perfectly functioning revolving door and skipped down the steps of 16 Lancaster Gate. A wave of the hand and a black London cab pulled up alongside the kerb. "St. Pancras station, please mate," Taylor said to the cabbie. "As fast as you bloody can."

Back in his own office, Sir Harold sat ashen-faced when a couple of random committee members from a random committee entered. Sir Harold reached for a whisky bottle and poured himself a large one.
"That was outrageous," he stammered. "I have never been treated so deplorably in my life. Ignorant, he is. Taylor's has no breeding whatsoever."

"The people love Clough and Taylor," said the first committee member.
"They hang on their every word," confirmed the second committee member.
Sir Harold swigged the whisky in one gulp. "Get out of here, whoever you are," he snapped.

The pool side at Hotel Bahia in Cala Millor boasted the usual lines of sun loungers and the hotel itself boasted a plentiful congregation of Germans.
 Clough arrived first, before he had had any breakfast, and began dragging sun loungers into a group formation. Some Germans arrived and informed Clough that they usually occupied those loungers. Clough informed them that they didn't anymore. Archie Gemmill came out with John McGovern and looked embarrassed as the Germans protested. But Clough was ignoring them and busying himself with his task.
"Come on lads, grab a seat," he said, "before there's an invasion."
A couple of other players began to arrive, along with the hotel manager who had been summoned by the head of the German contingent. The manager spoke. "We operate a first come, first serve system here, sir. We don't reserve places along the poolside."
"You do now," said Clough. "All these sun loungers here," he pointed out, "are for my lads. This is Nottingham Forest. We are currently sitting on top the toughest league in the world and I don't want anything to stop them from enjoying

themselves during our visit here. You can help by dragging that one there just a wee bit closer."

More players were arriving as the Germans continued their conversation with the hotel manager. "Come on lads, don't mind them," called out Clough, "they'll go away in a minute." The hotel manager approached the football team manager and said, "It seems you have some fans in Germany. They are football fans and want to know if they can get some autographs."

"Autographs," spluttered Clough. "We can do better than that. Gemmill, McGovern, Shilton, come on lads, get up and let these people sit down."

The players started to shuffle sun loungers around. Clough spoke to the manager. "Be a good lad and go get a note pad and pen. Hotel notepaper would be good." The hotel manager disappeared.

The Nottingham Forest party made room for the Germans and Clough insisted they bring their children in amongst the players.

"This is the captain, John McGovern, and he'll introduce you." The hotel manager returned with an official hotel notepad and pen which Clough gave to McGovern.

"Now, John, take these bairns along and get everyone to sign their autographs for them. And don't miss anybody out."

McGovern set about his task while Clough called the hotel manager over. They joined the German adults.

"Now, these people here," he said, pointing to the Germans, "are the guests of Nottingham Forest Football Club. Allow them to add any drinks, sandwiches, anything they want, to our bill. Now, sit down with my lads and enjoy the sun. If you want anything, just ask a member of the staff or tell my captain there. The one introducing your kids to the players. His name's John. He's a good lad, but don't tell him I said so."

As Clough went to leave, Peter Shilton sidled up to him. "Excuse me, gaffer, I have a routine where I have to do some exercises and some goalkeeping practice every day or I'm not happy. Don't get me wrong, I like being by the pool, and the sunshine and everything, but it's kind of a ritual I have."
"I know that, Peter," said Clough. "You have one of the most professional approaches I have ever seen in a footballer. I am very satisfied by the way you go about your business and your profession. Because that's what it is, a profession."
Shilton looked pleased with himself.
"That's why we bought you," continued Clough. "And furthermore, when we've finished with you, you might just be able to call yourself a decent goalkeeper. To be fair, you've only been with us for five minutes. I'll come back for you in an hour and I'll whack some balls at you. In the meantime, you do your exercises yourself. Swimming's good. Have a swim." Clough left Shilton, one of the best goalkeepers in the world, with a bemused look on his face.

As the Forest players rested by the side of the pool, ordering drinks when they wanted to, dipping in and out of the pool when they wanted to and enjoying the sun when they wanted to, a hotel guest arrived and pulled up a lounger alongside Larry Lloyd.
"That's was Brian Clough, wasn't it?" said Tim Cox. "Is he always so generous with strangers?"

"Depends on his mood," said Lloyd. "You never know what mood he's in."

"Sounds like he's in a good mood today. I think I'll order a beer."

"I wouldn't do that if I were you," said Lloyd.

"Why not?" asked Cox. "He included all those people there."

"Because he knows everything that's going on. Believe me, he can tell when you need to fart. He'll know exactly who's had what to drink and eat today. And he didn't personally invite you. So I wouldn't bother if I were you."

"You like Brian Clough, don't you?" asked Cox.

"Can't stand him," said Lloyd.

"Why do you play for him?" asked Cox.

"Because we win. Say what you like about him, he knows how to put out a football team."

"But, surely, if you can't stand the man, you must want to poke him in the eye, so to speak."

"Not really. I'll put up with his shit if it gets me some medals. And he said I should be playing for England."

"What difference does that make if you can't stand the man?"

"Do you know much about football?"

"Not really."

"Well, we're top of the league. He says we can win the title. I believe him. If he says I should be playing for England, I believe him. I might not like him, and if he walked into a pub I'd walk out but I respect him when he talks about football."

"But as a man, as a person, as a bloke…"

"He's an arsehole."

"He's married though, isn't he?"

"Yes."

"And he's got kids."

"Yes, three. Why?"

"Just wondered." Tim Cox paused. "I just wondered that if he was such an arsehole, maybe he treated his family badly too."

"I wouldn't go down that route with him. I've never known a bloke so family orientated. He'd kill you if you said anything bad about his family. Mind you, I've heard him tell his boys off and it made me wince. Poor little buggers."

"Does he hit them?"

Lloyd laughed. "No he doesn't hit them. Of course he doesn't."

"But they're frightened of him."

"I'm not so sure they're frightened of him but they do as they're told."

"He's a family man, then. So you won't see him tapping up some bird out here?"

"Good God, no. I've seen him flirt but that's because he likes attention all the time. Doesn't matter whether it's men or women. Big head, but he'll tell you that himself. I'm off in for a beer. Do you want me to bring you one back?"

"What about Clough?"

"It's all right if I get it. I'm allowed. But if anybody takes the piss, they'll be in for it."

Larry Lloyd got up from the sun lounger and walked off to the hotel to get a couple of beers, but he stopped at the sun lounger occupied by John McGovern. "That bloke over there," Lloyd said to his skipper. "He's asking questions about the gaffer."

"What do you mean? What kind of questions?"

"Bit nosey really. Not football stuff."

"Who is he?" asked McGovern.

"Don't know. Didn't ask him." Lloyd started to move off.
"Anybody want a beer?" he called to the rest of the players but nobody took him up on the offer.

After a while Clough appeared by the poolside again and summoned Peter Shilton.
"Come on Peter, I've found us a spot of grass you can field some balls on. I managed to get a couple of plastic ones from a shop up the road."
"Plastic!" said Shilton. "They're like balloons."
"That's the idea," said Clough. "Make you more agile, twisting every which way, not knowing where the ball is going to go."
Shilton looked at the rest of the players and rolled his eyes skyward but walked away with Clough anyway.

John McGovern wandered along the row of sun loungers and sat down beside Tim Cox on the sun lounger that Larry Lloyd had vacated. "Hello, mate. Enjoying the sun?"
"Yes. Just the job."
"You here on holiday?"
"Yes."
"Where's your missus?"
"Oh, she's back in London. She's expecting. Travel and all that, you know."
"You're here on your own. On holiday on your own?" said McGovern surprised.
"Yes, why?"
"What have you come here for? There's not much to do. Or at least there's not much that we're allowed to do."

"So I understand from Larry Lloyd. He says he doesn't like Clough."

"I suggest if you bump into him you refer to him as Mr. Clough."

"I can understand what you are saying but I'm not one of his players. What do I care what Big Head, as Larry called him, has to say? I don't have to answer to him."

"No you don't. I'm just warning you. Don't upset him while you are round any of his players."

"I appreciate your thoughts but it's not as if Clough, Mr. Clough, is of any importance to me."

"Just saying. So your missus is expecting?"

"Yes, in about six weeks."

"Don't you think you should be with her?"

"Well, yes and no. I think she needed to have a bit of space if you see what I mean. I'm only here for a couple of days anyway."

"Make hay while the sun shines, eh? While the cat's away…."

"My missus won't be getting up to much. You wouldn't believe how big she is. Having said that, there's a corking bird in the kitchen. Spotted her when I was having breakfast. Might have a crack at that. In fact, while I think about it, I might go and tap her up for tonight. You never know."

"Well, as I say, make hay …"

Tim Cox rose from his sun lounger and made his way into the hotel as John McGovern spoke to the rest of the players.

"Watch that bloke. I'm not sure what he's up to. He's not a normal football fan. He's gone to ask one of the waitresses out. I'll give a fiver to anyone who can get a photo of him with the waitress. Or any woman for that matter."

There was a general murmur of assent from the players as Larry Lloyd returned with two glasses of beer.

"Hey, where's that geezer I was talking to?"
"Gone to ask one of the waitresses out."
"Fuck me, I fetched him a beer. Never mind, I'll drink it myself."

***

Back in Nottingham, at the City Ground, McGovern had approached Taylor after training and asked for a discreet word. "There was a bloke in Spain, at the hotel, asking questions about the gaffer. Not the usual football questions. Being a bit nosey. Asking about the gaffer's family. Dodgy. Reporter."
"What did you tell him?"
"Well, nothing of course. There isn't anything. But I did ask the lads to see if they could get a photo of the bloke with one of the waitresses he was after. I offered a fiver. Archie came up with four photos and wanted twenty quid but they were all the same photo. Anyway, here's the one I got off him. The bloke's got his arm round the lass and they are getting in the lift at the hotel. The bloke told me he had a pregnant girlfriend back in England. Not a nice bloke."
Taylor scrutinised the photograph, reached in his trouser pocket and pulled out a fiver which he gave to McGovern.
"I'll keep this," he said. "Good lad."

After the few days away in Mallorca, Forest had drawn at home to both Merseyside teams, first Liverpool, then Everton 1-1, and sandwiched two away wins at Newcastle and Bristol City. There then followed a 0-0 away draw at Derby and a home win against Arsenal to avenge the defeat earlier in the season. The next scheduled home match was against Wolverhampton Wanderers.

Clough still had a good feeling about the League Cup competition. Aston Villa had been disposed of easily 4-2 at home in November in Round Four and Bury had been trounced 3-0 away in Round Five. This left a two-legged semi-final with Leeds United to negotiate.

Two wins in Rounds three and four of the FA Cup, at home to Swindon and Manchester City, had left Nottingham Forest handily placed in all three major domestic competitions.

The Football Association Challenge Cup, commonly known as the FA Cup, is a knockout cup competition in English football and is the oldest association football competition in the world. As its name implies it is organised by the Football Association. The FA Cup was first held in 1871-72. Entry is open to all teams who compete in the senior leagues, and those leagues just below that, as well as selected teams just below those. This means that clubs of all standards compete, from the largest clubs in England and Wales down to what amounts to amateur village teams. The tournament has become known for the possibility for minnows from the lower divisions to become giant-killers by eliminating top clubs, and even theoretically win the Cup, although lower division teams rarely progress beyond the early stages. The qualification rounds and a system of byes mean that the very smallest and very biggest teams almost never meet.

Nevertheless, the FA Cup is rightly held to be the most prestigious cup competition in the world. To Brian Clough, that was a load of bollocks. It was just another few games and, therefore, another competition that might as well be won.

At this time Forest had been top of the First Division since early October and showed no signs of slipping.

So much for a mid-season break being the idea of a madman.

Peter Taylor entered the office of Brian Clough and pointed something out. "You know we've got Leeds in the first leg of the League Cup semi-final."
"Yes."
"Well, there's a slight problem."
"Problem? We'll piss on them."
"The second leg falls on the twenty second."
"So what?"
"There's the England game against Germany that night. The friendly in Munich."
"Shit. I was looking forward to pissing all over Leeds. Twice. These two legged semi-finals are good for that. Fuck it." Clough thought for a moment. "Right, I'll have to do the England stuff so you'll have to do the League Cup. I'm not missing out completely though. Get Jimmy up here." Taylor left to summon Jimmy Gordon.

Jimmy Gordon had first met up with Clough and Taylor when he was a coach at Middlesbrough. A steady player himself, without reaching great heights, Bill Shankly once said of him, 'If you had to play against Jimmy every week you would never sleep at night.'
He was the buffer between the players and Clough and Taylor but, apart from that, he was loved and respected by all football people.
He was conscientious, firm but fair, a stickler for fitness, and his shrewd instruction and skilful preparation of the players was admirable.
Yet that did not represent the most onerous or valuable aspect of his duties at Nottingham Forest.

What made the coach's contribution so special was the way he coped with the club's hugely talented but undeniably eccentric management team of Brian Clough and Peter Taylor.

A man of unimpeachable integrity and always approachable, Gordon was an expert in rebuilding the confidence of young men whose egos had taken a battering from the tongue of the acerbic Clough.

Though hard in his own way, expecting total dedication and ceaseless effort, Gordon became a much-respected father figure and go-between.

He played until he was thirty eight years old and regretted that he hadn't carried on till he was forty. He was a football man through and through.

Gordon was often left to supervise the day-to-day running of football matters at the club, a task he accomplished with calm efficiency.

In his own way he had become a legend within the football community. For a start he was the only person on earth who could claim to know how Clough and Taylor worked. He understood them.

Gordon entered Clough's office followed by Taylor.

"Ah, James," said Clough, "what team would you pick against Wolves?"

Gordon thought for a few seconds. "Shilton, Anderson, Barrett, Burns, Needham, Gemmill, McGovern, O'Neill, Withe, Woodcock and Robertson."

"Good lad. I'd have chosen the same. Why did you choose that team?"

"That's all we have. Frank and Larry are injured but we can have Ian and John as subs."

"That'll do me," said Clough. "You're in charge this afternoon. Peter and I have to go somewhere."
All three left the office, Brian Clough and Jimmy Gordon clear about the plan for the rest of the day ahead, but Taylor completely unsure of his role in the forthcoming proceedings.

Clough and Taylor arrived at the Leeds United Directors' entrance at the Elland Road stadium and approached the man on the door.
"We're here to look at Trevor Cherry and any other of your players who think they might be good enough to play for England."
The doorman responded, "I'm sorry, Mr. Clough, but I don't seem to have been given notice that you were coming today."
"You wouldn't have been," said Clough, "Peter only decided two hours ago that we should come here." Taylor raised his eyebrows, familiar with Clough's way of doing things.
"I'll go and find out if it's okay," the doorman said but Clough and Taylor brushed past him anyway.
"That's fine, young man. We'll go to the boardroom. I know where it is. I was here for a few weeks, not that long ago, actually," said Clough.
They made their way up to the Boardroom which was empty except for a barman stationed behind the bar.
"Two complimentary Scotches please. We're the England management."
"Ah, Mr. Clough and Mr. Taylor. Good to have you here. And, may I say, I'm glad you were given the England job. Although I work here on match days I never was a Revie fan.

"Mr. Revie to you, young man. But call us Brian and Peter."
"Make mine a double," said Taylor.
"That's a good idea Peter," said Clough. "Make mine a double too."
The chairman of Leeds United, Manny Cussins, the man who had appointed Clough to his ill-fated forty four days in charge of the Yorkshire club, entered.
"Brian, Peter, good to see you. If we'd known you were coming we'd have invited you to lunch. It's all gone now but we can send out for some sandwiches for you."
"That would be excellent," suggested Taylor. "I'll have chicken."
"Chicken's good," agreed Clough.
"Fine. The young man here will organise that for you. Haven't you got a game today?"
"Jimmy's in charge," said Clough.
"Excellent chap,' said Cussins. "I take it you've come to run your eye over our lads for England and, of course, for the semi-final. International representation is always an honour. And, do please come and join us in the Directors' Box to watch the game, won't you? You're always welcome. You know that." Cussins left the bar to go to his seat.
"Another Scotch please," said Taylor.
"That's a good idea Peter. Another for me too, please."
The barman also had an idea. "It's not long to kick-off. Do you want me to bring the sandwiches to you while you watch the match?"
"That won't be necessary," said Taylor. "We'll have them in here where it's warm. Double Scotch please."
"Go on then, why not?"
"Now then," Taylor said to the barman, "who do you reckon is the best Leeds player?"

"What, now or ever?"
"Both."
"Well, there was John Charles who is a legend round here."
"You're absolutely right," confirmed Taylor. "Another Scotch please."
"I'll go along with that," said Clough. "And I agree about John Charles, too. He tried to warn us about those cheating Juventus bastards when we were in the European Cup with Derby. We could have won it if it hadn't been for the shenanigans going on."
"John Charles saw Helmut Haller go into the referee's room twice before the kick-off and warned me," explained Taylor.
"We were good enough. We had the players. We had self-belief. We'd have been worthy champions," moaned Clough.
"We're going to keep Trevor Cherry in the squad. For now."
"That's good. He's a nice bloke," said the barman.
"Oh dear. That might not be any good for our defence. Ah, here's the sandwiches. Excellent," said Clough.
"They look delicious. Just need a small glass of red."
"To wash them down," advised Clough, as he and Taylor began to devour the sandwiches.
"What about you, Brian? Who's your favourite Leeds players?" asked the barman.
"Without a doubt, Giles and Bremner. Both brilliant. Class acts. But I wasn't here long enough to get them to play to the best of their ability. Never mind. It was a good pay day."
"Another Scotch, then we'll be on our way," said Taylor.
"Aren't you going to stay for the match?" asked the barman.
"No," said Clough. "We've got things to do. But do pass on our best wishes to the board. And tell them we'll see them for

the semi-final. Better get some more Scotch in to be on the safe side."

In unison Clough and Taylor drank their Scotches and left.

The game at the City Ground between Nottingham Forest and Wolverhampton Wanderers, with Jimmy Gordon in charge of the home team, had ended in a 2-0 win with goals from McGovern and Woodcock.

This allowed the Nottingham team to tick over nicely and set up a welcome return for the management to Elland Road for the first leg of the League Cup semi-final.

On a night of very little whisky, the visitors had carved out a 3-1 win with two goals by Peter Withe and one from John O'Hare. Barring a meltdown of catastrophic proportions, Forest had all but booked their place at Wembley in the League Cup Final.

The Leeds fans had started up a chant of 'Brian Clough and Peter Taylor', something that had been heard around all the nation's football grounds that Forest visited, ever since the newspaper polls had asked fans who they wanted to be in charge of the England team.

Cynics might say that those fans just wanted the best manager out of the way of their team, but there were a great many genuine football fans who wanted the best team to represent their country and, of course, that team would be picked by the best manager.

Football fans mostly fell into the type of person who would get very upset at their own team's disappointments but, such was their enthusiasm, could live with the highs and lows. Even though local derby bragging rights might be lost for a year, for example in Manchester or Liverpool or North London, your team was always the best, to be cheered through thick and thin. With England it was different. A defeat for the national team was a national disaster, shared and felt by fans of all clubs.

Back on the team bus as the coach pulled out of the Elland Road car park, Clough stood up and addressed the triumphant players. "Well done lads," he said. "That was a very good, workmanlike victory against a good team."
The Forest players nodded to each other, pleased with their efforts and the outcome. Clough continued. "But if any of you think you've got yourself a place in the final, you'd better start thinking again. I've got my eye on all of you and if I spot one flicker of daydreaming, I'll kick you up the arse so hard you won't sit down for a week. Withe, call yourself a centre forward? You scored two but I'll tell you what, if I'd been playing I have scored at least four with the chances you had. For missing the target that many times you should be shot. I'm pleased you got one John, and it was well taken too, but I'm mostly pleased because if I'd had anybody else fit you wouldn't have been playing anyway. Now, enjoy the rest of the journey home."

He sat down next to Peter Taylor and said, "I suppose we'd better start thinking about the England team. Who've we got? Shilton's a given. Why Greenwood couldn't decide I don't know. Shilton is head and shoulders above Clemence in every aspect of goalkeeping. It was the biggest insult to Shilton to alternate between the two."

"I know. I told you that," said Taylor.

"How can a football manager not choose between two players?" Clough continued. "Now, right back, Phil Neal or Mick Mills. Mills can play on the right or the left. Or there's Trevor Cherry."

Taylor said, "Neal's too set in his ways. Get Anderson in. We know he'll do as he's told. Cherry can cover centre or right back. Mills is a left back. What about Kenny Sansom?"

"I don't know anything about him."

"Young lad. Steady."

"Is that it?"

"All right, he's come through the youth team as captain at Crystal Palace, captained England Youth too. He's quick, calm, strong in the tackle and an excellent crosser of the ball."

"Bloody hell."

"He's a good lad. I think he likes a drink. Won't let you down though. Keeps himself fit."

"Not as good as Ray Wilson."

"No, you're right. He's not as good as Ray Wilson." Taylor paused. "Ray Wilson's 43."

"What about Trevor Brooking?"

"Stylish, clever, but won't win us battles. Typical West Ham."

"Floats like a butterfly," said Clough, pausing for effect, "and stings like one too."

"I told you that, too"

"Thompson?"

"He's all right alongside Watson but Watson isn't as big a thug as Lloyd."

"Anderson, Lloyd and Burns would be ideal. Our Frank's too old for left back so we'll stick with the Sansom idea."

"Brilliant," said Taylor, "except Burns is Scottish."

"I was kidding. So, Lloyd or Watson?

"Thompson's a player. Plays the ball out the back well. I'd put Lloyd alongside. Lloyd's evil. Lost his place to Thompson at Liverpool so he'll want to show who's best."

"Coppell I like. Fast, works hard. Gets his crosses in. Who else we got? What about Hoddle?"

"Two footed. Very, very skilful. Needs to be allowed to play, though. Can score goals, open or set piece. McDermott's good, but mostly a runner. Useful to have. Scores great goals."

"Can Hoddle play on the left?"

"Yeah. But he has odd ideas. He's besotted with his own image. If he was an ice cream, he'd lick himself."

"We can knock that shit out of him. Sounds good. If we get Wilkins to start playing the ball forward, we'll make him captain."

"Yes, captain material."

"Captain Material? He's not a bloody superhero."

"Keegan's captain."

"I don't give a shit. Wants the limelight. Always at the front when there's a camera about, have you noticed? Wilkins captain. Who've we got up front?"

"Johnson ...swift, Mariner...not a bad target, good header. Same Latchford. Kennedy, clever up front but I reckon he sees more from midfield. Keegan, of course. Woodcock, Withe, Trevor Francis, blistering speed. Peter Barnes, sometimes a bit wishy-washy, Laurie Cunningham, potential.

"We've about got a squad," Clough said as the two football men continued to bandy names about.

The next morning Viv Anderson knocked on Brian Clough's office door. He had been told before the morning's training session had started that he was to shower quickly afterwards and make his way straight there. Anderson had asked Jimmy Gordon what was going on but Gordon had assured him that he didn't think anything bad was in the offing.
"I can't think I've done anything wrong,' said Anderson, "so it can't be a fine."
Brian Clough called out to Anderson to come in and he was met by Clough and Taylor sat behind Clough's desk.
"Sit down," said Clough indicating the single chair placed as if he was about to be interviewed for a job. Anderson had noticed there was no envelope on Clough's desk which was a good sign, but not necessarily certain, that there wasn't to be a fine.
"What did I tell you to do when that Carlisle player called you a black bastard a while back?" asked Clough.
"You told me to call him a white bastard."
"And what did you do?"
"I called him a white bastard."
"And what happened?"
"Nothing. He didn't say it again."
"Good. Well, that kind of stuff is going to get worse for you because you are going to be the first black player to play for the full England team."
Anderson broke into a huge smile but didn't say anything. He felt like he wanted to jump up and go and tell his team mates but he knew it was right to wait until he was dismissed properly before he could shout his good news to the rest of the world.

"And I'll tell you this," said Clough, "you breathe a word of this to anybody, and I mean anybody, you won't get picked and you'll look like a lying twat. Now think on. And if I see you pulling out of any tackles, or doing anything that pisses me off, you'll be in trouble. Now, off you go."

Anderson jumped up. "Thank you Mr. Clough. Thank you Mr. Taylor, thank you," he said and he left the room barely able to suppress a smile.

However, he knew full well that if he told anybody, even his own family, Clough would find out somehow, he always did, and his dream of international honours would be ruined.

Taylor turned to Clough, "He's a good lad," said Taylor.

"Top class," said Clough. "Let's come down hard on him for the next few days. If he so much as farts, I want him fined. I'll get Linda on the phone to arrange for us to announce the squad for the trip to Germany."

"Are we going to London?" asked Taylor.

"Not bloody likely," said Clough. "We'll have it at the Blue Boar. It really pisses off those press lads from London to have to come up here. Bollocks to them."

Taylor got up to leave. "I'm off back to my office. When you've finished talking to Linda, ask her to ring me on my number."

Taylor left Clough's office and returned to his own. He sat there for a few minutes before his own phone rang and he answered.

"Hello, Linda. How are you?" he asked. "Good. Now, it's about this list of people you sent me that had visited Harold Thompson. Tim Cox. Find out what you can about him and I'll see you at the Blue Boar when we announce the England squad."

Taylor went back into Clough's office and suggested that since Forest were due to play Queens Park Rangers down in London in the FA Cup the weekend before the semi-final with Leeds, they could stay over, take the Forest lads to a show or something and tie it in with the announcement of the England squad at the FA headquarters at Lancaster Gate.

"Is Sinatra playing in London?" Clough asked.

"No, I don't think so," said Taylor.

"Then we'll go to the Blue Boar as planned," said Clough. "I like their full English breakfasts."

***

A few days later, the national press arrived at the Blue Boar, eagerly anticipating the announcement of Clough and Taylor's first England squad. They were only kept waiting a minute or so while Clough helped himself to an extra Lincolnshire sausage which he ate as he approached the table that had been set out for himself, Peter Taylor and Linda. As Clough sat down, a hush fell upon the room.

Linda spoke first. "Morning gentlemen," she said. "Peter will give you the provisional squad and then Brian will answer a few questions."

"But not many because I'm a busy man," said Clough. "I've got to get back home to see to me house plants. Peter, go on."

Peter Taylor began to read in, a monotone, from a sheet of paper in front of him. The reporters read the same from sheets of paper that they had just been handed. "Anderson, Barnes,

Bowles, Brooking, Cherry, Clemence, Coppell, Cunningham, Currie, Francis, Johnson, Keegan, Kennedy, Lloyd, Mariner, McDermott, Mills, Neal, Sansom, Shilton, Thompson, Watson, Wilkins, Withe, Woodcock."

A seasoned football reporter began the questioning. "Did the squad selection give you any headaches?"
Peter Taylor responded. "I don't get headaches as a general rule but there was one problem."
"What was that?" the reporter asked.
"We weren't sure whether McDermott should come before Mariner," said Taylor. "In the end we decided not to do it like the phone book because there isn't actually a letter 'a' in McDermott. So Mariner came first. You see, it's not MacDermott it's McDermott."
"So it's just alphabetical."
"Tricky, isn't it?"
Another reporter started, "Mr. Clough, this might be a difficult quest…"
Clough cut him off abruptly. "Young man, if this is about football, you can't ask me a difficult question."
"Sorry, um, you've picked Bowles in the squad. He's never featured much before. Why did you pick him?"
"First of all, his name is Stanley Bowles. He's a very good, very talented footballer. I've heard he can also be an idiot, but I'll be the judge of that. When he's on England duty you won't see him being an idiot. If he, or anybody, does anything wrong when he's with me, he'll be out of my squad immediately."
"Is the reason you gave out the squad in alphabetical order to prevent us from guessing your first choice team?"

"You'll try to guess anyway," continued Clough. "But the real reason we gave out the squad names in alphabetical order was to make it easier for the players to see if they're in it. Footballers aren't that bright you know, and I include myself in that assessment."

"Shilton or Clemence?"

Peter Taylor responded, "Anderson or Neal."

"What do you mean?" asked a reporter.

"Oh, I thought it was a word game," said Taylor.

The first reporter came back into play. "There's a rumour you are taking the squad to Wembley to train before flying out to Germany. Is that true?"

"No," said Peter Taylor.

"No, it's not true?"

"No, it's not a rumour."

"You say it's a provisional squad but this is supposed to be the announcement of the actual squad to the press. Why is that?"

Clough broke in. "It's provisional because I'm not sure whether to leave the Forest lads out. We have a League Cup semi-final second leg against Leeds that night. I might keep my lads back. I haven't decided yet but if I do leave them out I'll have to get somebody else. So it's provisional. There you are gentlemen. Off you go and make something up. Now, you will excuse us. We've both got dogs and neither have had a good, long walk while Peter and I have been carting round the countryside watching football games."

After a brief pause, Linda spoke again. "Thank you once again for coming, gentlemen. The squad will assemble at the Hendon Hotel on the Sunday night before the game. There will be a training session on Monday morning and Monday afternoon and the squad will fly out on Tuesday morning. If you need any further information you can get me at Lancaster Gate. My phone number's on the press release you've been given."

***

On the way back to the City Ground, Clough pulled his Mercedes into the car park of the Nag's Head, a large pub near a roundabout on the edge of Nottingham.
"I've always liked the look of this place," said Clough, "I just never had the chance to pull in here before."
The two football men entered the lounge bar. It was empty except for an old gentleman in the corner with half a bitter in front of him as he read the ***Sporting Life***.
Clough approached the barman who was replacing an optic.
"Two Scotches, young man, please, with just the slightest hint of water in one of them. Thank you," said Clough.
Taylor spotted the man with the racing paper and asked him if he had any tips. The old man looked up, shrugged and returned to studying the form. The barman placed the two drinks on the counter.
"You can put your own water in," he said, placing a small jug on the bar. "I'd like to give you those drinks myself but I have to account for every penny and I've no money on me."
"Then you'll have a drink with us," said Clough.
"I'm sorry, I'm not allowed to drink on duty," said the barman.
"You are now. Just the one won't harm you. If somebody comes, don't worry, I'll grab it," said Clough.

"Thanks Mr. Clough, Mr. Taylor," said the barman, clearly delighted. "Cheers. You're announcing the squad today, aren't you?"
"Just come from there," advised Peter Taylor.
"I take it Shilton and Clemence are in. Who will you pick?"
In unison, Clough and Taylor said, "Shilton."
"No doubt about it," expanded Clough.
"Got to be," confirmed Taylor. "He's the best by a mile."

Back at the City Ground Linda reminded Clough that she had rearranged the flight to Germany according to his instructions and that she had misinformed the press appropriately. She had left out important bits of information, a situation that had also allowed the FA hierarchy to remain in the dark.

When visiting Taylor's office afterwards, she was able to tell Peter Taylor that Tim Cox was a freelance journalist who had visited Sir Harold Thompson for a reason that was not noted in the visitors' book. She also said that Tim Cox was not a name that was on the accredited list of journalists who were allowed entry to England's press box.

Wembley Stadium was empty apart from Brian Clough, Peter Taylor and the England football squad who all stood in the centre circle.
Brian Clough spoke. "This is what it's all about gentlemen. Playing on this velvety surface in front of the best part of a hundred thousand fans. There's no better feeling. Some of you already know that. The ball rolls so true. Not all pitches are as well looked after as this, and I doubt whether you will have

this luxury on Wednesday in Germany. Wembley is renowned for its perfect surface. Get down and kiss the turf. It's your friend."

Anderson, Lloyd, Shilton, Withe and Woodcock immediately got down on their hands and knees.

Stan Bowles had other ideas. "I'm not kissing any fucking grass," he said.

Clough turned to Peter Taylor. "Peter, you better go and telephone one of the replacements. Mr. Bowles is injured."

"I'm not injured," said Bowles.

Clough moved menacingly towards Bowles, his fist clenched. "You will be," said Clough. Bowles dropped down immediately. "And while you're down there, you'd better kiss the grass or you won't be getting another fucking chance to play for your country."

The rest of the England squad dived to the sacred Wembley turf and began to kiss the grass.

***

The England team bus arrived outside Terminal Two at Heathrow Airport and, as it came to a halt, Brian Clough stood up and faced his players. He spoke in a sombre tone.

"Gentlemen, you may have wondered why I have brought you here three hours before we are due to fly to Germany. Well, you see, you will spend the time mingling with the other travellers. And if anyone asks for your autograph, because they think you are important, then you'll sign for them. And you'll spend time and have a chat with them because they pay your wages week in week out. And don't talk about your bloody selves. Now, Linda, bring your Mam and Dad and sister, you're coming for a drink with me." He led his party to the nearest bar.

Len Shackleton, his wife and an assortment of Derby County and Nottingham Forest supporters were already at the bar.
"Ah, Leonard, Mrs. Shackleton what can I get you?" asked Clough.
"We're all right, Brian. Just got one in," said Shackleton.
"Are these the lads you brought from Derby and Nottingham?" asked Clough.

The Derby and Forest supporters gathered round Clough upon his arrival, as if he was some kind of messiah and they were his disciples.
'Who is the greatest in the kingdom of heaven?' they seemed to be wondering. For a moment, their imaginations were running riot. They expected the messiah to call one of the youngest of the supporters towards him and have him stand in front of them.
Surely he would say, 'I tell you the truth, unless you change and become like little children, you will never enter the kingdom of heaven. Therefore, whoever humbles himself like this child is the greatest in the kingdom of heaven. And whoever welcomes a little child like this in my name welcomes me.
But if anyone causes one of these little ones who believe in me to sin, it would be better for him to have a large millstone hung around his neck and to be drowned in the depths of the sea. Woe to the world because of the things that cause people to sin! Such things must come, but woe to the man through whom they come! If your hand or your foot causes you to sin, cut it

off and throw it away. It is better for you to enter life maimed or crippled than to have two hands or two feet and be thrown into eternal fire. And if your eye causes you to sin, gouge it out and throw it away. It is better for you to enter life with one eye than to have two eyes and be thrown into the fire of hell.'
Except Clough didn't say anything of the sort.

"Yes," said Shackleton. "There's a couple of lasses among 'em somewhere."
Brian Clough spake. "Ladies and gentlemen. Glad you could join us as ambassadors of the Football Association. Now, I will not tolerate hooliganism, and there will be some idiots who will go to Germany just to cause trouble. But we'll not be part of that will we?"
The supporters all answered together. "No, Brian."
"Well, just to make sure there's not a couple of cloth heads among you, I'm putting these young ladies in charge. And you have strict instructions to tell me if any of these so much as blows their nose without your permission," he said to the ladies.
"Yes, Brian," said the disciples. They began raucously chanting, "Brian Clough's England Army."
"Now, please," Clough broke in. "Think about it. We're going to Germany. I don't think that's at all appropriate, do you?"

***

A day later Professor Sir Harold Thompson, various Football Association committee members, and their families, arrived at

a first class check in desk at Heathrow airport for the trip to Germany.
Thompson looked angrily at the young lady clerk at the desk. "What do you mean the Football Association's charter flight left yesterday?" he snapped.
She responded authoritatively. "Yes, it was moved forward a day. It was definitely authorised by your office."
Sir Harold Thompson turned to his assembled committee members and their families and said, "Brian Clough is a bastard."

***

On the match day, the England team bus was slowly making its way through the crowd near to the Olympic stadium in Munich. Clough stood up to speak to his players. He had been reading from a pamphlet he had picked up from the front of the bus. "Get a good look at this stadium, lads. The design, with large sweeping canopies of acrylic glass stabilised by steel cables, was to imitate the Alps. Does it bollocks! It was built for the 1972 Olympics and was to symbolise the new, democratic, optimistic Germany reflected in the official motto 'The Happy Games'. They were really happy games. Those terrorists shot all those Israeli athletes. The best thing about this stadium is that it was built in a pit made by our bombs in the Second World War."
German fans started banging on the side of the bus and chanting. Clough was only momentarily startled.
"Driver. Stop this bus," he shouted. "Stand up gentlemen. Get your stuff we're walking to the stadium."
Without stopping to think, everyone got off the bus and started to walk through the astonished crowd.

A young German punk rocker, with an outrageous, spiky hairstyle bellowed in Clough's face. Clough grabbed him by the hand.

"Now then, young man," he said. "I don't know what you're saying because you're not speaking English. More's the pity. But whatever you're saying sounds very interesting, so you can walk to the stadium with me, hand in hand, and we'll see if you have anything else interesting to say."

The punk rocker attempted to escape Clough's grasp but failed because Clough had him in such a vice that his knuckles had gone white.

"You might as well enjoy the walk young man because you're going nowhere without me."

***

In the bowels of the Olympic Stadium, the England players were ready to go out to play Germany but the missing ingredient in the whole mixture was the England team manager. Players were in various stages of preparation, some doing warming up exercises, some going to have the tenth pee in as many minutes, some tying and retying their bootlaces, some having rub downs.

England's physio was a Londoner called Fred Street who had started in the job for Don Revie and this credential had prompted Clough to interview him with a view to keeping him in the role.

"I'll tell you about you," Clough told him, "because I've asked a few questions here and there. Frankly, I'd prefer Jimmy

Gordon but I need him at Forest and he's Scottish which doesn't help."

Clough then began to tell Fred Street what Fred knew anyway, but probably not as well as Clough did.

Street had been a Physical Training Instructor in the Royal Air Force and, as a patriotic serviceman, believed in the ethos of Queen and country. He believed in fair play and regarded teamwork as far more important that the individual. He was level headed, not swayed by opinion and was exactly the sort of person you'd want alongside you in the trenches. Without trenches, the England dressing room would have to do.
If you threw in the added, excellent, ingredients of old-fashioned English virtues of the stiff upper lip, integrity, loyalty and sportsmanship, you'd have the sort of man that Clough wanted in his team. Fred Street, despite having worked for Arsenal and been appointed by Don Revie, displayed the right qualities.

After the RAF he had trained as a chartered physiotherapist on the advice of his friend Bertie Mee who was later to be Arsenal's physio before being made manager. That's when Mee persuaded Street to join him at the Gunners. Except he was working for Stoke City at the time and Street, being the straight-as-a-die character that he was, refused to be poached unless everything was done properly and above board. Nothing devious or underhand at all.

So it was that Stoke City's physio was sold to Arsenal for five thousand pounds. When Revie became England manager he asked the Arsenal chairman, Dennis Hill-Wood, if he could borrow him for England games. Hill-Wood thought it was a tremendous honour, a bit like having a double-barrelled surname, and readily agreed.

Clough had asked Street what it was like working for Revie and he had replied that Revie was a great professional and a terrific bloke to work for. Clough informed Street that he was an even greater professional and an even more terrific bloke to work for. The excellence of the work side was expected.

Street had explained to Clough, when he was able to interrupt his own interview, that he was more fascinated by the players' different approaches to games than by the medical side of things. He could tell a player's quirks and sense their fears before a game. It was this that took Clough's greatest attention - someone that could instinctively understand a player's sense of humour, whether they needed a consoling arm around them, whether they needed a kick up the backside, whether they had courage and how they dealt with stress. This intrigued Clough. The difference between Clough and Street was that Clough worked on, and with, the players' foibles whereas Street knew it but just rubbed liniment into limbs or put strapping onto joints.

Street, having been with England a few years, knew the players at the top of the English tree who were likely to be picked for their country. He had an insider's knowledge. He knew which players would need to punch the dressing room wall shouting "Come on!" before going out to play and he knew which players would want to get a kip in the corner. He knew which players were thoughtful about the game and how its intricacies would develop, and who would just turn up and play. Those who would be irritating to others and want noise.

"What's Ray Wilkins like?" Clough asked Street, "when he gets injured during a game?"

"He tells you which bit is hurting him," said Street, and added, in order to explain, "because some of them don't even know which is the bit that's hurting them."

This had given Clough the idea to make Wilkins captain because he was the sort of player who could think while he was on the pitch.

What had impressed Clough most about Street was what Clough had said about him. His qualifications in the field of physiotherapy were fine and also he wasn't particularly a football fan. He should stay out of all that crap and not get involved in the histrionics of the game. Just deal with the players if they fall over.

Clough insisted that, as manager, he would be the one who dealt with all the emotions, Street could handle the technical side, treat the injuries. He would be allowed to encourage and give them support but all the loose cannon stuff was Clough's domain.

Hardly anyone had said anything until Kevin Keegan broke the silence. "Where's Mr. Clough?" he said to nobody in particular.

"He'll be here in a minute," said Peter Shilton, who continued to stretch his legs and arms by pressing them against the dressing room wall.

There was a long pause before Brian Clough entered and threw the captain's armband at Ray Wilkins.

"Here you are Raymond. Enjoy it," he said.

There were a few shocked looks on the faces of the players, especially Kevin Keegan since he had not long been made captain after Emlyn Hughes had been discarded.

Ray Wilkins looked embarrassed, but proud in equal measure, and had the good grace to look at Keegan and shrug his shoulders in a knowing, apologetic manner.

Clough spotted a Football Association official stood in the corner of the dressing room.

"Who the hell are you?" he asked with more than a hint of annoyance in his voice.

Fred Street explained that he was an FA employee who always travelled a few days ahead of the team on foreign visits and liaised with the host football association as the official representative.

Clough eyed him warily for no more than half a second. "You don't belong in my dressing room. Now fuck off."

The FA official left the dressing room hastily and without looking back.

"How do you want us to play? Tactically?" asked Keegan, concealing his hurt, though maintaining his team ethic and willingness to do his best for his country.

"Tactics!" scoffed Clough. "You're international footballers. You're playing against Germany. Now get out of here and play for England. Tactics. Bollocks."

As the players were kicking in, Clough called Anderson over. "Now, young man, you're the first black man to be picked for the full England team. How to you feel about that?"

"I'm very proud."

"Good lad. So you should be. And what if one of their players calls you a black bastard?"

"I call him a white bastard."

"No you don't. You kick the bastard into the stand. This is international football."

Clough made his way to the dugout after the teams had been presented to the dignitaries and lined up.

Phil Thompson turned to his central defence partner, Larry Lloyd, and asked, "What's the difference between how you go about things at Forest and how we do things at Liverpool?"

"I haven't got a clue," said Lloyd. "You know me, I know my football, and I know how I want it to be played. Sometimes I have an idea, and I think I'll put the idea forward when I get in to training but when I get there Clough or Taylor, or both, I don't know, has already decided to do it. Or we get told to run through some fucking nettles or something."
"What?" screeched Thompson.
The referee blew the whistle for the start of the match.
"I'll go for the high balls. You tidy up," said Lloyd.

After an uneventful first half the England team returned to the dressing room fearing the worst from the tongue of Brian Clough. They had gone a goal down to their hosts and they sat down, dejected. Brian Clough entered breezily.
"That player who scored against you, his name is Worm. Worm! What kind of a name is that? Ray, don't do anything but play the ball forward. You shouldn't even have to look up. You know where your forwards should be. If there's nobody there, that's their fault and I'll deal with that. Is Woodcock listening? Kevin, you are our only class act up front tonight. You deserved three. If you don't score tonight, I'll strangle me grandmother. I mean it."
Clough looked round at the still dejected faces.
"What's up with you lot? Get a grip of yourselves. This game is there for the taking. We're going away from here with a win, don't worry about that. Lloyd, Thompson, spot on. Get the ball to Coppell. He knows what to do with it. Anderson, what are you going to do when you get the ball?"
"Give it to Steve," said Viv Anderson.
"Good lad," said Clough. "That's the ticket. Now, let's go and win a game of football. I've told you, they shot me Dad. Have a thought for me grandmother, too. Bless her. Off you go. First

round's on me afterwards. Worm! Comical that, isn't it? Well, it would be except you let him score against you."

The team left the changing room noticeably happier, Anderson and Coppell deep in conversation as they went to line up for the second half.

The game, from England's point of view, increased in tempo and there was a constant movement of the ball out to the right wing from the midfield and forward from Anderson at right back.

If it was difficult for Wilkins, who patrolled the centre of midfield, to get the ball out to the wing, by virtue of the German midfield pressing, he would thread it through the channels to the inside right or inside left positions.

Clough was right. There was no need for him to look up in those harassed moments because Keegan and Woodcock made themselves available at every opportunity.

One such build up saw Wilkins play a beautiful cross field ball to Coppell who used his speed to go past the German full back and put the ball in to the near post. Keegan was hurtling in and got his head to it. As he fell to the turf he watched as the ball looped over the German keeper to draw England level.

Further sustained pressure by the England team in the second half saw them gain control, and their reward came when Woodcock was on hand to stab in the rebound from a long range Wilkins piledriver.

After that, the England team kept the ball, restricting the Germans to one half chance and, as the final whistle blew, they shook hands with their opponents and left the field with a more confident step than they'd had at half time.

The team entered the changing room after the game followed by Brian Clough. "That was a tremendous victory, gentlemen," he said. "We beat the Germans on their own patch. Not for the first time, mind you. Shilton, you won us the game."
"Thanks, gaffer," said Shilton.
"Don't let it go to your head, young man, because you had Lloyd and Thompson stopping everything coming at you in the second half. You only had one save to make but that's why I picked you. And you cocked up on their goal anyway."
"Yes, gaffer," said Shilton.
Clough continued. "Raymond, you passed the ball forward. Good lad. Get it to the front lads. They'll stick it in the back of the net for you. Sometimes, it was all very pretty and silky but your job is to get it to Coppell. He's a far better player than you might think. I don't care what you do as long as the ball ends up with Coppell. Got it? All right, well done lads, now get showered and let's get back to the hotel. I don't trust these Germans."

Clough left the dressing room and went to the room designated for the after match interviews.
"Good evening gentlemen," he started. "What can I do for you?"
An English reporter opened the inquest. "How satisfying was that performance, Mr. Clough?
"It was a win," said Clough. A win away from home is always good. The overall performance was so-so. Keegan and Woodcock, brilliant. If Trevor Francis could learn from these two lads, we might have a decent chance in front of goal."
A second reporter asked, "Who was your man of the match?"

"Their central midfielder," explained Clough. " Can't pronounce his name. Beautiful player. Lovely through balls. Made our captain look like a novice."

The same reporter attempted to clarify his question. "I'm sorry, I meant man of the match for England."

Clough scowled. "We didn't have one," he snapped.

"Why did you make Wilkins captain instead of Keegan?"

Another scowl came from Clough. "Their names are Raymond Wilkins and Kevin Keegan. And why I made Raymond captain instead of Kevin is nothing to do with you."

"I just thought it would be in the public interest," continued the reporter.

"Well it isn't," snapped Clough. "The public want to see a winning team. They're not interested in who's in the team as long as it's winning. We won tonight so the public should be happy. We beat the Germans on their own soil. They're one of the best teams in the world. Did you know that?"

"Yes, I agree," said the reporter.

Clough warmed to his theme. "Then you go along to any bar in Munich tonight where there's an England football fan and you'll see a happy person. Thank you, gentlemen. It's been a pleasure."

Back at the hotel, the England team strolled into the bar. "Come on, get yourselves a drink lads," said Clough. "I always keep a promise. The first one's on me."

Kenny Sansom sidled up to Clough and said in subdued tones, "I've twisted my ankle a bit. I think I'd better let Fred have a look at it."

"No you haven't," said Clough. "Sit down there. I'll bring you a pint." He shouted over to Linda and her family. " Linda, get yourselves a drink and bring you Mam and Dad and sister over here with Mr. Sansom. He's feeling a bit poorly."

Kevin Keegan had left the bar and went back out to the hotel foyer where he picked up the pay phone and dialled a number. After a few seconds he spoke. "Hello love. Did you watch it? He took the captaincy away from me."

There was a pause as Keegan's wife, on the other end of the line spoke. Keegan continued in an increasingly incredulous tone. "He said what? Did he? He did what? You're joking. Bloody hell."

After saying goodbye to his wife, Keegan made his way back to the bar and joined Peter Shilton. "Hey, Shilts, I just phoned our Jean. She said a bouquet of flowers arrived from Cloughie at half time for her."

"That means he thinks you're ok," explained Shilton.

"He took the captaincy off me," moaned Keegan.

"He'll have had a reason. You'll get it back. That's his way of telling you he's in charge. Don't say anything about it and I bet you a tenner you get it back."

Ray Wilkins came up. "Well done lads," he said." Cracking save Shilts. And a well taken goal, Kev. I think we just about deserved it in the end."

"Nothing against you, Ray," said Keegan, " but Shilts just bet me a tenner that Clough makes me captain for next game. He knows him better than us."

"I never said the next game," said Shilton. "What makes you think that either of you will be in the squad for the next game? Or me, for that matter. It doesn't work like that."

Keegan and Wilkins, confused, looked at Shilton and decided it was best to take his word for it.

The aeroplane carrying the England party had landed back at Heathrow and taxied to the gate before Clough spoke again to the assembled players.

"I didn't want to mention this until we got back but its twenty years this month that the Busby Babes were in that plane crash at Munich. You lads are lucky. You are here to ply your trade. And if you don't make the most of what you've got, you are idiots. One of the players who died in that plane crash was a lad called Duncan Edwards. Now there was some player. He had everything. He had strength, character, it just oozed out of him on the field. If he had lived he might have proved himself the greatest player ever. Maybe. Better than Pele, Best, Law, Charlton, Greaves, Charles, di Stefano, whoever, you name it. The thing is, he was better at every aspect of the game than anybody – heading, tackling, defending, attacking, whatever. Matthews and Finney, and they could play a bit, both said they'd never seen anything like it. If he'd have been a goalkeeper he'd probably have been better than Shilton and Clemence put together. Do you get my drift? Well, think on. Make the best of your talents. Now, there's a game against Brazil coming up in April at Wembley. We all want to play them, don't we? At Wembley. Get back to your clubs and bust a gut. Me and Taylor will be watching."

While Clough was saying that, back in England, Peter Taylor had been watching his Nottingham Forest team beat Leeds United 4-2 at the City Ground with two goals apiece by Bowyer and O'Neill. This meant they had confirmed a place in the League Cup Final in a month's time at Wembley. The opponents would be Liverpool.

In the meantime, league duties took over and a thrilling 3-3 draw away at Norwich was followed by the trip to Wembley for the 1978 League Cup Final. Clough still had a good feeling about this competition despite being underdogs.

Forest withstood plenty of pressure from the current league and European champions but forced a 0-0 draw that led them to a replay at Manchester United's Old Trafford.

Forest won with a John Robertson penalty and added a trophy to the cabinet to join the Anglos-Scottish Cup that had had plenty of polishing in the last year or so. The penalty decision was arguably harsh if you were from the Liverpool area but cast iron if you were from Nottingham.

Peter Shilton was cup-tied, having played for Stoke earlier in the season, so Clough had promoted the now 18-year-old Chris Woods to the team and he gave an outstanding display at Wembley to take the game to a reply.

Not only were Gemmill and Needham also ineligible but captain McGovern was injured, making way for John O'Hare.

In the replay four days later, Woods' heroics again kept the stars of Liverpool at bay and it was O'Hare, again in for McGovern, who was chasing a through ball from Woodcock when the controversial penalty decision took place.

In the corridor outside the changing rooms after the game, a TV interviewer asked Phil Thompson, the Liverpool defender, what had happened to make the referee award a penalty because it didn't seem clear cut.

"I had to pull him down," explained Thompson, referring to John O'Hare as he chased the ball through the middle. "Any professional would do it. I brought him down outside the box." As if a magic lamp had been rubbed, Peter Taylor appeared and was asked a pertinent question. "What about the penalty?" "Obvious penalty," snapped Taylor. "I think John would've stuck it in. No one's doubting it, surely."

The reporter wavered on the side of reason. "Well, on the replay it looked as though it was outside the box."

Peter Taylor, the fount of all knowledge and wisdom, was equal to this taunt. "No, definitely inside."

Rather fortuitously for the reporter, John Robertson, the scorer of the penalty, arrived.

"Let's have John in," said the reporter, invoking the rule of truth and witness. "Let's have his story of it. How close were you when the trip took place, John?"

"I was quite a bit away actually. Left hand side when Tony put it through. It looked to me if it was inside," said the Scottish truth merchant.

'What was John O'Hare's feelings about it?"

"He says it was certainly inside. Certainly," confirmed Robertson.

Peter Taylor looked slightly bemused by this questioning. "Your cameras will catch it, surely," he said, slapping the coup de grace on to the reporter.

"And I think they show it was outside," was the wholly unreasonable response.

"It also shows we've got the cup," responded Taylor.

And who couldn't vouchsafe that? For indeed the red and white ribbons of Nottingham Forest were tied around the 1978

League Cup. Nobody mentioned they could easily have been the red and white of Liverpool.

Forest, who had last lost a game the previous November, continued to dominate the league and looked down on the chasing pack but not with any particular worries.
They continued with home wins against Newcastle, Chelsea, Leeds and Queens Park Rangers and had managed to squeeze in away draws at Manchester City and Middlesbrough and a win against Aston Villa at Villa Park.
So it was all looking good as Forest sat astride the league table coming in to the final handful of games.

The next big game on the agenda for England was the visit of Brazil to Wembley in front of a full house. It was always a full house when and where Brazil travelled. This would be no different.
Although no longer World Champions, Brazil was always going to be ranked in the top teams. They were the Harlem Globe Trotters of the football world – everybody loved their exciting play. It didn't matter who were current World Champions, Brazil was always the bench mark. Clough entered the press meeting.
"Morning gentlemen, what can I do for you?"
"Morning, Mr. Clough. Will you be trying out any new players for the visit of Brazil and prior to the Home Championships next month?"
"Maybe not against Brazil. They're bloody good, you know. We'll have to be at our best to beat them. They're better than us, they're faster than us and they're more skilful than us. They kill the ball instantly when it comes to them. We'll be

lucky if we get a kick. They've won the World Cup three times, you know. It's because they've always got the sun on their backs. Makes you feel better. The secret is that they play on hot sand. Not like Skegness, or Blackpool or Redcar where it's wet and flat. Their sand is hot and dry and bumpy. So when the ball lands it squirts off in any direction and they have to learn to control it instantly. Brilliant technique."

"So you're not confident?"

"Oh, no. We'll win. But it's going to be just a wee bit more difficult than usual. We'll have to be careful, that's all. I might try some new players in the Home Championships because we'll win that anyway. That's only Ireland, Scotland and Wales for Christ's sake."

"That's not going to endear you to their supporters."

"I know. That's why I said it. Look I've got players, good players, from those countries at Forest. I say it to irritate them. It might make them play a bit better against us. Make it more of a challenge."

Another reporter intervened. "You've managed to keep Forest boiling even though you are only here with England part-time. How do you divide your time?"

Clough bridled. "First of all, young man, I don't do this job part-time. It's a doddle, I admit, but I give it as much thought as I give to Forest or tending my roses or walking the dog. Or making sure I remember to take some flowers home to Barbara. The Forest job's nearly finished anyway. We'll wrap that up next week, possibly away at Ipswich's lovely ground. And don't forget I have Peter Taylor working with me. If I didn't have him with me, I wouldn't be half as successful. I've said before, if I'm the shop window, he's the goods in the back. Never underestimate the importance of Peter Taylor to this set-up. He's absolutely essential."

Another reporter joined in. "Your first match in charge of England was a victory away to Germany. Your second match is against Brazil. It doesn't come much harder than that."

"You're right. But if we want to be the best team in the world, and we will be, then we'll have to beat the best teams in the world. After we've won the Home Championship, we'll begin qualification for the European Championships in 1980. But I haven't decided yet whether to stay on at Forest another season so that Peter and I can win the European Cup."

There was an audible gasp of astonishment.

"Will Forest let you do that? Will the FA?" asked an incredulous reporter.

"I'll not bother to answer that," said Clough. "And where's your tie?"

The new reporter to the gathering responded, "I'm sorry, I didn't know it was obligatory. It won't happen again."

"You're dead right," said Clough. "Gentlemen, somebody help him out."

A seasoned reporter pulled a tie from his pocket and handed it to the new guy.

"That's better. Now you are properly dressed," Clough advised.

In the England dressing room at Wembley, the team sat ready to go out but once again were minus their manager.

Suddenly, Clough burst in. "Gentlemen, I've just had a drink with Pele, the greatest footballer there ever was or ever will be.

Absolutely stunning. Nothing he couldn't do with a football. He could make it talk. If I rolled all of you together into one, you still wouldn't be a patch on him. And that includes you, Shilton. But, you know, what people often overlook is that Pele could look after himself. And that's what you've got to do tonight. Don't bother about anything fancy they might try. They're not Pele so just clatter into them. Lloyd, give 'em a snarl in the tunnel. They'll shit 'emselves. Now, Raymond, you're too much of a gentleman to be captain tonight so I'm giving the armband back to big head here."

Clough handed the armband to Keegan. "And don't think it's yours to keep," he reminded him.

Shilton looked at Keegan and suppressed a smile.

The game was a brutal affair with both Edinho and Ze Maria lucky not to be sent off, mostly because the referee, a Dutchman called Charles Corver, was basically inept that night.

Brazil did have Cerezo to display the traditional silky samba skills but he was played too far back to cause England any real headaches.

Though they had a few special moments, the only one that counted was from right winger Gil who accelerated, twisted, and smashed the ball home.

Indeed, if anyone had a flair-o-meter that night, England might have just edged it. A Keegan equaliser was the best they could manage.

Afterwards, in the dressing room, an in-depth investigation began as the England team filed in. Peter Taylor began it. "Well done lads. You deserved a draw. Deserved it," he said.

Clough came in soured faced. The players waited for him to don his black cap.

"Hey, if you hadn't let that bloke with a girl's name score against you, we'd have had that. What was the name? Gill. Raymond. You were brilliant. Good lad. Lloyd, you're a thug. Well played. But I saw you argue with the referee. I never, ever, want to see that again. From any of you. The referee's your friend. If we didn't have a referee we wouldn't have a game. Remember that, gentlemen."

"The ref was crap," whispered Keegan.

"No he wasn't," whispered Shilton. "Never."

Peter Taylor took off to the after-match press conference leaving Clough to pour himself a large Scotch and offer one to anyone else if they wanted it. Nobody took up the offer.

"What did you think about that?" asked the first reporter.

"About what?" responded Taylor.

The same reporter tried again. "About the game."

"I didn't know what you were talking about the game. Could have been anything. Could have been that horse I backed yesterday. That was useless. We weren't. We drew with Brazil. Could have won. Should have won."

Another reporter tried a different tack. "You kept the same line-up tonight as you did against Germany. Will it be your policy to keep a settled side?"

Peter Taylor stuck his tongue in the side of his cheek as he contemplated the enormity of the question.

"Of course. As much as possible. We pick the best players available. That's these eleven at the minute. Things could change. Instantly. Football's like that."

"So this eleven will start against Wales in the Home Championship next month," suggested a hack.

Peter Taylor seemed unsure. "I don't know that," he said.
Another reporter butted in. "But you just said you'd like to keep a settled side."

"I did. And we do," said Taylor. "But one of them might drop dead. I don't know that. You might drop dead. You look a bit pasty."

Clough and Taylor's insistence on keeping a settled side, if at all possible, was partly due to the fact that they trusted their players to do the jobs for which they were picked.

If the team was successful, the players wanted to play, and even wanted to play if they were struggling with a slight injury. Jimmy Gordon always knew what was going on with the players' bodies, and would tell Taylor, who knew what was going on in their minds.

This meant that injuries were kept to a minimum because any player who was injured but lied because he wanted to play would be found out. That would leave Clough, with regard to club football, no option but to pull the plug.

Playing an unfit player, even if it was a minor injury and, despite a game being of major importance, would exacerbate the injury and probably result in a longer, enforced lay off.

In other words, it was stupid. From England's point of view it was different but only slightly so. Basically, you still pick the eleven best players that fitted into the system you wanted to play.

With Derby, and now Forest, Clough and Taylor's teams were manned by an uncompromising defence, a diligent but creative midfield that included wide players who could get the ball

accurately into the penalty area where there would be forwards who weren't afraid to put the ball in the back of the net.
In essence, for England, Clough and Taylor had the pick of the best English players from all clubs. The best players available could be picked to play in the system that Clough and Taylor had found so successful. It seemed an easy problem to solve. What happened when Revie was in charge made Clough's blood boil – as indeed, most of what Revie did.
The facts speak for themselves. The England teams in the Revie era were as changeable as the English weather. During the period he was in office, Revie had to pick twenty-nine England teams.
The only time he ever chose and unchanged team was for the last game he was in charge.
Prior to that he had made seven changes to the team on five occasions, six changes on six occasions and five changes on four occasions. Hardly the stuff of a settled side.
With all those changes, the players must have wondered what was going on or even who was going to turn up.
Only three players managed more than twenty starts during Revie's reign – Kevin Keegan, Mick Channon and, in goal, Ray Clemence who, in Clough and Taylor's eyes, was not as good as Shilton.
Of the other games, only a couple of others notched up starting appearances into the teens, most notably Colin Todd and Gerry Francis.

An exasperated fourth reporter, more or less to change the subject, asked, "Do you think that Larry Lloyd was overly aggressive tonight?"
"No," Taylor said.

The reporter pressed on. "But he left their right winger about three rows up in the stands."

"I know," commented Taylor. "He got a bollocking for that. Shouldn't have been anywhere near the touchline. That was Sansom's fault. He got a bollocking too."

"What about Keegan's goal?" asked a reporter, homing in on the positive.

"It was well taken," said Taylor. "But that's his job. What else would I expect?"

Just then, Clough entered which gave the assembled reporters a lift. At least with him they could be guaranteed some copy, a quip, a snippet, or some insight on which to hang a story or fashion a headline. Anything would do.

The first reporter fired off, "Mr. Clough, what was your highlight of the night?"

Clough, nicely warmed against the chill night with his tot of Glenlivet, responded, "Nice tie. Well done, lad. My highlight of the night was meeting Pele in the hospitality bar before the game. Best player there ever was."

The reporter pressed home his advantage. "Anything about tonight's game you want to say?"

"No thanks," said the England manager. "I think Peter will have said it all. In fact, I'm not even thinking about tonight's game anymore. It's over. I'm thinking about taking my Forest team to Ipswich next week. We could win the title there on Bobby Robson's patch. That would be nice. If, in fact, we don't clinch it at Coventry on Saturday."

Jimmy Gordon had looked after the Forest team the night before England's Brazil game and a Robertson penalty brought a 1-0 home victory over Queens Park Rangers.

That win meant that only Everton and Liverpool could match Forest's 58 points, so one more point would bring the league title to the City Ground.

On the Saturday, Forest went to Coventry looking for that point and came home with it, due mostly to a phenomenal display by Peter Shilton in goal.

Forest's keeper had already produced a string of fine saves when he made a spectacular, almost miraculous, point blank save from the Sky Blues' centre forward Mick Ferguson's fearsome header.

"He was only doing his job," Clough said afterwards and Taylor quietly pointed out to Shilton that he had made saves like that, many times, on this very ground when he was playing for Coventry.

The visiting fans went wild, not for the first time that season, and Forest had clinched the most prestigious league title in the world just one season after having been promoted into it.

And by a huge seven point margin over their nearest rivals, the current League and European Champions Liverpool. It was the first time that the First Division title had been sown up so early in the season.

There were wild celebrations too, of course, in the Forest changing room and it was no surprise that Clough was able to crack open the champagne, although he drew a line at spraying it around as that would have been a terrible waste.

Although the league was now won, Forest had a proud unbeaten run to protect and did so with a win at Ipswich.

In an unfamiliar dressing room, painted predominantly in blue and white, the Nottingham Forest players were readying themselves for the game.

Brian Clough entered the changing room carrying a crate of beer. "Right lads, there's plenty for everyone," he said. "Get stuck in. We've only half an hour before kick-off. Come on."

"I'm all right, gaffer," said Archie Gemmill.

"No you're not. Get a drink," said Clough.

"I'd rather not," protested Gemmill.

"I don't give a shit what you'd rather or rather not do. Get a beer," ordered Clough.

Larry Lloyd chipped in. "If he doesn't want a beer, he doesn't want one."

"Who the fuck asked you to stick your nose in? If Kenny Burns wasn't the ugliest footballer in the world, it would have to be you, Lloyd. Now get a beer."

Lloyd continued. "Do you know, if you walked into a pub I was drinking in, I'd walk out."

"Aye," said Clough, "and it wouldn't bother me one bit."

The players did as they were told but those that were seen putting the beer to their lips were going through the motions and not drinking at all. When it was safe to do so, Jimmy Gordon was tipping some of the beer into the sink, or others were taking theirs to the toilet with them and disposing of it that way.

An uneventful first forty five minutes saw both teams have half chances before the Forest team returned to the dressing room for a pep talk.

It went along the same lines as the start of the game. As the Forest players entered, they noticed there were plastic cups laid out on a table.

Gemmill, who had run tirelessly throughout, as usual, was the first to take one and dash the drink straight down. He gasped and spluttered violently.

"Frigging hell," was all he could manage.

Clough explained. "Just a little vodka and orange to calm the nerves."

Martin O'Neill made an observation after he had tasted a sample. "There's not much orange."

Peter Taylor became a voice of reason. "McGovern, get a grip of these lads and don't let them off the hook for one minute. The season isn't over."

The players did as they were told because a 2-0 victory was sealed in somewhat unlikely circumstances.

Left back Frank Clark, who had come on as a substitute, scored not only his first goal of the season, but also his first in around five hundred league games. The away team's advantage was doubled when the Ipswich centre forward, Mariner, back trying to help his own defence, put through his own net.

Bobby Robson, the Ipswich manager, had the good grace to visit the opposition dressing room, amid the celebrations, and wished Clough, Taylor and the Forest players his heartfelt and sincere best wishes.

In amongst all the commotion, Archie Gemmill sidled up to Brian Clough and Peter Taylor.

"Well played, wee man," said Taylor. "Feels good to be a champion again, doesn't it?"

The balding Scotsman, the architect of so many of Forest's goals during the season, had had an idea which he now offloaded to the management. "Aye, it does," he said. "I was thinking, gaffer. Now that we've won the league, I was thinking that maybe I deserve some more money."

Clough snapped, "You're not getting a penny more."

"I'm not happy," said Gemmill.

"Which bloody dwarf are you then?" said Clough, which effectively ended the salary negotiations.

Following the capture of the league trophy, there followed three final games of the season which turned out to be draws. A dull 0-0 at home to Birmingham City was brightened by the players showing off the league trophy to their fans, followed by two away games. The first was a 2-2 at West Bromwich Albion where Robertson took his season's tally to twelve, a penalty, which made him joint top scorer with Withe, and one from the ever reliable Bowyer. It was perhaps fitting that Forest's last game of the season was away to Liverpool where they once again proved the Merseysider's bogey team, escaping with another goalless draw at the Anfield fortress.

It had been another routine day at newly crowned First Division champions Nottingham Forest.
They had spent most of the morning kicking a ball about in a practice game and being bellowed at by Brian Clough whose propensity for vicious verbal attack wasn't directed at anyone in particular even though it was taken as a personal insult by each of the players individually. It was a special knack that he had.
Whenever he was around, the players paid more attention to what they were doing. It wasn't that they showed less respect for Peter Taylor or Jimmy Gordon, it's just that they knew that with Taylor and Gordon there was an element of leeway if a mistake was made.
It was different with Clough. It was as if he thought that if you scored an own goal, even if it was in training, it was your fault, and possibly deliberate too.

With Taylor and Gordon, an own goal would be regarded exactly for what it was. A genuine mistake. Nobody would set out, after all, to score a deliberate own goal.

But despite Clough's reputation for vitriol, the players knew that their medals were as much, if not more, down to him as their efforts themselves.

To a man, they would have run through a brick wall for the man. It was utterly inexplicable.

The Forest players strolled off the training ground and entered the changing rooms followed by Clough and Taylor. There was none of the usual dressing room banter. The players sensed something was up.

"Gentlemen, we've come to a decision," said Clough.

The players became silent. This was serious.

"Peter and I have had a chat and we've decided not to be with you for the league campaign next season."

There were looks of disappointment and astonishment, and groans of disbelief in equal measure..

"But what we've decided to do is win the European Cup with you," Clough said in an upbeat manner.

There were confused looks on the faces of the players.

"We should have won it with Derby," continued Clough, "but that bastard of a referee cheated us out of it. Everybody knows that. So they won't dare give us bent referees again. Anyway, we've decided to win it with you lads. But we're also paid to get England up to scratch. That's why we're not bothering with the league, just the European Cup. We'll come in for the European Cup games only, got it?"

John McGovern, as captain of Nottingham Forest, had a very valuable comment to make. "What about the league games and the other cups?"

"We've decided to appoint a couple of you to look after that side of things," Clough explained.

At this, Larry Lloyd began to stand up in anticipation.

"You can sit down for a start," snapped Clough. "You haven't got a chance. It's your job just to be ugly. And you and Burns are the best in the business at that. We've decided that Frank Clark and Martin O'Neill will be in charge."

"But you don't like me," said a startled O'Neill.

"You're right. I don't," confirmed Clough. "In fact, I can't stand you. You're more intelligent than me for a start. But this way, you might stand a chance of getting in the team."

Peter Taylor joined in. "The rest of you just do as you're told and you'll be all right."

Clough continued to outline the plan. "McGovern stays as captain because he knows what to do on the pitch. In fact, he's the only one who knows what to do on the pitch. But you, Clark, and you, O'Neill, will organise the team. You'll have final say in team selection, Frank."

"What's the chairman said about this?" asked McGovern.

"We haven't told him yet," said Taylor.

Clough and Taylor sat in Clough's office and decided that they had better be seen more and more around Lancaster Gate because the place bothered them.

After Taylor had been to visit the FA offices in London, when Clough had taken the Forest team for a mid-season break in Mallorca, he had reported back to Clough what an utter shambles the place was.

Overlooking the Machiavellian attitude of Sir Harold Thompson, Taylor had pointed out that the place was achieving things by default rather than design.

There seemed to be very little structure to the proceedings. He had come across committees, in big rooms, that had very little to do with the day to day reality of football.

An upstairs, downstairs attitude pervaded the whole building and organisation.

Upstairs were volunteers who were trading on their ability to organise committees in order to get free tickets to international matches or the FA Cup Final, for themselves and their friends, or their respective County Football Associations.

An even better bonus was that they could also participate in the junkets to England's away matches. This worked because a lot of the volunteers were self-made wealthy businessmen who had got themselves elected to positions of authority on local football association committees, and the benefits had duly fallen into their laps.

Downstairs were the FA officials who were salaried to carry out secretarial duties, public relations assignments and so on. This domain also included the positions of the England team managers, of course.

The biggest cheese in the hierarchy was Professor Sir Harold Thompson himself, the chairman who lorded over all his minions. To him, the salaried people were more or less people who had to be tolerated.

Another one of the most important people in amongst all this Football Association interference, as Clough and Taylor viewed it, was Charles Hughes.

He was the Football Association Deputy Head of Coaching and England Amateur Manager. His views on football were the complete antithesis of the Clough and Taylor edict that the ball should be got to the ground as soon as possible and played to a teammate.

Hughes, on the other hand, could provide statistics to prove his points. Clough and Taylor thought he was a nutcase.

Hughes had studied the statistics from over a hundred games and liked to pore over the figures. They made sense to him and the facts were there for all to see. Whether it was games involving the current European Champions, Liverpool, or major international teams like Brazil, West Germany and Argentina, or from a whole host of amateur games, the facts were there.

His statistics proved that most goals were scored from less than three passes. Since most goals were scored from inside the penalty area, he argued that it was best to get the ball into the opposition box as soon as possible and the chances are something would happen.

What this overlooked was all the stuff that went on in between. Like passing to teammates, tackling and winning the ball. Clough's assertion to his players to 'get the ball' was based on nothing other than the fact that 'if we have it, they haven't'.

Hughes would go on to his teams about Positions of Maximum Opportunity or, as he liked to call it, POMO. His theory was that if the ball was played into POMO enough times, players would score a goal. Clough was more likely to be heard shouting from the sidelines during training, "You are the best header of a ball in the club. What are you taking a corner for? Get in the box, you idiot."

Hughes constantly reiterated the importance of getting the ball into the box and so did Clough.

Except, Clough was a prolific centre forward who knew how to put the ball away.

He hadn't been particularly bothered about how he received the ball but knew it was easier to score if the ball was cut back from the byline as he was running in.

So he encouraged Robertson and O'Neill to do that at Forest for Withe and Woodcock.

Taylor, being a goalkeeper, also knew that a ball going away from the keeper caused more trouble than that coming on to him.

The coaches that followed Hughes' long ball policy inevitably had players that had little skill other than to lump the ball up field.

If a player had done that for Clough he was likely to be met with, "You ever do that again, young man, you'll not play for this club anymore."

Clough's players knew how to control the ball and knew what to do with it when it came to them.

Clough had met Hughes before when he had first been chosen by Walter Winterbottom for the England squad.

Hughes was regarded at the Football Association as an exceptional coach and, for a scientist like Professor Sir Harold Thompson, Hughes' theories made perfect sense.

Clough didn't have a scientist's analytical brain. All he had was a footballer's brain.

What Clough despised most about Hughes' ideas was that the ball was always in the air. Clough was always ready to spout

one of his favourite sayings: 'If God had wanted us to play football in the clouds, he'd have put grass up there'.
This opposite ends of the football philosophy spectrum brought about a decision by Clough and Taylor to get themselves into the FA headquarters and start a revolution. But how were they going to do this?
"We'll fuck Hughes off out the way," suggested Clough.
"That's a good idea,' agreed Taylor.

However, neither Clough nor Taylor could dispute the facts. Hughes' statistics stood up to scrutiny.
Eventually it came down to the idea that when the supporter comes to the game he wants to see more than just the ball going in the back of the net.
"It only takes a second to score a goal," Clough was often quoted as saying. But he could have elaborated.
By that reckoning your team could score six goals and not concede any but that would amount to six seconds out of the ninety minutes.
Clough, as well as anybody, knew that goals win matches but for the other 89 minutes the fans would want to see some decent football.
So, get the ball on the ground to create some quality passing movements that would ultimately lead to a goal.
From Clough's point of view, as an egotistical and brilliant centre forward, he would want the ball played to him at any time during a game.
What he preferred was that the wingers got to the by-line and pulled the ball back, preferably for him to be there to knock it in. The record books would prove he had done so with alarming regularity.
This made sense when you brought that argument into play with regard to the country's best players. Why would a national football manager want to choose people to play for

their country who could only kick the ball up in the air and into the opposing penalty area as quickly as possible?
What if the opposition was adept at keeping the ball on the floor? Your team had better be able to do that too, but even better.
Clough and Taylor knew that as long as their team had two commanding centre backs then an aerial attack could be neutralised. Therefore, it was simple. Get the ball on the floor and play attractive, inventive, effective football.
In the end Clough and Taylor came to the conclusion that they would have to infiltrate Lancaster Gate in order to get rid of the Hughes influence and build a coaching system for England that would be based purely on skill alone.
Goals would come naturally after that.

Clough and Taylor had entered the FA Briefing Room that had now been painted white and had had that horrible wallpaper removed.
The room had been the scene of some concern to Professor Sir Harold Thompson some weeks earlier when Taylor had visited.
On that occasion, when Thompson had entered the room to find the two painters and decorators hard at work stripping wallpaper off the walls, he had tried to assert his authority.
"What the hell is going on in here?" Thompson had shouted, with an air of one who should have known.
The first painter, the one who seemed to be in charge, informed the FA Chairman, "We've instructions to take the paper off the walls and paint them white."
Thompson raged. "That paper cost thousands. I chose it."
The second painter calmly apprised Thompson of the situation. "Brian Clough ordered us to do this and if he says do it, we're doing it. And we're on bonus the quicker we get done. So, clear off whoever you are."

And that before Thompson had been given short shrift by Taylor. That day hadn't been Thompson's best day at the FA.

Now, the room was full of reporters awaiting the entrance of the England management team in the persons of Brian Clough and Peter Taylor.

The first reporter off the blocks opened with, "Are there going to be any surprises in the squad for the Home International Championship?"

"The only surprise will be if we don't win it," said Clough.

A second reporter said, "In the last couple of months, you won the League and the League Cup with Forest, and you've beaten West Germany away and drawn with Brazil for England. That's not a bad record, is it?"

"It's not a bad record, thank you young man. The only niggle I have about it is that we should have beaten Brazil. We were careless and I will not tolerate carelessness."

A third reporter broke in, "To what do you attribute your success, Mr. Clough?"

"Look, I've said it before. It's simple. The things that are hard work to other managers are not hard work to me," Clough said. "The discipline side, the judging of players, the training and coaching. These are not problems as far as I am concerned."

The first supporter said, "The players seem to respond to you."

"Of course they do," explained Clough. "Because they want to win"

"There must be more to it than that," the scribe continued.

"There is," said Clough. "I know my players. The moment I see the players in the dressing room I can tell their moods. Or if I don't spot it, Peter Taylor will. I know whether a player is off colour, had a row with his missus, or just doesn't fancy it. I know who needs to have his arse kicked and I know who to leave alone. It only takes a minute to score a goal, and it takes less than a minute to change someone's outlook with a word or two. You have to really know your players. It's a special kind of coaching that only very, very good managers are capable of…. like me."

Although they made hard work of it, England had somewhat predictable wins against Wales at Ninian Park, Cardiff, 3-1, and two 1-0 wins - Northern Ireland at Wembley and Scotland at Hampden Park.
Ray Wilkins, Steve Coppell and Trevor Francis were the pick of the bunch and those victories brought the Home International Championship to England as Clough had confidently expected.
The victory in Scotland was notable, not just because of the away win on the auld enemy's soil in front of a crowd of nearly ninety thousand, with Coppell scoring, but more because of an incident that took place at half time.
The England team entered the dressing room followed by Clough and Taylor. Clough strode up to Trevor Brooking and smacked him very hard on the nose, after which he turned round and left the room.
As he was entitled to, Brooking asked, "What the hell was that for?"
"Ah," said Peter Taylor, "you passed back to the goalkeeper. He hates that." Turning to Phil Thompson, Taylor said, "You better not do that. If he punches you, your snout'll be spread all over your face. Even more than it is now. Fuck me, that's a big nose."

Afterwards, having secured the victory, Clough reappeared in the dressing room. "Excellent performance gentlemen. Well taken goal, Steven. You should be scoring more like those. See you lads up in the hospitality bar. And be quick. We don't want to be hanging around Glasgow too late after we nicked that off the Jocks. Bless 'em. Come on Peter."

That was it. There was no mention of the back pass but it was also noticeable that there weren't any in the second half.

The FA Committee members were already sat around the large table in the FA Briefing Room when Clough and Taylor entered and sat down.

"Now, Mr. Clough, Mr. Taylor," began Professor Sir Harold Thompson. "We've called this meeting because of a few incidents that have taken place that are not the regular way we do things at the Football Association."

"You mean we won a competition?" quipped Peter Taylor. "The oldest international football competition at that. Been going nearly one hundred years, you know."

Peter Swales was quick to congratulate the management. "Yes, that was excellent. I enjoyed that. Especially beating the Scots up there."

"Just a piss pot really," said Clough. "Nothing but a training exercise. I'd rather be watching that young Botham play cricket. He's good, he is. But thanks, anyway."

"I don't mean that," snapped Thompson, adding grudgingly, "although that is in the minutes."

"Minutes sound good," said Taylor. "We don't want to be hanging about here a minute more than we have to. Brian and I are busy people."

Thompson was ruffled. "Look, this is important. We've had a formal complaint from Leeds United that you two turned up at Elland Road, abused their hospitality and didn't even bother to watch the game."

"That was ages ago," said Clough.

"Abused their hospitality! I think it was the other way round," huffed Taylor. "We only got chicken sandwiches. I may be mistaken, and forgive me if I am, but I firmly believe the directors and chairman of Leeds United had a sit down roast lunch. And I think they must have had wine judging by the number of empty bottles on the tables. I'm no detective but, to me, that was a clue."

"But you didn't even watch the game," complained Thompson.

"Don't have to," explained Taylor. "We know how they play."

"Then why did you go there?" asked Thompson.

"Why did we go there? Why did we go there?" said Taylor, seemingly astonished at the stupidity of the question. "Duty, of course. Our duty is to England, one hundred per cent. This is our country and we intend to scale the pinnacle of world football. If you'll let us, that is. Mind you, we're playing catch up, because you've cocked it up for years."

"I think this is unacceptable behaviour," huffed Thompson.

"You'd best tender your resignation then. Pop it into the office. I'm sure somebody out there will deal with it. Young Linda's very good at admin."

"That's another thing..." spluttered Thompson as Taylor butted in.

"Are we now on item two?"

"Um, well, yes."

"Aren't you supposed to say that we've moved on to item two? The committee members might not know what is going on."

"Item two," continued Thompson. "The cancellation of our chartered flight to Germany."

"The chartered flight to Germany was not cancelled," said Taylor. "We just moved it forward a day."

"Nobody told us."

"That's the thing about football," said Taylor. "You've got to keep your ear to the ground. Essential. People do things behind your back if you're not careful. You of all people, Harold, should know what's going on round here. You are the Chairman of the Football Association, for Christ's sake."

"Don't let it happen again," snapped Thompson. "We were left looking like absolute idiots. Laughing stocks, all of us."

"Now there's a thing."

"I don't like your attitude Mr. Taylor."

"I don't give a shit what you think," said Taylor. "Our player, Kenny Burns, is the Football Writers Association Footballer of the Year. Our player, Peter Shilton, is the Professional Footballers Association Player of the Year. Our player, Tony Woodcock, is the Professional Footballers Association Young Player of the Year and my esteemed colleague here, Brian Clough, is the League Managers Association Manager of the Year. We know about football. You don't. Now, if that's it."

Thompson wasn't finished. "Wait. This European Cup thing with Nottingham Forest. What's all that about?"

"We haven't won it yet," Clough began. "We should have done with Derby County but we were cheated out of it by those cheating Italian bastards. We've got a tough tie in the first round, so we won't be down here much in September.

Except to take England to Denmark for the European Championships qualifier on the twentieth. Never been to Copenhagen before. Since some of my Forest lads will be in the England squad anyway, I think I'll take the rest of the Forest lads too. You see, the first round games are the week before and the week after the England game. It makes sense to keep us all together. It'll make a nice break. But we'll make sure Forest pay for the lads who aren't in the England squad."
Clough and Taylor rose to leave but this prompted Thompson into action again.
"Just a minute," he squealed. "We haven't finished yet."
"That's all right," said Taylor generously. "Take as long as you like. I'll ask Linda to organise some sandwiches for you. Chicken's best, if you ask me."
Clough and Taylor left the FA Briefing Room.

As luck would have it, Nottingham Forest's first opponents in the European Cup turned out to be their fellow English First Division club, and reigning European champions, Liverpool. Despite having finished seven points clear of Liverpool in winning the League Championship, Forest were still heavy underdogs, but they were to take their doubters by surprise in the first leg of the first round match at their City Ground stadium in Nottingham.

The Forest players were gathered round Clough and Taylor after a gentle work out on the training ground. Clough spoke first. "It's a big night tonight, gentlemen. You are playing the European Champions, Liverpool, at home in the first round of the European Cup. Superb team. It's vital we get a win to take to Anfield. I really don't know who to pick."

John O'Hare piped up. "We beat them in the League Cup Final. I got us a penalty."

"Aye, you cheating Jock," Taylor reminded him. "It was never a penalty. It was miles outside the box. I saw it."

Clough had an idea. "Now lads, get a football each and kick it as far as you can into that field over there."

The players looked bemused but got a ball each, just as they were told.

"Go on, belt the things as far as you can, over the hedge," Clough commanded.

The players kicked the balls over the fence into a cow field adjacent to the training ground."

"Now, go and retrieve a football each," he said. "Don't worry if you don't get the one you kicked. Just get a ball and bring it back here as fast as you can."

Robertson complained, "There's all those nettles in the way."

Clough ignored him."The first eleven back with a football get to play tonight," he shouted. "Off you go."

The players set off at pace and, unable to avoid the nettles, had to wade through them. Upon their return a couple of minutes later, the players took to scratching their legs violently.

"That fucking hurts," moaned Robertson. "I'm covered in stings. Have we got anything to put on our legs?"

"What do you want, tights? You poof," said Taylor.

Martin O'Neill then joined in. "I don't wish to be pedantic," he said, "but can I point out that Shilton was not one of the first eleven back with a football? Therefore, we don't have a goalkeeper tonight if you follow your own rule."

"I've just changed the rule," said Clough. "And since it's you that's challenged my rule, smart-arse, you don't play tonight. Shilton does."

Clough turned to Taylor and quietly asked him what pedantic meant.

As for the game itself, it was a closely fought affair, as expected from the top two teams in the country.

Garry Birtles, Clough's squash partner, had scored for Forest before Liverpool took a grip on the game. However, they were unable to breach the defence where Lloyd and Burns were at their intolerant best.

Birtles again proved a worthy replacement for Peter Withe, who had somewhat surprisingly departed for Newcastle. Following a cross from the left into the box, the ball was headed back into the path of full back Colin Barrett who scored with a thunderous shot past Clemence in the Liverpool goal.

A two goal lead before the second leg was more than could be hoped for by Forest fans, though Clough and Taylor merely marked it down as a job well done.

After the Liverpool game, Clough and Taylor had taken the England squad to Copenhagen, along with the rest of the Forest lads who were allowed to join in England's training session if they wanted to.

None of them did, preferring to do some sightseeing inside the bars of the Danish capital.

The whole touring party met up at the team's hotel on the eve of the match and, as they settled into their evening meal, they were ambushed by Clough.

"Do you know," said Clough, "that it was just off the coast near here where Horatio Nelson defeated a fleet of Danish and Norwegian ships. Nelson was only a Vice-Admiral then, not an Admiral, and his boss, Admiral Parker, told him to withdraw. But Nelson famously put his telescope up to his blind eye, so he purposely didn't see the signal to cease fire, and went on to destroy a lot of the opposition ships. It was an even tougher fight than Trafalgar apparently. You lot wouldn't disobey my orders would you? Anyway, we've had enough of Admirals with that crap kit that Revie brought in."
There was a general murmur of agreement.

The game itself was exciting to watch for the fans but a nightmare for the management of both sides.
Keegan and Brooking gave decent performances and so too did Shilton in the England goal mostly because he had to. Even so he let in three Danish goals because the defence played like a bunch of fairies in front of him according to Taylor.
Luckily, according to Clough, England managed to score four, with Keegan on target twice, and so too the young Steve Coppell.
All in all, though, it was a dire performance but sealed the points in what was a European Championship Qualifier.

In the after-match press conference, Clough praised Keegan, Coppell and Brooking and said that if it wasn't for Shilton England would have been in the shit. And he offered the press that as a quote.
However, when a member of the tabloids criticised Wilkins for what he perceived as an overly timid approach, Clough asked the reporter what professional club he had played for.
When the answer arrived in the negative, Clough advised the scribe to go jump in Copenhagen Harbour. Further, he suggested he stay there and get acquainted with the little mermaid that hung around in that area and that if he wrote any fairy tales, like Hans Christian Andersen, about the match, he would grab him by the balls and not let go until he apologised. This excited some of the Danish press, thinking that Clough was familiar with the work of their most celebrated children's writer, until he quashed their enthusiasm by saying that he regarded their pastry as pretty much as it is described, that is to say 'poof pastry'. And that come the return a year hence, in front of a full house a Wembley, England would piss all over them.

The second leg of the European Cup at Anfield, where Forest were to defend their 2-0 lead from the City Ground, soon came around.
Liverpool were still favourites to go through, but the tie was now set up perfectly for Forest.
It should have been a nerve wracking experience except that Clough and Taylor contrived one of their unusual pre-match arrangements.

Leaving Nottingham late morning on the day of the match, travelling to Liverpool for the evening kick-off, the Forest squad was pleasantly surprised when Brian Clough stopped the bus and ordered the team into a pub on the way. There he bought them all a pint.

If that wasn't enough, when they sat down for lunch upon arriving at the team hotel in Liverpool, Clough insisted everyone have a large glass of wine. Red or white; they had a choice.

The players were then sent to bed where they snoozed all afternoon, before waking fully refreshed and free from worrying about the important match about to take place.

As it was, the Forest team easily held the reigning European champions to a goalless draw and progressed to the next round of the competition that Clough and Taylor were desperate to win after that cheating scandal of half a dozen years previously that they remembered so well.

Clough and Taylor had been summoned to the Football Association headquarters in Lancaster Gate and, though they had no idea what was likely to be on the agenda, they weren't worried. It was their intention to spend more time at the FA anyway because they wanted to instigate some changes without the FA knowing.

It was a matter of how to go about it. Having found out that there was a warren of committees upstairs they wanted to know what use they were, if any.

Their business was downstairs where they wanted things to be done with as much haste and as little fuss as possible.

On their arrival by taxi, Linda was quickly out to meet them. As Clough was besieged by waiting press on the steps of the grand establishment, Linda was able to take Taylor aside and inform him that Tim Cox had entered the building half an hour before and had gone into a private meeting with Harold Thompson.

What transpired in Thompson's office, in his meeting with Tim Cox, was not what Thompson had hoped for or expected. He had thought that all this time, digging about in Brian Clough's past would have unearthed more than the fact that Clough drank more than the normal person and probably much more than was good for him.
There was no womanising, gambling, peeping through windows or whatever Thompson had hoped for. Nothing. If this was not good news for Thompson, it certainly was not good news for Cox, who had hoped to improve his career as well as his bank balance, especially with the fatherhood thing going on. Thompson was annoyed and made his feelings clear to Cox that he had let him down and that he had better look for a new profession since he was clearly incompetent at the one of his choice.

As Cox came disconsolately down the stairs from Thompson's office, Taylor grabbed hold of him and drew him to one side.
"Ah, Mr. Cox," said Taylor. "Glad of you to come. I've been meaning to speak to you."
Cox was startled. "How do you know me?" he asked.
"None of your business," said Taylor. "But you are my business. I know what you've been up to, trying to drag up some shit about Brian. But you won't do it. His idea of getting up to something naughty is letting his kids splash water about

in the bath without his missus Barbara getting to know. So, basically, you've been barking up the wrong tree. Sadly, for you, you should have covered your own back."

Taylor took the photograph that McGovern had provided from out of his inside jacket pocket and showed it to Cox. "You wouldn't want your lass to see that, would you?"

"Look, I am just trying to make a living. It's tough without regular work."

"You're working for me now," said Taylor. "I'll give you some stories you can sell and I'll make sure you travel with England and Forest. Just keep your head down and you'll get your job."

Cox was overwhelmed. "I can't believe what you've just said. Thanks. Thompson's just kicked me out anyway."

"He would. He's an arsehole. Now, think on. Brian wondered what you were up to in Cala Millor because he sees everything but he never quite figured it. Play your cards right and you'll be fine. With me."

"I don't understand," said Cox. "Why help me?"

Clough left the reporters on the steps of 16 Lancaster Gate and joined Taylor just inside the revolving doors, pausing briefly to say hello to Linda before the England management team made their way up the stairs to the committee room.

The committee members had been joined by Professor Sir Harold Thompson and were now sitting round the large table in the middle of the room.

Clough and Taylor sat on chairs away from the table, the regulation distance apart, so that the committee members would have to look from side to side, in Clough and Taylor's usual tactic to control the conversation.

Sir Harold Thompson opened the proceedings. "I've called this extraordinary meeting today because, Mr. Clough and Mr. Taylor, there is some disquiet in the press about the time you are spending here at the Football Association headquarters."
"We'll soon put a stop to that," said Taylor. "Disquiet, you say. Not sure I've ever heard that word before. Sounds wrong. I presume it's not very nice. Anyway, we won't come here again if that's how you feel."
"He's only joking, gentlemen," said Clough. "Of course we'll come here again. When it's necessary. We won't be coming as much as we have, that's all."
Thompson huffed sarcastically, "You're hardly ever here as it is."
Clough retorted, "I know. Waste of time here. By the way, we're off on holiday next week to Greece. We're playing AEK Athens. I don't know what AEK means. Maybe it's the noise they'll make when Lloyd and Burns show up in their tunnel. Anyway, we'll nip over to Ireland for the European Championship qualifier in between the two legs. Then there's only the friendly against Czechoslovakia and it's Christmas."
Peter Taylor mused, "I like Christmas. My favourite time of the year. Unless it snows. Can do without that shit."
Clough continued, "You're right as usual Peter. Sun on your back, that's what we need."
Taylor seemed to be enjoying the conversation. "I'm looking forward to Greece. Might even take a look round Athens. I've heard it's quite interesting. Old buildings and stuff like that."
Clough and Taylor rose to leave, considering that the business was done.

There was a final parting shot from Clough, "Well, if we don't see you at Wembley at the end of November, have a happy Christmas. And don't overdo it on New Year's Eve."

The weather was pleasantly warm as the Forest players strolled around the centre of Athens on the morning of the first leg of round two of the European Cup.
An early morning bus tour had taken the team to the Parthenon and a pretty young lady on the bus with a microphone told the Forest lads in a funny accent that the place was built as a temple to the Greek Goddess Athena who was regarded as their virgin patron.
A few players pricked up their ears at the sound of the word 'virgin' but made out their interest was because of the attractive accent.
The young lady explained that it is the most important surviving building of Classical Greece. The Parthenon, she went on, was regarded as an enduring symbol of Ancient Greece and one of the world's greatest cultural monuments. Its decorative sculptures considered the epitome of the acme of Greek art.
Kenny Burns asked, on behalf of the team who had made a few interested murmurings, why the Greeks hadn't looked after the place since it was that important.
The young lady revealed that in 1687 the Parthenon housed an ammunition dump and it was ignited by a deliberate bombardment. The damage was extensive, although some of the exquisite sculptures survived.

However, in 1806, Thomas Bruce, the Seventh Earl of Elgin, removed some of the surviving sculptures. These became known as the Elgin marbles which were sold in 1816 to the British Museum in London where they are still on display. "Thieving English bastards," shouted out Burns, much to everyone's delight, as evidenced by the laughter of all except Brian Clough and Martin O'Neill.

Clough was annoyed that his team had shown some disrespect to the young lady and he told McGovern to stand up and apologise.

Before McGovern could carry out his employer's wishes, however, O'Neill stood and pointed out to the class of Greek scholars that it was, indeed, widely regarded as theft, and that the Greek government has been committed to the return of the sculptures to Greece but, so far, without any proper consideration from the British government.

He also pointed out that Thomas Bruce, the Seventh Earl of Elgin, was Scottish.

Kenny Burns suffered the indignation of hideous verbal abuse from his team mates. Martin O'Neill momentarily basked in the glory bestowed on him by all in attendance.

Even from Clough, though he didn't show it.

Following that excursion into the heritage of the city and country they were visiting, Clough and Taylor shepherded the team to a pavement bar, Clough suggesting, to a waiter's obvious annoyance, that they drag the tables together so they could sit apart from the other clientele.

A few bottles of wine were ordered though the players were advised that a one large glass would probably be sufficient, but also the minimum expected.

Clough and Taylor sat apart from the players and, as Clough sipped his wine, he mused. "You know, Pete, looking at all these world famous buildings, it makes me think that I'm a bit like a Roman Emperor. Emperors are thought to be a notch higher than kings, you know. These lads look upon me as an emperor I reckon. Good that, isn't it? "

"We're in Greece," said Taylor.

"So what?"

"You're on about a Roman Emperor. Roman is Rome. Italy."

"I thought they got all over the place."

"They did but I don't know about here. You've seen these ancient buildings and I reckon you're thinking about Greek gods. You think you're a Greek god."

"Some of them were all right, in fact I should think all of them were all right, or they wouldn't be gods, would they?"

Zeus, the king of the gods, the ruler of Mount Olympus and the god of the sky, weather, thunder, lightning, law, order, and fate," stood up and said, "Right lads, get them down your necks, it's time to get back to the hotel for a nap."

Martin O'Neill sidled up to Peter Taylor and whispered, "I heard what the gaffer just said. He may be getting confused. For example, Byzantium was an ancient Greek city founded by Greek colonists and named after their King Byzas, hundreds of years ago, hundreds of years before Jesus Christ even. In fact, Byzantium was renamed Nova Roma, by Constantine the Great although it was popularly known as Constantinople. Even so, it became the imperial residence of the classical Roman Empire and, subsequent to that, it became the capital of the Byzantine Empire for more than a thousand years. Of course, the Byzantine Empire was the Greek-speaking Roman Empire of late Antiquity and the Middle Ages. And, as we all know, Constantinople became Istanbul in 1930 after the establishment of modern Turkey."

"So it's not really round here then?" said Taylor.

"No."

"Well for Christ's sake, don't tell him any of that."

As it happened, O'Neill had either been in or out of favour with Clough, for one reason or another, or injured, and he was to sit out this game despite his extensive knowledge of ancient history.

Although the hosts managed to get a goal, so too did Birtles, who had been bought a couple of years before from non-league Long Eaton United for £5000.

Clough had regarded that as a good piece of football business and, also, Birtles had got fed up of purposely losing to Clough at squash, so had earned his inclusion in the team on merit.

Forest secured a 2-1 away win with a rare goal from team captain, John McGovern.

The trip to Greece was a decent break for the Forest team and, although they had to work hard for their victory, the away win set up the return leg nicely.

This meant that for the rest of the trip, Clough and Taylor could think about the upcoming England game in Dublin, another European Championship qualifier.

The match at Lansdowne Road was scheduled for the following Wednesday so there wasn't a great deal of time to prepare.

They were due to meet the England players at the Hendon Hotel on the Sunday night but wasted no time in getting down to discussing the team in the airport bar before leaving Athens.

"I'm not keen on Guinness if I'm really honest," said Taylor as he ordered himself and Clough a double Scotch each.
"Me neither. I mean, I'll have it if there's nowt else."
"What about the team for Wednesday? Same as last time?"
"Yep, barring injuries, of course," agreed Clough.

So, despite the performance in Copenhagen being less than what was required of an England team by Clough and Taylor, they had independently come to the conclusion that it would be wrong to kick the players when they were down.
After all, it was their decision to pick them in the first place so it was their fault that they had not performed well.
Clough's assertion that, 'If a chairman sacks the manager he initially appointed, he should go as well,' was a principle he applied to himself. And anyway, the Danes had been a bit lucky.
Therefore, it stood to reason, in terms of their preparation, they must have got something slightly wrong.
They agreed to mull it over which they did. But not for long.
A propos of nothing in particular, Taylor turned to Clough and said, "We drink too much, you know that, don't you?" Clough nodded in agreement.

Come the night before the game, in the bar of their hotel in Dublin, the England players gathered after their evening meal and were offered an almost endless supply of Guinness. They served it properly in the hotel bar. Clough had insisted. The barman poured a perfect two-part Guinness pour.
"Lloyd, get over here," shouted Clough. "Get behind this bar

and pull me a pint of Guinness like this young man's just done. It tastes brilliant when it's poured properly. Different to what I've had before in Nottingham."

"But I'm not a barman," protested Lloyd.

"I know. But I know you've had Guinness before," said Clough. "Too much. I've seen you."

Larry Lloyd shrugged his shoulders and took up a position behind the bar.

Clough looked pleased with himself for putting Lloyd in an awkward position.

"The first thing to remember," said Lloyd, picking up a clean, normal size pint Guinness glass and tilting it to a 45 degree angle, "is that it is a two-part pour."

He proceeded to pour the liquid until the glass was about three quarters full.

"Now allow what's known as the 'surge' to settle until there is a clear delineation between the head, which should be about an inch, and a light cream colour at the top. This is known as the bishop's collar."

Clough looked as much bemused as Lloyd looked smug.

"Now, holding the glass upright, fill it to the top with the final quarter pint of Guinness."

"How did you know all that?" asked Clough.

"Martin O'Neill taught me," said Lloyd. "A perfect pint of Guinness should take exactly one hundred and nineteen and a half seconds to pour. Isn't that right, barman?"

"Piss off," said Clough

The match was not as good as the Guinness in Dublin but it wasn't for the want of trying.

The midfield included both Wilkins and Brooking, where Brooking proved himself inventive to Wilkins' conservatism.

Though the match ended in a 1-1 draw, the venom of Clough's tongue was aimed at the defence because Gerry Daly was left unmarked from Liam Brady's free kick.

It only takes a second to score a goal, Clough might have said. Or he could have said that it only takes a second to lose concentration for the opposition to score a goal.

Instead he said neither, and the collective ears of the England defenders glowed hot as Clough ranted so much in the dressing room afterwards that some thought the building was shaking. Although the English attack had spurned enough opportunities to carve out a handsome victory, it was the solitary conceded goal that made the journey back to the hotel remarkable for its periods of silence, then anger.

The players did not know when Clough would explode. And he did, several times, on each occasion singling out a particular defender or midfielder for his part in the blunder.

It was inconceivable to Clough that international footballers could be so incompetent that they leave a player unmarked in the penalty area. That was the unforgivable part.

It was acceptable to be outclassed by a higher jumper and a better header of the ball, for example, but to leave someone unmarked was reprehensible.

At one point his daughter Elizabeth was described as being a better defender and he wasn't sure that she was even interested in the game.

The reason that the forwards came away remarkably unscathed is not that they only scored once, through Latchford, but because they had got themselves into positions to score.

Missing chances was not a sin; not having the guts to get into the position to miss was what Clough couldn't stand.

So on the bus journey, the forwards sat glumly, hoping and praying that the volcano sitting in the front seat alongside his pal Taylor wouldn't erupt again and cause their teammates more anguish.

Although Shilton could not be held responsible for the goal, he was guilty by being an accessory to the fact in that he was regarded as a fully paid up member of the defence.

When, finally, after one more apoplectic explosion, the captain, Kevin Keegan, decided to say something on behalf of the players so he approached the front of the bus.

He stood alongside, but slightly behind, the management seats and whispered quietly to Peter Taylor, asking if he could possibly have a word with Mr. Clough.

Taylor said he could, without even consulting the enraged one. Keegan put forward the argument that the players, especially the defence, were extremely sorry to have made mistakes, and sorry not to have won a game that they should have won, but that were trying to win and that they would always try to win for England.

It was an honour to be picked for their country and, for both Mr. Clough and Mr. Taylor, they wish they could change things if they could.

He finished by asking if they, and especially Mr. Clough, would forgive them on this occasion and that they hoped it would never happen again.

Clough, who had sat through all this with his head in his hands, gave a barely audible grunt, and Taylor indicated that the apology had been accepted.

After Keegan had returned to his seat, and still without looking up, Clough said to Taylor, "Are they shitting themselves?"

"Smells like they have," replied Taylor.

"Job done," said Clough.

The return leg of the European Cup, round two, second leg against AEK Athens was a formality as expected.
Forest were in scintillating form on their own ground and pasted the Greeks 5-1 with Birtles netting two of the goals and his strike partner Woodcock getting on the score sheet too. The other two goals came from defenders – Anderson, and Dave Needham, deputising for the injured Kenny Burns.

As for England, at the end of November, in a friendly against Czechoslovakia on an icy pitch at Wembley, there were no defensive lapses and although England were again restricted to a single goal, this time from Coppell, the performance was positive.
Coppell was congratulated on his incisive finish because he was in the right place at the right time when the Czech keeper, Pavel Michalik, made an error.
Shilton was reminded afterwards that he could easily have slipped up like that if he didn't concentrate.
Shilton protested that he concentrated for the full ninety minutes whereupon Clough bollocked him for not concentrating on the match for the whole of the daylight hours leading up to kick off.

It was dark, around 5pm, as Clough was driving his Mercedes through the edge of the village of Quarndon, Derbyshire. A young boy, about ten years old, standing on the pavement, threw a snowball at the passing car.

Although it hit the car, it was not a malevolent throw, more of a gentle toss that could not miss because of the closeness of the passing vehicle.

It was a boyish prank, nothing more.

Clough drove round the corner, out of the boy's view, pulled up and got out.

He slowly made his way back round the corner where the boy was about to throw another snowball at another passing car.

The boy did not see him approaching.

Clough caught the boy by the arm and clipped him round the ear before the boy could react.

"Hey, young man. Throwing snowballs is good fun if you're with your mates. But if you do that to drivers, they might swerve or something and then you might cause an accident and somebody could get hurt."

The boy apologised and Clough asked him where he lived. The boy gave his address, as if he was being interviewed by a policeman.

Clough then informed the boy that he should go home immediately and tell his Dad that Brian Clough was coming round to see him at six o'clock.

The boy ran off as carefully as he could so he wouldn't slip on the snow. Clough smiled to himself and made his way back to his Mercedes.

Not much further through the village, the Mercedes pulled into a long drive and made its way to the front door where Clough parked up and got out.

Clough's wife, Barbara, was at the kitchen sink preparing vegetables when she heard the heavy front door close. "That you, Brian?" she called out.

"Yes, dear," he said. "Something smells nice."

"I'm doing hotpot, it's so cold outside. Be an hour or so."
"Perfect," said Clough. "I've got to go out soon for a short while, but won't be long. Only in the village. I'll just have a beer then I'll go see to it."
"What's going on in the village?" Barbara asked.
"Just some bloke I've got to see about his lad. Only take a minute."
Clough went into the lounge and turned a cassette recorder on. Frank Sinatra was singing 'Fly Me To The Moon'.
Clough joined in, singing the words perfectly, his phrasing a little bit earlier than Ol' Blue Eyes would prefer, as he poured himself a glass of beer from a chilled drinks cabinet.
The phone rang and Clough answered it. "Who? Never heard of him," said Clough. "What's he want?"
It was Peter Taylor on the phone telling Clough that there was a young, struggling freelance reporter trying to get some regular work and needed a helping hand.
Clough agreed with Taylor that they could throw something his way as long as he wasn't an arsehole.

After a short return journey into the village, Clough pulled his Mercedes outside a cottage, the address that the young boy had given him.
Clough's knock at the door was instantly opened by a man, evidently the boy's father.
"Please come in Mr. Clough. Our Oliver said you were coming. I have to say he doesn't know who you are. I do apologise for his behavior. Now, what can I get you? You like Scotch don't you?"

Clough was quickly furnished with a large glass of Jura as the man began telling Clough how much of a Derby County fan he was and what a great team Clough and Taylor had produced to clinch the First Division championship six years previously.

Alcoholism, the broad term used for people who have problems with alcohol, and largely used to mean compulsive and uncontrolled consumption of alcohol, usually to the detriment of the drinker's health, personal relationships, and social standing, had reared up in Clough and Taylor's faces, mostly in the shape of a whisky glass.
Both Clough and Taylor had become aware of this and had talked at length about how they should deal with the problem. The trouble was they weren't talking often enough, and if they were in different places then the conversations wouldn't take place at all.
Clough had read up about various causes like stress, social environment, mental health, family history, age, ethnic group, and gender which were all regarded as influences in the risk for developing the condition.
He brought the subject up with Taylor when they did have chance to sit down together at what was going to be a slack period in their lives for a little while. The next European Championship qualifier with England against Northern Ireland at Wembley wasn't until early February and the quarter-final first leg of the European Cup games with Forest wasn't until next March.
The subject was broached in the lounge of Clough's house at Quarndon on New Year's Eve.
As Barbara, and Taylor's wife Lillian, were putting the finishing touches to some hors d'oeuvres or, as Clough

preferred, 'nibbles', in the kitchen, Clough and Taylor were listening to Sinatra in the lounge.

Clough explained that he had had a glorious childhood in a great family, he had no mental health problems that he was aware of, and there was no past history of alcoholism in the family that he knew of. Age and gender he dismissed as part of every scenario and were, therefore, irrelevant. He took ethnic to mean black and he was positive that there were no black Cloughs in the cupboard, skeleton or otherwise.

"Then it's down to your injury," said Taylor. "Be fair, when you did your knee, and you were hobbling about for months, you did start knocking it back a bit then. And then, even after you'd tried to come back and they gave you that coaching job, you were hammering it a bit. Anyway, that's what I heard."

"Bang on," said Clough. "So it must have been the stress bit that started me off. Young family, career and knee in tatters. Time on me hands. It's bound to send a man to drink. What started you off?"

"You," said Taylor.

Clough gave Taylor a scathing look but realised he was at least half-joking.

"Look at our lifestyle," said Taylor. "We drink every day because it's there, and it's an excuse to relieve the pressure of always having to produce winning teams. It's constant. Once one game is over it's on to the next. Win, win, win or you are out. That's what's happening to us."

The Clough and Taylor kids were carting around the house, mostly upstairs ignoring the adults when the doorbell rang.

A few seconds later, Barbara poked her head into the lounge and announced that their gardener had turned up, as Clough had requested, for a New Year's Eve drink.

"Go steady, Brian, at least while the bairns are still up," said Barbara, as she let the gardener into the lounge.

"You're absolutely right, my love, as usual," said Clough. "Now, Pete, have you met my new gardener. Brilliant with roses. Just set him on. Good with lawns too."

"I suppose his manure delivery is worth watching," said Taylor.

Clough put on a different cassette of Sinatra and *The Bells of Christmas* came on. "That's funny," said Clough. "These Manager of the Month gallons are handy."

He then topped up the glasses of his best mate Peter Taylor, and his new mate, the gardener.

The first European Championship Qualifier of the year, against Northern Ireland at Wembley in early February, in front of another sellout crowd, went satisfactorily enough in terms of goals and proved a welcome respite in the 'winter of discontent'.

Keegan managed two with Coppell notching another and Larry Lloyd opening his England account with a towering header from Coppell corner.

The team work ethic, according to Clough, was more than acceptable and was the difference between the two teams. Taylor suggested that the players were beginning to develop an understanding of the pattern of each other's play.

However, Brooking's performance, though inventive was regarded as not being damaging enough, and he promised he would try to play more incisive through balls in the next game. Clough pointed out that that would be a fine aim to hold in his thoughts as long he was selected for the next game.

Clough and Taylor had seen enough of Birmingham striker Trevor Francis on England duty to want to sign him for Forest's European Cup campaign.

The only problem was that he wasn't eligible for three months, due to UEFA rules, so that a transfer was nothing short of a gamble that they would get to the final in May.

Except that, having sized up the teams left in the competition, Clough and Taylor decided it wasn't a gamble at all.

The transfer made the news, inevitably, because it was the first million pound transfer and Francis was duly introduced to the waiting press at the City Ground.

The press corps was kept waiting for Clough and Francis to arrive. When they did arrive, Clough told Francis to take his hands out of his pocket. He also announced that they couldn't stay long because he'd arranged a game of squash with Birtles. Asked why he had signed Francis for a Forest team he, ostensibly, no longer managed, Clough informed those present that Francis was an understudy for his excellent centre forward Garry Birtles who scored more goals than Francis, was a better team player, and probably a better squash player too.

Also asked whether the record fee was ego on his part, as the first manager to break that barrier, Clough agreed that it was another record in the books against his name.

A month later, Forest entertained Grasshoppers of Zurich in the quarter-final first leg of the European Cup at the City Ground. Obviously, new signing Trevor Francis couldn't play but he wasn't needed anyway as Birtles popped up again, followed by Robertson with a penalty, and Gemmill and Lloyd to establish a 4-1 advantage.

A few days later Forest retained the League Cup with a thrilling 3-2 win against Southampton at Wembley.
Buoyed by the success of having a few drinks before the Liverpool match, Clark and O'Neill decided to follow the Clough and Taylor modus operandi before the Wembley showpiece.
The night before the game, the Forest lads were ordered to meet for a team talk in one of the hotel's side rooms.
Since Clough had never bothered talking about the opposition, the players thought that their new management team had changed things but they were there waiting for them with a crate of champagne.
The doors were locked and the players were told that nobody was going to bed before it was all gone.
John O'Hare protested that he only drank bitter, so ten pints of ale were delivered.
It was a team proclamation. Tony Woodcock, not the heaviest of drinkers, had to be carried to bed.

Although now, technically, not part of the domestic competition management team, Clough insisted that Peter Taylor lead out the team for the final.
It was much deserved and a fitting tribute for what he had achieved on Forest's behalf without the same acclaim that his management partner had received.
Although Southampton scored first, Birtles had surfaced twice in the second half to put Forest 2-1 up. A third goal by Woodcock did not, however, put the game out of reach. Southampton scored late on and set up a tense final few minutes. Fortunately, Forest survived and became the first team to successfully defend the League Cup.

Two weeks after their first leg victory, Nottingham Forest found themselves in one of the world's leading financial cities, Zurich, for the return leg of their European Cup quarter-final at Grasshoppers Stadium.
Grasshoppers is the oldest team in Zurich and, though nobody knows the origin of their name, local legend says that it is because of the energetic celebrations when a goal is scored. Clough was not impressed with that explanation.
Neither was he impressed when Martin O'Neill mentioned the Kunsthaus because he thought he was on about a brothel and Clough was insistent he would not have any member of his team catching anything other than a late tackle.
Even though O'Neill explained that it was one of the most important art museums in Switzerland, and indeed Europe, with fine examples from the Middle Ages to the present day, and that it housed predominately Swiss art, Clough thought he was making it up.
Despite all that, O'Neill was selected to play and scored Forest's goal to secure a 1-1 draw and a safe passage through to the semi-final.

When that first leg of the semi-final came round, against FC Cologne, it was held at the City Ground in Nottingham.
The game was set to be a classic and it was.
There was some fantastic attacking football but, unfortunately for the home side, it came from the opposition.
Forest were shocked when the Germans went two goals up. The first, a low shot that eluded Shilton and hit both posts before going in, was like pinball in slow motion.

Forest fought back magnificently and Birtles headed one in before Bowyer levelled with a low shot through a crowded area.

Then Robertson, with a diving header nonetheless, put the home side ahead only for the Germans to bring on a Japanese substitute to equalise.

Tim Cox's preferred headline 'Japanese Sub Sinks Forest' was frowned upon by Clough.

Despite the goals from Birtles, inevitably, Bowyer and Robertson, Forest were always chasing the game.

The fact that the opposition scored three away goals, meant the attempt to surpass Derby County's semi-final effort half a dozen years before seemed to have foundered.

In the Press Room afterwards a downcast reporter said, "They scored three away goals. Is that the end of the dream Mr. Clough?"

A breathless Clough was only able to splutter, "What a great game of football! This is what people come through the turnstiles to see. Absolutely first class game of football. We've got to thank both teams for that. Especially Cologne, to come to our patch and put on that kind of a display. But, no, don't talk rubbish. I hope anybody's not stupid enough to write us off. We'll get a result over there and we'll be in the final. Looking forward to it."

Then he left and, genuinely, could hardly wait for the second leg to come round in a fortnight's time.

Clough was in his office at the FA Headquarters in Lancaster Gate awaiting the arrival of Tim Cox.

Precisely at the appointed hour there was a knock on Clough's office door. Upon the instruction to enter, Cox opened the door and poked his head round expectantly.

"Come in, young man," said Clough. "Now, what can I do for you?"

Cox explained that he was looking for a few interviews, if possible, so that he could impress the editor at the paper he had been freelancing for so that he might get himself a permanent job. He explained he could get the same stuff as the others at the general press gatherings but he was really trying to make an important enough impression that might help him along the way. Cox also acknowledged that he understood that Clough had no reason to help him out and that it was good of him to allow him a few minutes of his time anyway. And that he might be able to cobble together a saleable piece about just being in the inner sanctum at the FA headquarters.

Clough leaned back in his chair, narrowed his gaze at the young reporter, clasped his hands together and said, "Can I trust you?"

"I think you can, Mr. Clough. I'm really getting worried. I've a young kid and, well, I'm about messing myself. It's very stressful not having a full-time job."

"I know what you mean, young man." Clough said.

He rose from his seat and fetched two whisky glasses. "Do you want a drop?" he asked.

"No, that's okay. I'd better not."

"That's very wise. But you'll have one anyway. I don't like to drink alone." He poured out two generous measures.

"Now what if I give you something about the Football Association?"

"That would be excellent. Anything that I could use."

"How about if I gave you my thoughts, call it my blueprint for the development of football in England?"

"Superb. Like how you would want to see things develop during your tenure as England manager."

"Not exactly, no. I will tell you how it will be developed. Not possibly. I'll tell you what I want and I will assure you that it will happen. You can consider this an exclusive."

"This is incredible."

"Right, get your sports editor on the phone now and tell him what I just said."

Tim Cox rang his sports editor and, judging by Cox's reaction, it was obvious the editor seemed reluctant to believe that the freelancer would be able to deliver what he said he would deliver, and that it would require a more senior reporter to deal with that, and even get access to Brian Clough anyway.

The young man's face was crestfallen, a state that was immediately picked up by Clough.

Clough snatched the phone from the young reporter's hand.

"Oi, I don't know who you are but this is Brian Clough. I am going to give this young man an outline of how the coaching at grassroots level in this country will be developed from now on. And I will give it to this young man only. Now, I'll tell you what you are going to do. You are going to give this young man a permanent job following the England games for your newspaper. I don't want anyone else. I don't give a shit what you give him to do at other times but when there is an England game he will have a press pass along with everyone else. I take it you've understood that. Well, you busy yourself and get him a contract sorted, and don't take the piss with regard to his wages."

Clough put the phone down and turned to Tim Cox. "Right let's get started. No more messing about."
"So this will be the way you see the coaching of England's youngsters," Cox said.
"Correct. Now when I say coaching I am talking about the skills that the young people of this country do not have. Coaching at professional level is different. Good coaching at professional level is telling Roy McFarland to get his hair cut. I'm not talking about that. Look, I know when my players are about to fart. I know you can't write that but you won't have to because we're not talking about that, we're talking about youth. Grass roots. School kids.
Look, there are too many arseholes round here who have been hanging about too long. Charles Hughes and his fucking POMO are going straight out the window. There's too many people been sitting in their little cubby hole offices issuing do this and do that shit when they haven't got a clue about football. Sitting on their fat arses thinking they know how to bring our game up to scratch. Well, here's what will happen. Me and Taylor will choose somebody to oversee the whole of the technical coaching in England. There are plenty of good lads out there who know how the game should be played. And it starts in schools with the teachers.
Our technical coach, and by that I mean the very basic stuff, trapping, passing, heading and what have you, will send coaches round to schools and tell them, no, show them what the teachers should be showing and teaching the kids. Simple stuff, simple exercises to practice skills, practice and practice and practice. Stanley Matthews, Tom Finney, Len Shackleton, those lads, you kick a ball at them and the control was instant.

Why is that? I'll tell you why, because they had a ball, sometimes just a tennis ball, but it was constant practice. The teachers should be showing them how to trap and pass and so on. You learn technique when you're a kid.

And, you know, teachers do a grand job but they are only doing what they can in the time they have available.

The governments don't help, doesn't matter which government is in power, their attitude to sport has become nothing less than disgraceful. Money should be thrown at sport in schools, then we might produce some decent players.

Do you know there are some professional players who don't know how to kick a ball. How the fuck does that happen? Or who picks them? No, what we'll do, Taylor and me, is to make sure that there are enough coaches taught how to coach the basics, and those coaches will travel the country teaching the teachers how to coach. None of this tactics bollocks. That's a different thing and comes later anyway.

This is for kids starting out and learning the game. Here's another thing, though. When these really young kids start to learn the game, the emphasis should be on the ball skills. You can get them to play little games against each other. It doesn't matter at that age if they win or lose. Obviously, you encourage them to try to win, or else there's no point in taking part, and if anybody tells you any different I'm telling you that you are talking to a complete idiot.

What I am saying is that the winning is not the be all and end all at that age. Important, and to be encouraged, but not the be all and end all. The essential thing is to learn to play the ball about on the floor.

When I was youth team coach at Sunderland, after I knackered my knee, I used to get my team ready for the Saturday game by doing stuff that involved the ball.

At Middlesbrough we used to play head tennis, that sort of thing, all ball work.

I was lucky when I was a kid because I had a tennis ball and used to kick it relentlessly, for hours on end against the wall of these garages at the end of the street. Right foot, left foot, constant. Side foot, instep, whatever. It got to the point where I could hammer the tennis ball at a certain point on the garage wall. I was good, I can tell you, but it was all down to practice.

I'll tell you how I got to be a good header of a ball too. There was this pantile roof on one of the buildings next to those garages so I would toss the tennis ball up on to the pantiles and I would know, I had learned, and I could anticipate which way it was going to bounce down. So I would have to control the ball, however it came to me, and belt that ball as if the garage wall was a goal.

Sometimes if the ball bounced high off the pantile roof I would have to head it. That's where timing came in because to get a tennis ball some distance, you have to get the timing right. I'd get these coaches I'm on about to develop little games and strategies like that.

Incidentally, I was one of the youngest qualified coaches in this country. Mind you, I didn't take any notice of those idiots at Lilleshall who thought they knew about football but didn't. Charles Hughes was one of them. I'm surprised I passed because everything I did was to prove him wrong. I got my coaching qualification but a lot of what we did had fuck all to do with football. I went along with it just for the badge.

Bits of paper don't necessarily mean anything. I knew a kid at school could pass every exam going, brilliant he was, answer any question in class, but he was still an idiot when it came to the real world, if you get my drift.

Now, if you get kids at school learning the techniques of kicking a ball at an early age, those skills can be transferred to local leagues. It stands to reason that kids with good, basic technical skills will likely as not want to play in local leagues. Obviously, some kids will be more naturally gifted than others, so they will stand out anyway, but they will then go up to the higher, representative sides. You know, you play for your school, then your town, then your county and so on as high as you can. But we want a structure right from the ground level up. We will, through our coaching system, and working with the schools and teachers, have knowledge of the best talent in the country. I'm not saying that doesn't happen to a certain extent now, but we want to have it more refined. I don't want to miss the chance of seeing a diamond just because it wasn't seen sparkling somewhere.

Which brings me on to professional clubs. We will have each professional club introduce age group coaching sessions for those boys, and girls for that matter if they're interested, who stand out from the crowd in terms of ability. Not many of them will go on to be professional players, that's the nature of the way it is, the strongest shall survive type of thing, but everything is coming down to getting a structure that encompasses all possibilities.

Eventually, the professional clubs will benefit, and the England set up will benefit because we will then have the cream for our representative sides.

Here's the thing though. Right from the start, kids will be taught to get the bloody ball on the floor. On the floor. Practise control to get the ball on the floor. I wish this country was surrounded by hot, dry beaches like they have in Brazil. That's why they can control the ball instantly. Ball bounces over there on the beach, you don't know what direction it's going to go in. Doesn't bother them because, right from the time they can kick a ball, they've been learning how to control it, however it comes at them and at whatever height too.

Going back to this winning thing, at the very youngest it is about developing skills. There should be no pressure from parents or teachers to win games. The point is to develop the love of the game. Playing for twenty minutes, here and there. We did it in the street where there were few cars. Fair enough, you can't do that now, but that was enough to learn the basics. Teachers should just let them play. Let them develop as players as they want to be. Express themselves is the modern term. Then, when they get older, letting them transfer those skills into a game situation. Trying to be big headed and take on players, that's what I did.

There's never been a Football Association plan, for everybody, all ages. Everybody's been left to their own devices.

But you'll never get that at senior level in the clubs because there will always be some idiot who wants to pump the ball into the clouds. And if the clubs get it wrong like that then those players will never end up and an England team.

And, mark my words, Me and Taylor will be keeping our eyes on every England team at every age group. That way we can encourage. If my old manager at Middlesbrough had had any wits about him he would have made me a better player than I became and that would take some doing.

On my debut, he should have said something encouraging as I went out and I would have probably scored. As it happens he didn't, so I never scored on my debut away at Barnsley. If he had said something positive, my record would have been even better than it was. Our policy will be to instil the right philosophy from the bottom up, or the top down, depending on which way you look at it and then it's up to the individual clubs, or their managers, to fuck it up.

That's because the FA can't tell clubs how they should play. Shame, though, that you might get a talented, very gifted player, crippled by his own manager. Of course, this will be revolutionary here at the FA because they've lived so long with their head up their arses they wouldn't know a good thing if it reared up and bit them in the face. Well, I'm here now, and I'm hungry so I'm ready to bite. Understand?

So, from the very basic skills, we will get a greater depth of quality and to achieve that we need the right amount of investment in our coaching resources, the correct planning and the right structure.

Me and Taylor won't be able to do that ourselves but we will make sure it happens as quickly as possible. And, you ask, where does the money come for these coaches? Some of it will come from here at the FA. There's enough money wasted here by old farts going on freebies but this place hasn't got enough money for what I have in mind.

Therefore, the government's going to have to put its hand in its pocket. That means more money for sports in schools, not just football, and so on and so forth. And when I've finished with them, whoever is in government will be gagging to get money into sport.

Look how Harold Wilson kept his job as Prime Minister because Alf Ramsey won the World Cup for England.

All that financial crisis going on at the time. Everybody forgot about all those worries when Alf brought the World Cup here.

And on another point, never overlook the fact that there might be late developers. Otherwise, Jackie Charlton would never have been a World Cup winner.

Now, take it from me, the government will fund all this, or most of it anyway. But these old buggers here shouldn't get away with everything.

Also, I will have a national academy built that will also be a school, like a boarding school. All the best age group youngsters in the country will be offered the chance to attend that school.

There you will have better coaches who will be able to coach the better, more talented young players. And we'll have to pay them properly. What is it? If you pay peanuts you get monkeys, that sort of thing.

So, you are now talking about proper youth coaches, the ones on the bottom rung if you like going round the schools as a proper full-time job. None of this part-time shit as if it is a hobby. Full-time and all teaching the same stuff so that, especially when they get to academy level, or at club level youth teams, you get them all playing skilful, on the ground football.

Another thing on that point is that coaches should be experts in their chosen age group level. It's like some teachers teach younger kids better and some teachers can only teach older age kids. That's how it is. Teachers have different talents. So we have a vast army of well paid age group expert coaches. The pinnacle would be head coach at the national academy. And you know who will be telling him what to tell his coaches, don't you?

Now, to break that down even further, you've got your coaches, who are teaching the teachers the proper way they should be introducing the game to the youngest school kids, but, as the kids get older and they come through the age groups, then you start to splinter into specialist coaches like heading, trapping, passing, shooting, tackling and so on.
And we'll not forget fitness at the national academy and professional clubs because you are dealing with older kids and players.
Professionals, that's another thing. Do you know, when I was at Sunderland, they had us playing a game against nobody. Nobody! The manager, Alan Brown, I rated because he taught me about discipline but, for fuck's sake, what's the point of playing a practice game against no opposition? That never happened on a Saturday afternoon at Roker Park in front of thousands. Jesus, think how good my record would have been if that was the case.
I could go on forever, young man, but I'm sure you can get something out of that, and maybe next time if you prepare a question or two then I'll explain things a bit more. Will that do you for today?"
"Actually, that was fascinating, Mr. Clough. And may I say that I hope that you persuade the FA to implement what you have spoken about today because it seems just the fantastic start England needs to get it out of the doldrums at all levels really."
"Call me Brian. And don't worry about any of that happening. You can take it as read. They say Rome wasn't built in a day but I wasn't on that particular job."
Tim Cox laughed, not just because he'd heard that Clough quip before, but because he felt very happy and secure. He had the notes for a fascinating piece, an exclusive by a real football

person who was about to revolutionise English football, and he had a full time job to go home and tell his girlfriend about.

"Thanks, Brian," he said as he reached the door and opened it. "I can't tell you how grateful I am."

He was nearly out the door when Clough interrupted his departure.

"Oh, young man. Just one thing."

"Yes," said Cox intrigued.

"You try and shit on me again and I'll grab you by the balls and dangle you out the window."

Cox looked shocked. "I'm sorry, did Mr. Taylor tell you what…?"

"No he didn't, actually. Let's just say this. I see everything and I hear everything …. But I don't always let on. Peter Taylor is very shrewd. He is very calculating. He rarely does anything off the cuff, without thinking about it beforehand. Peter Taylor is a genius. We are the best of friends. People might think we are as different as chalk and cheese. But I know him better than anybody. And I knew he was up to something. The thing I also know is that, whatever he was up to, he would be doing to protect me. Listen, I'm a genius too. So I worked it out. Now clear off. And marry that girl."

When the second leg of Forest's European Cup semi-final against FC Cologne arrived, everyone knew it was an insurmountable task. But the Forest management had travelled to Germany with confidence.

Clough spoke to the players before the game. "You reckon you've got big task ahead of you. Well, you haven't, I can tell you. It's a piece of piss when you compare it to what happened in the Second World War right here in this city. It was the first time that the RAF sent out 1000 bombers in one night. The idea was that it might knock this place out of the war or at least give the Germans something to think about. But it didn't. Still, it did enough to get some support for Bomber Harris to go on and build his bouncing bombs. We did bomb the shit out the centre of the city though. Anyway, you'll have an easier time tonight than those brave young lads did that night all those years ago. Lots of them didn't make it back and most of them were younger than you. Can you imagine that? And you reckon you've got a problem. I bet those young lads wished they had a job like yours. Coming in to work at half past ten in the morning. Your biggest worry is that you might lose a game of football or the wife hasn't forgiven you for being the arsehole that you are some of the time. Think about it. Those young lads, bless 'em, were the bravest of the brave. That whole raid, never knowing if they'd be alive the next minute, lasted about as long as the game is going to be tonight."
During the two weeks since the first leg draw, Clough and Taylor had worked on their team and convinced them that they were a better team than the Germans anyway and could score more goals than them.
"Get a goal tonight and fight like hell to keep a clean sheet," was Clough's advice.
"We only need one," said Taylor.

It was 3-3 from the first leg and FC Cologne, having scored three goals away from home, only needed a draw and they were in the final.

The only people who thought Forest had a slim chance were idiots, the Nottingham Forest management and the players. Clough and Taylor didn't allow a shred of doubt.
Forest defended stoutly, occasionally trying the breakaway that would give them the decisive goal.
After 65 minutes Robertson took a corner on the left, a perfectly worked set piece for Birtles to flick on.
Bowyer, coming through a crowded penalty area, found himself in a surprising amount of space and stooped low to head the ball past Schumacher in the German goal.
Thereafter, it was backs against the wall for Forest and they held out magnificently.
Shilton, in the last minute, made an astonishing save at the near post to send Forest into the final at the end of May.
Clough thought it amusing that Forest's goalscorer, Ian Bowyer, went by the nickname of 'Bomber'.

The FA committee was sitting round the large Brazilian mahogany table when Clough and Taylor entered and sat down, carefully separating their chairs so that the committee members had to do the 'tennis spectator effect' if either of them spoke.
"Are you aware that we haven't seen you here for six months?" said Professor Sir Harold Thompson.
"Bloody hell. Is it that long?" said Peter Taylor. "Did you have a good Christmas? We did. "
"I was here not long ago," said Clough. "The trouble with you lot is that you get stuck in these little rabbit warrens of your offices, messing about with these pretend committees and pretend that you are actually achieving something. But that

will be changing. Anyway, gentlemen, enough of the pleasantries. We've got the British Championships coming up in the space of a week so we want to get that won and out the way because, I don't know whether you spotted it, but we're taking Nottingham Forest to the European Cup Final in Munich at the end of the month. With regard to the Home internationals, if you're interested, we've got Northern Ireland away, Wales away and Scotland at home. Come if you want to. Just ask Linda to get you some tickets. And if you want some tickets for friends and family you can buy them from her as well."

Sir Harold Thompson broke in. "Mr. Clough, we've never had to buy our own tickets before and, frankly, we find it goes completely against the grain for Football Association officials of some years standing to be subjected to the degradation of having to purchase tickets from an administration assistant."

"I hope you are not saying that you are above Linda in the pecking order," said Clough. "She actually works here. If you're saying that, I'll chop your balls off. Anyway, here's the thing, we won't be competing in this Home International championship again after we've won this one because, with Thatcher now in charge, this country's going to have plenty of shit going on. We're not going to bother upsetting the Welsh, the Scots and particularly the Irish by pissing all over them in a tin pot tournament. We've got to go to Belfast as it is in October for the European Championship qualifier. Can't avoid that, but after this one we'll not bother."

The committee members shared indignant scowls and wide-eyed looks of disbelief, accompanied by audible huffs from the FA Chairman.

"The 'do' at Brian's house on New Year's Eve was a cracker," said Taylor.

The Home International championship came and went with predictable wins, 2-0 against Northern Ireland in Belfast, with Lloyd and Coppell scoring, a minor blip in terms of a 0-0 draw with Wales at Wembley as Clough rested his Forest lads, and a 3-1 Wembley win against the Scots, again the Forest lads rested.
But goals by Kevin Keegan and wingers Steve Coppell on the right and Peter Barnes on the left was enough to see off the Scots.
Noticeably, the England team trooped off with gentlemanly shakes of the hand rather than indulging in excessive celebration.

That was the season's end for most of the players but the Nottingham Forest contingent had one more game to play.
The European Cup Final, to be held at the Olympic Stadium in Munich, pitched them against the Swedish side Malmo.
To most managers, the team selection might have been a problem in that all the players had declared themselves fit for the end of season showpiece to decide the best club team in Europe.
Not Clough. He had spotted, with advice from Taylor and, especially, Jimmy Gordon, that Archie Gemmill and Martin O'Neill had been carrying injuries.
Clough would not pick a player if he thought a niggle could damage that player further. His own experiences would never allow that, and he suspected these two were trying to get a game because of the importance of the occasion. He could understand their thinking.

Clough was squatting on a football on the morning of the game after a very light workout, with the players sitting on the grass in front of him.

Gemmill and O'Neill told Clough that they were in perfect condition and Clough announced that he was delighted for them but that they weren't playing that night.

Both were unhappy, Gemmill reacting with a barely audible stream of vitriol directed at his manager while O'Neill took the hump big time and sulked silently.

On the way to the stadium, on the team bus, Clough plonked down a crate of beer, with the instruction for anyone to get one if they wanted one. Some did, some didn't. Clough and Taylor did.

In the changing room of the Olympic Stadium, prior to the game, Clough asked if the players had noticed the magnificent canopies of glass supported by steel cables.

He pointed out that it had been designed like that to imitate the Alps, in an elegant attempt to forget the Summer Olympics of Hitler's Nazi regime. He also pointed out that the stadium was built in a pit made by bombings in the Second World War.

O'Neill sat in the corner and said nothing.

Clough told Birtles to go and shave his beard off and Birtles protested that it had taken him ages to grow it.

Clough said it looked scabby and there would be lots of cameras about so that he must look his best.

Birtles went off to shave off his beard and Taylor nodded to Clough, realising that Clough had made him do that to occupy the young striker's mind, if only for a few minutes, to take it off the game.

Forest were considered favourites because the Swedes had lost influential players in midfield general Bo Larsson and defenders Roy Andersson and Krister Kristensson.

The night before the game, their captain, Staffan Tapper, broke his toe but decided to play on.

From the start, Malmo packed their defence as Forest attacked with freedom but without result.

The truth is, it was a dull game, with many offsides. The tall Swedes had been instructed by their English manager Bob Houghton to stop the flowing moves of Forest and snatch a goal on the counter attack if they could.

The one moment of magic came when John Robertson - as Clough had once described, 'A very unattractive young man, but give him the ball and a yard of grass and he is an artist' - went past two Malmo defenders and swung over a perfect cross.

The one million pound man, Trevor Francis, making his debut in the European Cup, stooped and stumbled to head firmly into the roof of the net before crashing down on the concrete discus circle just behind and alongside the goal.

Francis had got on the wrong side of Erlandsson to score after a great blind side run.

Birtles' story was also remarkable coming from such a different background to the former Birmingham City wunderkind Francis.

It was only three years previously that Birtles was playing non-league for Long Eaton, so to be in that prestigious final was unbelievable.

Birtles remembered afterwards that the Swedes were all six feet plus tall and impossible to beat in the air. None of his family noticed that he had shaved his beard off for the final.

163

For the record the victorious team from Nottingham was: Shilton, Anderson, Lloyd, Burns, Clark, McGovern (captain), Francis, Bowyer, Birtles, Woodcock, Robertson.

After the final whistle and the wild celebrations on the pitch, the Forest team and the management returned to the dressing room where champagne was opened.

The screaming, shouting, punching the air and hugging that attends such highly emotional football occasions was brought to a halt when Brian Clough called for quiet.

"Fantastic lads," he started. "Got to be one of the most satisfying moments of my, our, career. So, well done. But now, it's time for Peter and me to bow out and concentrate on the England job. We've shown you how to win the League, the League Cup and now the European Cup. Now go and win the League again and the European Cup again. You can win the League Cup whenever you like. But, for us, it's time to go."

There was a total hush as the players looked at Clough and Taylor in disbelief and then at each other.

It was something that they couldn't readily take in.

Martin O'Neill, who had remained moodily silent after his exclusion from the team, but had joined in the euphoria with his team mates, sparked into life

"In the midst of all this celebration," he asked, "might I challenge the timing of this announcement, devastating as it is for us as a team and as a club."

"I wouldn't expect anything else from you, young man. But my timing is as impeccable as ever," confirmed Clough. "And let me tell all of you. When we arrive back in Nottingham we will be in our club blazers looking like a football team and not a bunch of jaded rock stars. Have a drink, but go steady."

A few days later, Clough and Taylor were sat in their usual chairs near to the large Brazilian mahogany table with the FA committee members sat around expectantly.
Clough spoke first. "Good morning gentlemen. Thank you for attending this meeting. You may have noticed that we won the European Cup the other day with Nottingham Forest. We have now severed our ties with that lovely club and we are going to devote our energies to England. Of course, we would have done that earlier but that European Cup thing was bugging us. That's sorted now. And so we will concentrate fully on England. What you can do is keep out of our bloody way. If any of you think you will stop us winning games for England, I'll kick your arse and then throw you out of the nearest window."
This upset Professor Sir Harold Thompson. "Now Mr. Clough, you don't come in here issuing orders," he said, ridiculously.
Clough continued. "From now on, yes I do. And you Professor Sir Harold Thompson, you're reign of terror is over. I've seen the way you've bullied this staff. Well it doesn't happen with me.
How do you think it would be if I went round terrorising and bullying people? It doesn't work. Believe me.
You must have done some good round here at some point. Probably not by design but the law of averages says you must have got something right from time to time.
Don't worry, I'll be good to you. I'll bring you in every now and then, to let you know what's going on and bask in our glory. Because that's what's coming our way. Glory.

We haven't been here five minutes, we're undefeated with England, we've won the British Championship twice, and now we're going into the big league.
And we don't want you hangers on getting in the bloody way. Now clear off the lot of you, do what you want to do but I don't want any of you blazer brigade getting in the way. If you get a message from Linda to get something done, don't ask any questions, just get it done. And don't bother coming in here again until I invite you."
Clough raised his voice with that last sentence that caused an embarrassed shuffling of feet.
"Don't be hasty, Brian," said Taylor. "I've arranged for some sandwiches to be brought in. Chicken."
"That's a good idea, Peter. Have some sent to my office. I've a young reporter, Tim Cox coming in."
Thompson looked embarrassed, then attacked. "That's another thing, Mr. Clough. There are reports in the national press with information obviously coming from you that hasn't been passed by the Press Release Committee. Please ensure everything is vetted first," said Thompson.
"Shut up," replied Clough. "Make sure there's enough for two, please Pete."

Brian Clough was chosen for his only two full international caps in 1959, against Wales in Cardiff and Sweden at Wembley. It was scant reward for the prolific centre forward. Walter Winterbottom, the England team manager, was originally placed in charge in 1946 but, in reality, his position was nominal.

He had what was perceived as sole control, but the national team was, in essence, still chosen by a Football Association selection committee.
This inevitably led to officials of league clubs, who had managed to get themselves elected on to the selection committee, arguing the case for their own players so that it would bring credit and prestige to their club and, by proxy, themselves.

Winterbottom's first England team in 1946 saw him play Tom Finney on the right wing where the mesmeric Stanley Matthews had roamed for quite a while on England duty. Finney would have deserved a place in the team anyway, so it suggests some interference behind the scenes that the two were not included together, especially as Finney was equally adept on the left wing and went on to win many caps in that position. So it was, in truth, a long time before Winterbottom was able to have some semblance of autonomy, away from the interference of the myriad of Football Association committee members and councillors
By 1958, at the World Cup in Sweden, that is to say twelve years after he had first started in the job, Winterbottom had, by and large, got his way, and was allowed to choose the team himself.
Winterbottom preferred the bruiser of a centre forward from West Bromwich Albion, Derek Kevan, who scored very few goals and so was nowhere near as good a goalscorer as Clough.
The selection committee still existed but was basically a nonsense. It still kept those committee members fulfilling a

role of sorts at the FA headquarters, and ensured their free tickets to games and any other perks they could get their hands on. They still seemed to have an influence of sorts.

At least that's why Clough only got two caps, according to Clough.

It was a not going to be the same for Winterbottom's successor in 1962.

Alf Ramsey was the successful manager of rural Ipswich Town who he had led to the First Division championship by frugal, insightful management and clever tactics.

He wouldn't have taken the job of England team manager on the terms that Winterbottom had originally agreed.

Although Ramsey had trusted people to help him, Harold Shepherdson of Middlesbrough and Les Cocker of Leeds United, they had no input in the selection of the team.

Ostensibly, there was to be no interference from anyone at the FA.

Indeed, it was Ramsey who said on a tour of South America that he would rather have brought four more players, but at least the four FA committee members present allowed him to avoid official receptions.

Reluctantly on the FA's part, although the selection committee was abandoned, it merely resurfaced under another name as the Senior International Committee.

Ramsey was never forgiven for upsetting that particular sinecure.

By the time Nobby Stiles of Manchester United and Bobby Charlton's older brother, Jack, of Leeds United, made their

England debuts at Wembley against Scotland in April 1965, Ramsey had found his World Cup winning back six, though he probably didn't realise it at the time.

A little over a year later, Gordon Banks (Leicester City), George Cohen (Fulham), Nobby Stiles, Jack Charlton, Bobby Moore (West Ham United and captain) and Ray Wilson (Everton), were to be part of the team that held aloft the Jules Rimet Trophy for England.

Over time, Ramsey had tried various players and formations but, ultimately, didn't discover his winning formula until the 1966 quarter final against Argentina when Geoff Hurst played after Jimmy Greaves had suffered a serious gash on his shin during the group match against France.

After Greaves had reported fit, Ramsey's decision to leave out the finest goal scorer of that generation purely for team efficiency, was met with gasps of disbelief and apprehension. In the end Ramsey was proved right when Hurst scored a hat trick in the final against West Germany and was thus immortalised.

The England squad of 1966 was the product of a rather protracted winnowing process. FIFA required that each national side provide a list of 40 players before the end of May, and then a final squad of 22 players.

Typical of woolly FIFA thinking was that the final 22 need not have been among the original 40.

Ramsey named his provisional list of 40 players on April 7, almost two months earlier than required and then made another squad announcement on May 6, naming 28 players who would report for pre-tournament training to the Lilleshall National Recreation Centre in Shropshire on June 6.

Players in the original 40 were put on stand-by.

As it happened, Everton's Brian Labone, a centre half, but not first choice, withdrew from the squad because of injury and the fact that he was due to get married, so only 27 players reported for training at Lilleshall.

At the close of the training session on June 18, Ramsey cut five players.

Thereafter, following a break for a short, last visit home, the 22-man squad embarked on a four-match pre-tournament tour of Europe.

During that tour, in Copenhagen, Ramsey formally announced the England squad to FIFA and the press.

The numbers Ramsey assigned to the squad generally reflected his preferences, Nos. 1-11 constituting his first team and Nos. 12-22 the second string players.

Ramsey was never comfortable with journalists and didn't always treat them with the respect they thought they deserved. This included the occasional red herring.

If the numbers were correct, why did Ramsey hint he would field his first choice and then announce Hunt instead of Hurst, and Peters instead of Connelly in the final friendly against Poland before the World Cup competition started properly? The answer could be that Hunt provided a more team minded type of player (and Hurst had had a dreadful game against Denmark a couple of days before) and he had in mind to play an out-and-out winger, John Connelly, against the ultra defensive Uruguayans in the opening game of the tournament. When Ramsey was asked by a press member if he could then explain what Peters would bring to the team, Ramsey replied that he couldn't and left the room.

This was better than the response he gave to a Scottish reporter when Ramsey was welcomed to Scotland for a game at Hampden Park. "You must be fucking joking," snarled Ramsey, whose dislike of the Scots was unhidden.

As it turned out, that opening match of the 1966 World Cup Finals in England, a 0-0 draw, was dire and, for English fans, a great disappointment.

What Ramsey was after was the team ethic which is where his and Brian Clough's football ideals converged.

Ramsey had taken Ipswich from a footballing nowhere to the very top and Clough would do the same with Derby County and then Nottingham Forest. The team was the thing.

Ramsey had the luxury of five truly world class players in Gordon Banks in goal, Ray Wilson at left back, Bobby Moore defending, Bobby Charlton in midfield and Jimmy Greaves, the lethal finisher.

Clough had a better strike rate than Greaves and would have fancied himself in the England set up had he not suffered that career ending knee injury. But would he have ultimately fitted into Ramsey's team ethic? In the end Greaves didn't either, being replaced by the less prolific but more industrious target men Hurst and Hunt.

Ramsey's World Cup squad choice was easily evaluated by Clough and Taylor - Gordon Banks (1), arguably the best goalkeeper in the world at the time, George Cohen (2), a dependable right back who could get forward to put crosses over, Ray Wilson (3), more stylish than his right back counterpart, Nobby Stiles (4), a ferocious tackler and competitor, Jack Charlton (5), solid in the air, Bobby Moore (6), captain and superb game-reading defender, Alan Ball (7), tireless ball gatherer for Bobby Charlton, Jimmy Greaves (8), world class goal scorer, Bobby Charlton (9), the most influential midfielder in the world, Geoff Hurst (10), good target man and finisher, John Connelly (11), versatile, quick winger, Ron Springett (12), experienced international keeper, Peter Bonetti (13), young, potential heir to Banks, Jimmy Armfield (14), experienced international right back, Gerry Byrne (15), solid understudy to Wilson, Martin Peters (16), an exceptionally versatile team player, Ron Flowers, (17) experienced international defender, Norman Hunter (18), dependable, hard-tackling defender, Terry Paine (19), quick, elusive right winger, Ian Callaghan, (20), right winger and midfield cover, Roger Hunt (21), good target man, finisher and work horse, George Eastham (22), experienced and stylish international midfielder.

Both Clough and Taylor admired Sir Alf Ramsey, not just because he had won the World Cup for England but because of the way he had gone about his task.
Ramsey was single-minded, efficient, and supremely confident in his own ability and that of his players. He also knew football inside out.
Ramsey had originally started out as an inside right, signed for Tottenham from Southampton as a left-back for a record fee for a full back, moved to centre-half then into the right-back slot, where he remained for the rest of his career including 32 appearances for England.
Ramsey's move to Tottenham was important to the renowned push-and-run side under astute Spurs manager Arthur Rowe. He completely understood the style Rowe wanted to play and his tireless running and his accurate passing made him a vital part of the team when playing out from the back.
Ramsey was forward thinking in many ways but, ultimately, everything came down to what was best for the team.
He had taken a keen interest in the way the game was played and was known as an influential, dependable, thinking, player on the pitch. His nickname was 'The General'.
He also instigated set plays at free kicks and corners when they weren't commonplace.
 One of the most important games he played in was the famous 6-3 defeat when Ferenc Puskas' Hungary tore England apart to inflict their first ever defeat at Wembley.

What Ramsey remembered most was the passing and movement of their foreign tormentors. It gave him food for thought.

With Ipswich, using the players he had available rather than setting out to build a team from scratch, his side lined up with a player behind the main strikers. With no recognised wingers, he was able to fashion a team that tactically baffled the opposition.

Announcing a couple of years in advance that England would win the World Cup in 1966 was seen by many as arrogance but it was just his way.

The committee men at the FA were referred to as 'those people' by Ramsey and he had no time for most people on the periphery of the game.

After Stiles had committed a terrible foul against a Frenchman, Jacky Simon, in the group game, FIFA implored the Football Association to at least suspend Stiles for the next match. Ramsey was called before the International Committee who suggested a suspension as a symbolic penalty.

Ramsey pointed out that Stiles was an integral part of the team, he was not even booked for the foul, and that if he wasn't playing in the next match then he would not be the manager either. Then he left the room.

However, the England players had the utmost confidence and belief in their manager, who was loyal to them and would do his best to convince them that they were the better than their opponents, by good planning and excellent preparation.

This was part of a template that Clough and Taylor had been shaping over the years, taking bits and pieces from various sources and moulding them to their own.

Ramsey's victory over West Germany in 1966 was to be a standard by which he and all future England managers were to be measured.

England defended their title in Mexico four years later. Ramsey, again prepared in minute detail, including transporting their own tinned food.
The best preparation, however, couldn't account for the arrest of Bobby Moore for allegedly stealing a bracelet from a jewellers in the Colombian capital of Bogota on their way to the tournament.
He was proved innocent but it was unsettling to the squad. Ramsey also made some derogatory remarks about Mexico and upset the host nation, much like he had upset Argentina in 1966 by saying, "Our best football will come against the right type of opposition – a team who come to play football and not act as animals."
This time, Mexico supporters made incessant and raucous noise outside England's hotel until 4 a.m. to keep them awake. Then there was the stomach bug illness suffered by goalkeeper Gordon Banks on the eve of the quarter-final against West Germany which meant Peter Bonetti had to play.
Even so, England had been 2-0 up with goals from Alan Mullery and Martin Peters and England should have locked out the game.
But the Germans came back into the game with a goal by Beckenbauer.
Ramsey replaced Bobby Charlton to save him from the heat, thinking England were through, but seven minutes from time Uwe Seeler looped a back header over Bonetti for the equaliser.

With England now struggling in the heat, Gerd Muller grabbed the winner in the second period of extra time to put Germany through to the semis.

Many people thought that that England squad was a better squad than that which won the trophy in 1966, but the defeat was the beginning of the end for Sir Alf.

The qualifying games for the 1974 World Cup were disastrous. A defeat in Poland with Alan Ball being sent off and a home draw with Wales were the prelude to a game that became famous for Brian Clough calling the Polish goalkeeper, Jan Tomaszewski, a clown.

That clown kept England at bay, while Shilton allowed the one shot he had to save to squeeze under his body to produce a 1-1 draw and, for England, an exit from that World Cup.

The Football Association committee men were sharpening their knives and at the head of the queue was Professor Sir Harold Thompson.

Ramsey had spent most of his career at the very top of the game and had brought great joy and success to his club sides and his beloved country.

One thing the FA could never take away from him was the unflinching respect of his players.

Even Jimmy Greaves, so disappointed to be left out of a World Cup winning team, understood Ramsey's reasons for that decision.

Brian Clough sat with Tim Cox at the bar of the England hotel in Hendon.

The players and staff had long since gone to bed and Clough had purchased two bottles of whisky before the bar had closed for the night. One was nearly empty.

Clough was in a maudlin frame of mind but Cox listened intently.

Clough said, "The greatest moment in the history of English football came at about quarter past five that Saturday afternoon when Geoff Hurst shot left-footed, magnificently into the top corner of the net.

The German goalkeeper just stood and watched as it flew past him. I think it took a slight bobble which made it sit up ever so nicely for him and he cracked it cleanly.

That goal clinched the World Cup but the Germans were out of it by then. It was Hurst's third goal, England's fourth.

It prompted Kenneth Wolstenholme, who was a great commentator, by the way, to say what has now become famous, 'Some people are on the pitch. They think it's all over. It is now.' But, you know, he never said just that. What he actually said was, 'Some people are on the pitch. They think it's all over. It is now. It's four.' People always get that wrong. Bobby Moore got the ball in his own area, took the ball forward, cool as you like, looked up and planted the ball up to Hurst in the inside position, ten yards inside the German half. The referee was looking at his watch and some England supporters had come on to the pitch as Hurst collected the ball from Moore.

He sprinted forward with a German defender after him and then he scored.

At the final whistle, the scene was chaos, unforgettable. Stiles and Cohen collapsed in a tearful hug, young Ball turned wild cartwheels and Jack Charlton dropped to his knees.

You know what Alf did when that last goal went in? He told Harold Shepherdson to sit down and behave himself. He was the only English in the stadium not on his feet cheering.
One of the first people on the pitch at the final whistle to congratulate the players was Jimmy Greaves.
Great player Greaves. Great goalscorer. Better than me actually. Made it look easy. Passed the ball into the net.
I always thought that was brilliant of him to behave like that when that could easily have been some of his glory. Was Alf right to leave him out? Of course he was. The team came first.
I remember the crowd shouting Ramsey's name over and over again. It was his moment.
Everything he had thought and planned and worked for had happened for him.
Eventually Bobby Moore led the team up to the royal box to receive the gold Jules Rimet trophy from the Queen.
Wiped his hands on the cloth that covered the front of the royal box before he got to the Queen. You'd never catch Moore out. Immaculate.
Then the lap of honour began. The crowd chanting 'Ee-aye-addio, we've won the cup'. You don't hear that anymore.
Bobby threw the cup in the air and I thought for Christ's sake, don't drop it. But he caught it. No problem
That day, it was the end of July but it had rained earlier on, England were more determined, aggressive and had shown more invention that the Germans over the whole match.
They were all heroes but, for me, a few stood out. Hurst, obviously, Moore, every inch a captain, Bobby Charlton, if for no other reason that they made Beckenbauer shadow him and Beckenbauer was their best player, and young Alan Ball. Ran

his socks off. You couldn't give anybody Man of the Match except Hurst but, for me, Ball epitomised everything good about that team.

All of them played as a team. When they went one down and then later when they let in that equaliser with seconds to play, the whole of the team came together.

Yes, they were pissed off, probably with each other too, but it made them dig that bit deeper. They wanted it bad enough to take those setbacks on the chin, get up and start again.

Ball's work rate was phenomenal, Charlton's sheer class inspiring. But every one of the others responded superbly and nobody lacked courage or total commitment.

It's what old Harry Storer said to me, 'Once you're a manager, if it ever happens, do a quick check before away games. Look at your players prior to the coach leaving and count the hearts. If there are less than five, don't bother setting off. A team's no good without courage.'

England had plenty of courage that day. The Germans fucked it up for themselves by putting Beckenbauer on Charlton but that was their problem.

They tried their hardest but in the end England's spirit broke them.

Wembley was fired up that day with an atmosphere it had never known before. Massive crowd, chanting and singing.

It might have been Anfield. There can be no greater tribute to the Kop than that. And England did wear red.

When the band of the Royal Marines played the national anthem it was sung as if it was never going to be sung again. I remember thinking the Germans began a bit nervously, standing off and letting England's forwards move up to the edge of the penalty area.

Charlton and Peters were able to work the ball along the left with ease, Wilson helping out, and the Germans seemed anxious before the ball was cleared.

Bobby Charlton wandered all over the field, composed, smooth. England seemed to be playing what I've heard called 'total football'.

I'll give you an example. Early on, Hunt set Stiles clear on the right, yes Stiles, and his cross beat Tilkowski in the German goal before it was headed away. Bobby Charlton put it back in the middle and Tilkowski knocked himself out punching it away from Hurst.

England had chances. Jackie Charlton carried the ball forward and then, with a lovely diagonal pass, set Peters up for a quick, powerful shot from the edge of the penalty area.

Ball took a corner on the right and Hurst volleyed the ball but it went much too high.

Peters tried, coming in from the right to shoot the ball only just over from 25 yards.

Then, incredibly, in the tenth minute England found themselves one down. The crowd couldn't believe it.

If you'd seen that defence so far in the tournament, superb, it just couldn't have happened.

Their inside forward lofted in a high cross from the left wing and Wilson, jumping for the ball all on his own, headed it down to the feet of Haller, yes, that same Haller from that Juventus shit years later, about twelve yards out.

He had time to steady himself before hitting a right foot shot on the ground past Banks.

You could see they were pissed off. Stiles was bollocking everybody but he was really just mad at Wilson.

Luckily, it took England only six minutes to equalise. Bobby Moore was tripped up and I remember he grabbed the ball before the referee blew for a foul because he knew it would be given. See, he was even ahead of the ref.

Anyway, he took the kick himself. He'd spotted Hurst running in, something they'd practised at West Ham I suppose, and Hurst planted a perfect header, downwards past the keeper. I'd have been proud of that one myself.

Moore held one arm aloft just to signal that he meant it while everybody jumped on Hurst. One thing Greenwood did with West Ham was to work on stuff like that in training.

Bobby Charlton tried a left foot shot after running along the edge of the penalty area from the right and the German keeper took two goes to get it.

Their goalscorer had another slim chance but otherwise most of the attacking was coming from England.

Bobby Moore, very calm and assured, kept trying to join in attacks, that's how much we were pinning them back but they weren't able to get Bobby Charlton in to have a crack.

That lad could hit piledrivers with both feet. He'd scored three great goals up to the final.

Another time, Cohen crossed a long ball from the right and Hurst rose magnificently to slam in another header which the keeper scrambled away.

When the Germans did have a sniff it was cut out and I remember Jack Charlton sweeping in with those long legs to smother an effort. He looked like a giraffe with those legs. That was his nickname. Giraffe.

Hunt had a cracking chance to score, and I think he thought he had, left foot volley, almost point blank, but their keeper blocked it.

Then Bobby Charlton tried to put Peters away but he couldn't quite reach the ball to get a shot in.

Banks did have to turn the ball over the bar once. And it was a brilliant save, too. We needed him. You don't want your keepers to do much but if they have to, you want a bloody good one.

Bobby Charlton kept moving, Moore kept trying to put him through, Cohen was making regular runs down the right and putting crosses in but they were being easily cut out.

Nobby got a bollocking for throwing the ball down after what he thought was a harsh decision. I'd have bollocked him for that. Never, ever complain about referees.

Hunt was working as hard as anybody, making himself available. That's the sign of a good, honest pro. Some people miss that. I always rated him for the stuff he did that went unseen by most people.

It was him who had a hand in England's second goal. He laid a pass to Ball and the German keeper pushed his shot out for a corner. It was because of that corner that England scored. The ball came out to Hurst who jinked to go to his left, came back and hit it with his right.

It ballooned up off a defender and fell to Peters who slammed it into the back of the net from about five yards out.

I used to love the sound of the ball hitting the net. Like an ever so slight metal twang.

Anyway, I'm glad it went to Peters because just behind him was Jack Charlton who'd been up for the corner. If it had fallen to him the ball might have ended up the other side of London.

Then came that shitty German equaliser in the last minute. Jack gave away a free kick on the edge of our area but I'm not sure it was a free kick except it was because the ref gave it. The ball was played in, a ricochet, handball by a German, not given, spins across the area, then that Weber sticks it in. That was so demoralising. For the fans as well, not just the team. But Alf got them up for it because that was the end of normal time. Our lads were so down. It must have been terrible for them. So close and then they'd got to do it again.

What Alf said was brilliant. 'You've beaten them once, now go beat them again'. Brilliant.

To be fair, the Germans were out of their feet. Knackered. You couldn't stop Ball running though. He'd have gone on forever. If ever there was a young lad, I think he was only twenty, who saw an opportunity in life, perhaps the only chance he would ever have in a World Cup Final, and said to himself, 'I'm not wasting this.'

I read somewhere his Dad had said something like that to him before the game. If he did, well played, because it was spot on. Anyway, after that it was nearly all England.

You couldn't underestimate the Germans, the same with any game, it only takes a second to score a goal, but it was only us who really looked like scoring.

Ball had a shot tipped over, Bobby hit a long effort, then came that goal or no goal.

I personally thought it was a goal but then I'm a forward. The thing is I would never have had all this controversy because I would have kept it lower and not bothered with all that hitting the bar shit.

Great run by Ball to cut the ball back, good control by Hurst then he should have buried it.

When the ref gave it and most of the people in the stadium didn't know whether it was in or out, still don't to this day, I swear the sun came out.

Do you know how I remember all that so clearly? Because Hurst could and should have been me. Mind you, if it had've been me, there would've been no need for extra time.

One last thing. What Alf said in '63 about winning the World Cup '66, I am telling you the same. England will win the World Cup in 1982. Except you can't quote me."

So Clough and Taylor set about building a team to, ultimately, win the World Cup in 1982 but they realised the preparation for that had to be done immediately, before the 1980 European Championships.

With the earlier qualifying wins against Denmark in Copenhagen and Northern Ireland at Wembley, and the draw against the Republic of Ireland in Dublin, thoughts were now concentrated on the remaining qualifying games.

A week in June saw a qualifier in Sofia against Bulgaria result in a 3-0 win with goals from Keegan, Lloyd and Barnes.

That was followed by two friendlies, a 0-0 against Sweden in Stockholm and a 4-3 loss to Austria in Vienna in which various combinations were tried.

However, it was clear to Clough and Taylor that they were beginning to mould a squad that would do what they were told and play in the manner that they decreed.

A clear bonus was the emergence of young Kenny Sansom as a solid left back.

The game against Austria was interesting for Clough and Taylor in that they had asked the team to play with only two out-and-out midfielders in Ray Wilkins and Trevor Brooking. Steve Coppell and Peter Barnes were to push up on the flanks with instructions to stay high up the field in order to occupy the opposing full backs.
England's defence, however, conceded four having pulled back form 3-1 down equalise.
Asked afterwards whether that experiment was a mistake, Taylor explained that the experiment couldn't have been a mistake because they meant to try it.
He conceded that it might have been a failure but that it was his decision whether it was a failure or not and, as such, he hadn't made that decision yet.
Clough pointed out that the best part about the display was that the team had shown fighting spirit by coming back when it looked like all was lost.

***

Over a couple of glasses of Australian Shiraz, Clough and Taylor sat down at the Nag's Head to discuss the England squad for the remaining qualifying matches for the 1980 European Championships to be held in Italy the following summer.
Clough suggested that they go through the players one by one, player by player, and decide whether it was worth persevering with them.
Both came up with the same twenty two players as first choice squad members but also chose six players as stand by.
The choice of the wine was Taylor's on the grounds that he had decided he would become knowledgeable about the wines

of the world wherever they had played and where they were possibly going to end up with England.

The Australian choice was because there had been talk at the Football association of fixing up a couple of practice games, and a full international, in Australia the following summer prior to the European Championships if England should qualify.

Taylor pointed out that he had never been to Australia and that he fancied having a look at the Sydney Opera House.

With that in mind he had already primed Linda to arrange that the international match be played in Sydney specifically to accommodate that experience.

After all, they would have a settled squad by then, though the players themselves wouldn't know it, so it only remained for the team to qualify for the finals for that holiday ambition to be realised.

Taylor had convinced himself and Clough that learning about wine was a good idea and would be a welcome educational diversion from the whisky that they had started to drink, as snifters, sometimes before lunch.

It had been great winning all those gallons of whisky as Manager of the Month awards but their attitude was that the fruits of their labours should be regarded as part of the job specification and not just an occasional social loosener.

"This wine is a Shiraz," said Taylor, "It's exceptional. I think we should order another and maybe have a beef lunch here too."

Clough nodded in agreement and asked Taylor what had suddenly put him on to wine.

Taylor explained that he had seen a programme on television in which experts were talking about the wine and tasting it and discussing its relative merits.

"What do you mean?' asked Clough.

"Well," said Taylor. "Take this particular wine. It's a Shiraz because it comes from Australia though the grape is also known as Syrah in Europe and other places. It's a dark-skinned grape grown throughout the world and used to produce quite powerful red wines. This particular variety that we're drinking is, to me, a rich but heady blend with a fruity body. I am wildly attracted to its immensely enticing aroma that reminds me of summer evenings when I was courting my Lil."

"That's a load of bollocks," said Clough.

"I know," said Taylor. "Apart from the bit about our Lil, I read most of it off the label."

The European qualifiers resumed in September at Wembley against Denmark with a Kevin Keegan goal to produce a 1-0 win.

The following month, with the players beginning to blend as a team, they took apart Northern Ireland 5-1 in Belfast. Keegan with two more, Woodcock with a brace and an own goal cementing the handsome victory.

However, a sparkling performance from Trevor Francis was leading Clough and Taylor to believe they were finding themselves with a potent strike force to complement the sturdy defence and the elegant and creative midfield of Wilkins and Brooking.

A month after that, there was a return to Wembley which saw England defeat Bulgaria 2-0.

Brooking had pulled out with injury and Clough and Taylor chose to blood a youngster from Tottenham, Glenn Hoddle, in midfield.

Hoddle was the essence of invention but too many of his passes, according to Taylor, were a waste of time because they attempted to achieve the impossible.

However, he scored a stunning goal, right footed into the top of the net from well outside the area that he thought would cement his name on the team sheet for years to come.

"That was well taken, young man," said Clough afterwards, "but I'm glad for you it went in because if it hadn't I'd have grabbed you by the balls and twisted them as hard as I could. You had two runners up front, in better positions than you, and both of them were screaming for the ball. Think about what you are doing and what is best for the team."

"That was a bit harsh, wasn't it?" Taylor said to Clough.

"Not really," he said. "Let's face it. He's a superb passer of the ball and he can drop it on a sixpence from forty yards. He'll get plenty of caps but we don't want him to know how good he is just yet. He'll not play the next game, that's a certainty."

The final qualifier came the following February against the Republic of Ireland at Wembley, Keegan netting both in a 2-0 win.

It was pretty much a foregone conclusion and the management had decided to test another young midfielder in Bryan Robson. He had shown, at club level, the sort of combative and forceful skills that Wilkins could provide at international level.

Brooking and Hoddle lacked those qualities. So Robson was a very useful addition to the squad that had now qualified for the European Championship Finals in Italy in June.

In the England dressing room at Wembley after the game, Clough and Taylor walked in to find that the players were congratulating themselves noisily and vibrantly.

"What the bloody hell is going on in here?" shouted Clough. "We've won sod all yet. All we've done is qualify for the finals. It'll be a nice trip to Italy. Stand up those of you who think they'll be enjoying a trip to Italy."

Kenny Sansom started to stand up but, not seen by Clough, was pulled down by Shilton.

"That's it," said Clough. "You've got it. Nobody is safe round here. If you think your place is guaranteed then you'd better get that fucking idea out of your fucking head."

Peter Taylor brought some measure of calm into the proceedings as the players thought Clough was going to explode like he had done on many occasions before.

"Keep your heads down, do your jobs and you'll be all right," he said. "But, remember, we are watching your every move."

Kevin Keegan stood up and said that, on behalf of the team, he would like to thank Mr. Clough and Mr. Taylor for their efforts in guiding them through to the finals, particularly after the disappointment of missing out on the 1978 World Cup Finals."

Clough thanked Keegan for his words and pointed out that they shouldn't have missed out on the last World Cup. He laid the blame firmly in the court of the players themselves, deliberately avoiding the opportunity to take a pot shot at his predecessor Don Revie.

He also pointed out that, though Keegan was nominally the captain thus far, there were other players in the team who probably deserved that honour just as much, and if they thought they deserved to throw their hat in the ring then they had better make their intentions obvious by their attitude.

The next opportunity would be in the friendly with Spain the following month in Barcelona and then at Wembley against World Champions Argentina in May.
If anybody thought Clough's comments were a deliberate squashing of Keegan's seniority then they understood correctly.

"Rioja," whispered Taylor to Clough, who looked at him as if he'd spoken a foreign language.
"What?" said Clough.
"It's a Spanish wine from that region in Spain. I'll get some from the supermarket and bring it round. I've had some before. It's all right."
"Is it full-bodied?" said Clough.
"I expect so," said Taylor.

***

At the Nou Camp, Francis and Woodcock were in irrepressible form and terrorised the Spanish defence, both conjuring up a goal apiece.
With Keegan doing his bit by filling in just behind, the performance was an eye-opener for the hosts because they had been drawn against England in Group Two in Italy.
The defeat for the Spanish was more comprehensive than the 2-0 score suggested and sent out warning signals to the tournament hosts Italy who had also been drawn in Group Two along with Belgium.
Two others who had made an outstanding contribution that night were the ever reliable Coppell and Wilkins, both of

whom were steadily adding to their collection of international caps.

Special mention, too, was made by Taylor to Shilton who had made a couple of good saves against a Spanish attack that occasionally showed flashes of danger.

However, Clough and Taylor, in the after match press conference proclaimed themselves only reasonably satisfied so far and that it would be a better test against the current World Champions, Argentina, in May.

Clough also pointed out that there was still time for players to force their way into the squad and that no one should either count themselves in or count themselves out.

Birtles, for one, another Nottingham Forest player, deserved a chance as Clough suggested he had more nous as a centre forward than Woodcock, Francis and Keegan.

A whole host of others like Latchford, Mariner, Johnson and Withe were all encouraged to claim a firm place in the squad.

The game against Argentina marked the debut in the United Kingdom of the mercurial Diego Maradona who had arrived as a teenage prodigy and had been frightening defences since his introduction to the South American international team.

Clough and Taylor ignored the comments in the press that the kid was a boy wonder, a genius, destined to be one of the great players of all time. In fact, Clough and Taylor never mentioned him.

In a pre-match press conference, when Taylor was about to name the team, a reporter had pointed out that the little genius had power despite his stature, was as fast as any player he had ever seen, had unbelievable ball skill and the ability to go on mazy runs as if the ball was tied to his boot by a piece of string.

"So what?" asked Taylor.

"Will you be taking any specific precautions to nullify his threat?" asked the reporter.

"No," said Taylor.

"But surely," pressed the reporter, "you must have some plan to counteract the obvious threat."

"Don't need one," said Taylor.

However, just before the team left the dressing room for the game at Wembley, Taylor took England's defence, as a unit, to one side.

"If that tricky little midget gets near you, stick him up in the air. And, you, Lloyd, you stand next to him in the tunnel before you go out. Do that smiling look that you do, so that he shits himself."

The full house at Wembley saw Woodcock score twice and Keegan once to confidently beat the World Champions.

Maradona did help to create the only Argentinian goal by writhing past Sansom who brought him down in England's penalty area.

The experienced Daniel Passarella scored from the spot.

Afterwards, in the press conference, Taylor was asked whether he thought that Maradona had made a mark, especially in that he had earned the penalty.

Taylor explained that it should never have been a penalty.

A chorus of disbelief rose from the assembled press corps who pointed out that he must have been the only one in the crowd who didn't think it was a penalty.

"I didn't say I didn't think it was a penalty," said Taylor. "I said it shouldn't have been a penalty. Sansom should have had him before he got in the area. That's what I'm saying. I am also saying that if Sansom thinks he will be in the next team after allowing that to happen then he's going to have a few sleepless nights wondering about it."

Taylor ruminated silently for a moment before continuing. "It's hard enough trying to keep the ball out of the area as it is. Then you not only can't keep the ball out of the area you can't keep a squat little bugger like that out either. My missus could have stopped him getting in there. You can see I am not best pleased with Sansom. In fact, it was shocking. A stupid error like that could have cost us the game. If that wasn't enough, Shilton's attempt to save the penalty didn't show enough thought to me. When I was in goal facing a penalty, I could tell by the way a player ran up which side the ball was going to go. Shilton went the other way. It's all to do with body shape. I will be having a word with him, and Clemence too, because after that I'm not at all certain that Shilton deserves to keep his place."

A reporter pointed out that England had just beaten the World Champions and quite comprehensively at that. "Was there anything that he could take from the game that might be useful information going into the European Championship Finals in Italy in June?" he asked.

"I will be studying things carefully," said Taylor. "I will be sitting down and having a good think about Argentina, doing some research, and seeing what wines they have that might be of interest."

Peter Taylor returned to the changing room and told the England players that for the trip to Australia they would be looking to give a game to those who had not featured so prominently, so that they could stake a claim not only to be in the squad for the finals but to make the team too.

He said that he appreciated that it was a long trip, half way across the world, but that it was a good career opportunity for them and also that he had never been to Australia and that he wanted to see Sydney Opera House.
"We're looking at attitude. If you're fit enough, and you show us the right qualities, as men as well as footballers, you'll be on the plane to Australia. And if you're on the plane to Australia, it means you'll be having a holiday in Italy too. And we might as well win the European Championships while we're there."

Clough, who had been ruminating over the game with a large Scotch in the corner, woke from his stupor. "Thank you, gentlemen," he mumbled. "Now, be sharp and we'll see you up in the hospitality lounge. All the Football Association bigwigs will be there. Be nice to them. They pay our wages." The squad, without forgetting the possibility that someone could sneak in at the last minute looked like this: Shilton, Clemence, Anderson, Neal, Sansom, Mills, Lloyd, Butcher, Thompson, Cherry, Watson, Wilkins, McDermott, Brooking, Hoddle, Robson, Coppell, Woodcock, Keegan, Withe, Birtles, Johnson, Mariner, Francis, Kennedy.

The England squad was relaxing on Bondi beach, a few miles south of the stadium in the morning before the game against Australia that evening.
Clough had arranged for each player to carry two bottles of beer for themselves on to the beach in bags. He wasn't sure whether it was legal or not and didn't want to cause a stir amongst the locals or upset the police.

Needless to say, he instructed the players that if they didn't want their full quota of beer they were to return them to either himself or Peter Taylor to be dealt with as required. This was to precede the usual tactic of having a nap in the afternoon before the game.

As most, but not all, the players quaffed a beer as they sat around casually, Viv Anderson stood up and asked if he could make an announcement. Clough readily agreed.

"I don't why I've been chosen to make this announcement," Anderson said. "Maybe it's because I am the only black person here."

The players stopped chatting and listened intently as Anderson pulled a piece of paper from his pocket and began to read.

"Bondi or Boondi, is an Aboriginal word meaning water breaking over rocks or noise of water breaking over rocks. The Australian Museum records that Bondi means 'place where a flight of nullas took place'."

"What the fuck's a nulla?" said Larry Lloyd.

"Hang on a minute. I haven't finished," said Anderson. He continued. "For the attention of Larry Lloyd and anyone else who might be interested, a nulla is an Aboriginal hunting stick."

"Where did you get that paper from?" asked Clough.

"Martin O'Neill asked me to read it out."

They all laughed, especially the Nottingham Forest contingent.

"It still doesn't make sense," said Lloyd. "A fight of nullas maybe, but not a flight of nullas. A nulla isn't a fucking bird is it?"

Linda had booked England into The Hotel Bondi, just across the road on Campbell Parade.

Clough stood up, "Right," he said, "where we're staying is an important landmark on the Bondi Beach townscape. It has an excellent bar. We'll make our way over there now and have one more before retiring for the afternoon. And you, Anderson, if I can find a fucking nulla, you'll get a crack round the head with it."

At half time, with England losing 1-0 in what was a pretty dull game, Clough entered the England dressing room and slapped four players round the head. They were, in alphabetical order of surname Terry Butcher, making his debut, Glenn Hoddle, Paul Mariner and Bryan Robson.
Clough turned to go out the door, hesitated, included Anderson in the attack, then left.
England won the game 2-1 with goals from Hoddle and Mariner.
"That was much better," Peter Taylor said after the game. "But if you're not careful, you'll drive him to drink."

And so it was on to the European Championships in Italy. Clough and Taylor's first press conference had two salient points.
"I thought I ought to explain the crap performances in the British Championships. Although we won it, Peter and I were trying out a few players, some of whom didn't prove up to scratch. That's okay, that's down to us to see if they had the balls for international football. Some of them didn't. Doesn't matter. Doesn't make them bad lads. I can only think they were nervous but that's my fault. Fair enough, some of them

weren't good enough but you have to find out. You have to give people a chance. Anyway, we'll sort that. That's down to management. Maybe I took my eye off the ball for a minute, but I doubt it.

Mind you, I'm only telling you this because I know you've got it in for me. The British press always have. Just be aware I've got my eyes on the lot of you. So if you think you're going to pull any sneaky shit behind my back, then think again.

The other thing I want to mention is that there was some rioting by English fans in Turin apparently last night. Tear gas was used. I've sent out a message to the English fans, and you will print this in your newspapers or else, that there will be no hooliganism from English fans. And I want any English fan who is seen to be behaving like a hooligan to be brought to me. Then we'll see if he wants to carry on that behavior. Now, I'll answer one question then I'm off with my team to the bar."

"Mr. Clough, is it true that John Robertson has joined the squad?"

"Yes it is. John Robertson is Scottish, as you know. But I've brought him here on purpose. He thinks he's on holiday. But he's not. He's been brought here because of who he is. I wish he was English and could play but he's not so he can't. But let me say this. If any of my England lads get a bit uptight, a bit worried, then Robertson is here. That lad can brighten up a room just by walking in. Just ask some of the Forest lads. He's priceless. You couldn't fall out with him if he was knocking off your wife. I might even get him on the training ground to show my England lads how to play. Thank you gentlemen. See you after the Belgium game."

In that first group game against Belgium, England were up against a team of giants whose sole intention was to defend and defend and then defend some more.

It took a world class goal by Wilkins to beat them. Collecting the ball on his chest just outside the Belgian penalty area, he flicked the ball over two approaching defenders, ran past them, and allowed the ball to bounce before hooking it gently over the advancing keeper.

Against Italy, a Keegan goal was enough to take them into the final group game against the Spanish side that had been so comprehensively outclassed three months before.

Brooking, preferred to Hoddle because of his experience, and Woodcock sealed a 2-1 win to put England through to the final. Dani scored a penalty for Spain.

The England players left the pitch without any one of them acknowledging, let alone celebrating, the fact that they had reached a major championship final.

"That was perfect tournament play," said Taylor. "Now we're in the final we need to take a few days off to rest. We'll go to the coast."

"Good idea, Peter," said Clough. "A few days sitting by the pool and drinking a few beers. No better way to prepare. But remember, we haven't won yet. And don't forget we've got West Germany in the final. Good team, good players. But we've beat them before so we'll beat them again."

"And don't forget," said Taylor, "they shot his Dad."

Clough and Taylor took the England squad away to the coast for a couple of days where the players were told to do nothing but lounge around.

They could have as many beers as they liked as long as they also got as much sleep as they could. If they had a hangover it was their responsibility to get over it so that it would not impair their ability to train or be available for selection.
There was a games room at the hotel and the players were encouraged to play table tennis and pool and it was John Robertson's job just to be around the place.
Taylor joined Clough as he lounged by the pool side enjoying a beer.
"They think they know who's going to play," said Taylor.
"How do you know?" asked Clough.
"I can sense it. I can see it in their eyes," advised Taylor.
"Then, I'd better pull that rug from under them," said Clough.

Later that day, as the players were awaiting their early evening meal in the hotel dining room, Clough interrupted the usual banter.
"Gentlemen, you've done well to get us to the final. But it's come to my notice that some of you think that the tournament is won. And some of you think that you're already in the team for the final. Don't be so bloody daft. Most of you know I'm a bastard. So think on. I'll be watching you the next couple of days. One step out of line and you'll be on your way home. You won't even get to see the fucking final."

A few days later, at the Stadio Olimpico in Rome, Peter Taylor led out the England team to meet West Germany in the final of the European Championships.
It was a dire game that was in need of some inventiveness from either side, but the opposing midfields cancelled each other out.

England were without Trevor Francis who had suffered an Achilles tendon injury, so Clough and Taylor favoured the former Nottingham Forest pairing of Birtles and Woodcock up front, with Keegan tucking in behind.

The industrious Wilkins and the elegant Brooking could not prise any openings however, and the defence was able to deal with anything that the Germans could throw at them.

In the first half Shilton hardly had a shot to save which was a testament to the organisation at the back.

But, too many times possession was squandered when the ball should have been played out quickly to Coppell on the right as the management had instructed.

Time and again, in the dugout, Clough and Taylor screeched obscenities without any effect.

Though the players were trying hard, their efforts were being nullified by an efficient but negative German machine.

With fifteen minutes to go, a Coppell mishit cross was forced home by Woodcock for the only goal of a desperate final.

Still, it was the first major international trophy for England since 1966.

The England team: Shilton, Anderson, Lloyd, Thompson, Sansom, Coppell, Wilkins, Brooking, Keegan, Birtles and Woodcock .

The lap of honour was the most disconsolate ever run by a winning team.

"It was just that we couldn't get going against what was effectively a nine man defence," said Clough by way of explanation afterwards. "If the other team doesn't want to play, it makes it very difficult. On the other hand, we came away with as win so the fans will be happy. Unfortunately, those people back at the FA will not look on the fact that we've just given them the European Championship, they will look on the negative side, that it was not a great display, and, unfortunately, that is what you people will be writing in your newspapers. You see, they think you know something about football, and so do you. But, unless you are a former player, you don't. Your opinion counts for nothing. Go and write what you want to write but remember, the fans will only remember that we have the trophy in our hands."

Asked whether the team selection was right, Taylor said that the team selection was absolutely bang on but he did concede that there might be some changes for the World Cup qualifiers which were due to start in September.

***

In his office at Lancaster Gate, Clough sat with Linda awaiting the arrival of Tim Cox. When he came in Clough said that he was busy but that he was going to throw out some ideas that Linda was going to write down.

Cox could then use the information in his newspaper, but he would be required to draw up a proper document that Clough and Taylor could use to get Prime Minister Margaret Thatcher to invest in the centre of excellence.

Clough rattled his thoughts off the top of his head as he occasionally sipped a large Scotch.

"The purpose of my idea, the Football Association's idea, is to identify players of outstanding ability, preferably at an early age, and coach them in an environment that would also include education of various aspects of life. This will take place in a specifically designated place.

Everything would be monitored and league clubs who signed up would be given licences by the Football Association to make sure they were delivering the right training.

No kid would be made to travel too far by a club just because he was good. In other words, rich clubs shouldn't be allowed to pay for kids to come from a long way off in case it affected that kid's normal schooling.

And also, even if a club finds a diamond, it can't stop the kid from playing for his school. The education side must come first in the kid's interest and the parents must be told everything.

If a club has an academy, there should be only one person in charge of the academy.

Local leagues in age groups are not to be too big. Say, for example, youth football must have only about fourteen teams per league. Thirty games a season maximum.

Players will be taught the rules of the game and how referees interpret the rules.

Schools, local league clubs and county associations will have to liaise regularly.

Development of young players will always take into account what other countries are doing.

There will be special courses for defenders, special ones for attackers and so on.

Coaches and staff will be fully trained to my Football Association standards.

Everybody must be kosher – staff, drivers, scouts, no dodgy people involved. So, a specific person would have to be appointed for kids' interests and have talks by police, social services and the like.

It might be a bit like the national service.

The Football Association, in other words, me, reserves the right to award a licence to operate an Independent Centre of Excellence, for example, to a county football association, a local authority, schools associations, non-League clubs, that sort of thing.

This means everybody has to report to me eventually.

Kids must have a game at least once a week, even if it is a short game, on the coaching night.

The number of players in a coaching age group per coach must be limited. Say, for example, for a younger age group nine to twelve years, forty players maximum.

Thirteen to fourteen years, thirty players maximum.

Fifteen to sixteen years, twenty players maximum.

What I'm suggesting here is that the coaching becomes more concentrated the older the players get.

If clubs sign up to scheme, they must provide nine to eleven year olds a minimum of three hours a week.

Twelve to fifteen year olds must have five hours a week minimum.

Seventeen to twenty one year olds must have twelve hours a week minimum.

These are for good kids, not just anybody.

All age groups must have about twenty four small games a season. Thirty six for older kids.

Parents must be told honestly how their kids are getting on so that they won't be expecting too much.

There should be different age group coaching awards.

So, the seven to eleven years age group, for example, it would be a FA Youth Coach Award – Junior.

Twelve to sixteen years, it would be a FA Youth Coach Award – Schools.

Seventeen to twenty one years it would be a FA Youth Coaches Award – Youth.

Some good coaches would go on to an advanced coaching award.

If a coach wants to go on to a different age group, he would have to pass a course to get a licence for that age group.

This means I know what each age group is being taught and that the people doing the coaching are properly trained.

Coaches must be able to 'talk' to get message across. This is not as daft or obvious as it seems. If you can't get the ideas across it's a waste of time. Or the coach is a waste of space.

The number of coaches depends on the size of the academy. In other words, the bigger the academy, the more coaches there are.

Especially if the academy is large, there should be a physio, just in case.

Again, in a big academy, there should be a welfare officer to make sure the kids are okay.

The coaches should go on a refresher course every three years in case something new comes up, like from abroad.

There should be two coaches for every twenty players.

The same coaches should work with the same players every week. Then they get to know them.

All the very young age group games are to be played on a friendly basis. No leagues, no results published.

Reports should be made on how the kids are progressing towards achievement in technical skills.

There should be adequate insurance. I know about this bit from personal experience. There should be first aid at all representative games.

Clubs to liaise with schools and attach a coach and there should be a maximum number of schools for each coach. Goalkeepers will have specialist coaches for at least fifty per cent of the time."

Clough broke off to top up his glass, then continued.

"You knock that up into a document. Linda can put it on FA paper and all that crap, and I'll take it round to Thatcher and tell her I want it sorting. In the meantime, I'll think about a place where all the best youngsters can go."

Clough took a big swig of Scotch as Linda and Tim Cox withdrew silently from his office.

In September, the qualifiers for the 1982 World Cup began at Wembley with a comfortable 4-0 win against Norway.

With no Keegan, Francis or Wilkins to call on due to injury, Tony Woodcock was partnered up front by Paul Mariner who scored one, Woodcock himself netting another.

In midfield, Terry McDermott shone, making forward runs effectively. At the end of one fluent move, it was he who finished it off by scoring. Later, he took responsibility from the penalty spot after a penalty decision in England's favour. Sansom stood out for his steady play and Robson was ever more evident in midfield, interchanging with McDermott.

"What do you reckon?" said Clough quietly to Taylor in the corner of the changing room after the game.

"The defence is getting better every game," Taylor said. "I'm beginning to like it. And if somebody does get a shot in, Shilton is equal to it."

"Mariner bothers me," said Clough. "He's good enough to be here but he's never going to be anything other than a target man. That's all he's been taught to do. He can score goals but I don't think he realises that the main reason he is playing up front is to score goals. I've told him, and to be fair he got a goal tonight, but he should be more greedy. Great goalscorers are greedy. I was. When Francis is fit again, he and Woodcock give us much more sparkle and make things happen."

In the after match press conference Clough was asked about Mariner's performance. "Outstanding," said Clough. "The perfect target man. Scored a goal. What more could you ask for?"

The other two qualifiers that autumn, against Romania in Bucharest and Switzerland at Wembley, resulted in 2-1 wins, Woodcock and Mariner again sharing the goals.

But Clough and Taylor were not happy. There was a lack of verve about the team's play.

Robson, though, was becoming more and more prominent each game, influencing the passages of midfield play. Clough and Taylor constantly mulled things over.

"We miss players like Keegan, Francis, Wilkins and Brooking when they are not here," said Clough. "I think Hoddle could take over from Brooking, but not just yet," counselled Taylor. But these thoughts were kept to themselves, in private conversations and not relayed to the national press who continued their own agenda anyway.

The press began hounding Clough about what they perceived as dull displays and pointed out that the England team, without their most experienced players, was sadly lacking in replacements.

"You are an idiot," said Clough when one reporter suggested exactly that. "Who did you play for professionally?" he asked. When the answer came in the negative, Clough pointed out that you have to have squad players for international football. "Look, young man," he said, "we've had some players out injured it's true, players that we might have picked ahead of the ones who played recently, but the ones who came in did as they were told and we came away with results that have kept us going in the right direction. I am happy that some of them are making the players who were out injured look over their shoulders. We nearly have a settled squad. I'll tell you this, at this moment in time, if Taylor and me sat down and picked a first eleven, we'd pick different teams. Now, what would happen if we came to pick our first eleven and we had different choices, eh? I'll tell you what. We'd have to go with Peter's choice because he knows more about football players than I will ever know. Now, if you're not going to ask sensible questions, I suggest you don't bother at all."

The murder of John Lennon in December had left a huge, solemn black cloud hanging over the country and everything, even the football, seemed miserable.

For months the press dwelt only on negative aspects of football and life in general. It was depressing, and nothing that Clough and Taylor said seemed to brighten the prospects of the England team. As much as anything, the interest in Clough and Taylor's drinking habits was growing.

It wasn't until the following June that there was a brief shaft of light with the England football team, following a particularly fine away performance in Hungary in the qualifiers.

England won 3-1 with Keegan and Brooking returning to the fold, both getting on the score sheet, Brooking twice.
The first was a fine, four man move involving Keegan, Robson, Coppell and Anderson before Brooking tucked the ball away just inside the near post.
Brooking's second goal, a rising drive into the top left hand corner, got wedged between the stanchion and the netting, causing some Hungarian fans to wonder, momentarily, where the ball had gone.
After the game Taylor voiced his concern. "There's something wrong," he said to Clough. "There's something about the attitude I don't like. Complacency perhaps, but I don't really think it's that. We better get these last two qualifiers won because we've got some thinking to do. I can't put my finger on it yet, but I will."

The next game, against Norway in Oslo was exactly what England didn't want.
It was a lack lustre performance that had Clough and Taylor screaming, even more than usual, from the dugout.
Only Robson, who scored England's only goal in a 2-1 defeat, Clough and Taylor's first for England in a proper competitive game, came out with any credit.
Even Shilton in goal was not as commanding as usual.
There was a lack of movement in the England play and Norway carved out a famous victory that sent the Norwegian radio commentator, Bjorge Lillelian into a paroxysm of ecstasy.
He screamed on air, "We're the best in the world! We've beaten England 2-1 at football! This is truly incredible! We've beaten England. England, the fighters' birthplace. Lord Nelson! Lord Beaverbrook! Sir Winston Churchill! Sir Anthony Eden! Clement Attlee! Henry Cooper! Lady Diana!

We've beaten you all. Maggie Thatcher, can you hear me? Maggie Thatcher, I have a message for you in the middle of your campaign. Maggie Thatcher, as you say in your language in the boxing bars around Madison Square Garden - Your boys took a hell of a beating!"
In the changing room afterwards Clough poured himself a whisky and scowled.
The players sat silently, waiting for the explosion. It never came. He simply said, "Some of you think you are the European Champions and that's enough. Get that fucking idea out of your heads or you won't be coming to Spain. We will qualify. There's one game left in this qualifying group and by that I mean that you have to qualify for my squad. Think on."
He left and entered the press room where the Norwegian press were deliriously happy with their historic victory.
They played the radio recording from Bjorge Lillelian and asked what he thought of that.
"The bloke's a nutcase," explained Clough. "I hope he's not in here or I'll throw him out myself."

Three weeks later the football world was plunged into more darkness when legendary former Liverpool manager Bill Shankly died of heart attack.
Clough and Taylor liked and respected Shankly.
Clough summed up his thoughts about Shankly by saying that Bill always suggested that a man should do his best at whatever he was doing. 'If you're going to sweep the street, then make sure your street is the cleanest in town.' But Clough's favourite story about Shankly was when Shankly was listening to some nonsense from coaches at the National Recreation Centre at Lilleshall. Bill walked on to the pitch, grabbed the ball and half-volleyed it into the goal. "It's safer in there," he said.

The final game of the qualifying group was a 1-0 win at Wembley against Hungary with another Mariner goal but the hounds of the press were out and it was Clough and Taylor's throats they were after. There was barely even a token celebration from the players.

"Time for fresh faces?" asked one reporter in the press room after the game.

"You are absolutely right," said Taylor.

"Who?" the hack asked.

"Yours, for a kick off," said Taylor. "Fuck off."

Taylor stood up and began to approach the reporter who ran from the room, knocking other reporters out of the way in his escape.

"Look, lads," said Clough. "They haven't been playing as well as we want them to play but we'll get to the bottom of it. There's nothing more certain than that."

"There's something bothering them," said Taylor. "If they aren't happy playing for us then we'll get rid of them, or maybe, just maybe, we're doing something wrong. I'll find out."

A few days later, back at Lancaster Gate, Clough and Taylor were sat at the head of the large Brazilian mahogany table. The FA committee, sat round the sides.

"There we are gentlemen," said Clough. "We're going to the World Cup. Spain's lovely. Lots of sunshine. I hope you'll be able to make it."

"And Rioja," said Taylor.

Sir Harold Thompson chipped in. "Mr. Clough, I'd like to point out that there is still some unrest at the Foreign Office regarding your comments about Norway. Mrs. Thatcher's not very happy with you."

"I never made any comments about Norway," Clough explained. "The comments I made were about that Norwegian idiot commentating on the game. And, anyway, I'm not very happy with Mrs. Thatcher so that makes it even. I might take her job when I've done with this one. I'd make a better bloody job of running this country than she's doing."

Sir Harold pressed home his point. "For decades it has been tradition that Norway presents us with a Christmas tree for Trafalgar Square. Now they are threatening not to send one this year."

"I don't bloody care about that," said Clough.

"Is Norway the only place that has Christmas trees?" mused Taylor.

"Wait a minute. You're thick with Thatcher, aren't you?" said Clough. "Somebody told me you were at university together?"

"It's true she was a chemistry student of mine," Thompson confirmed.

"Well, you didn't bloody teach her very much, did you?" snapped Clough.

Sir Harold tried again. "All it will take is a public apology and everything will be back to normal. It'll help the situation."

"Bollocks," said Clough. "I'll tell you what you can do with that Christmas tree. Stuff it up Margaret Thatcher's arse. Or anybody else in her government if she's not available. Now clear off."

Clough went back to his office where Tim Cox was waiting for him. "Morning," he said. "How's that bairn? I bet she's causing you some mischief now."

Cox confirmed the child's joyful antics as Clough poured himself a Scotch.

"Now," said Clough. "I have a plan for the Football Association school of excellence, call it what you will. You can get your paper to run a competition perhaps, to name it. It will be somewhere in the middle of England so it's easily accessible. It will be a place with proper, paid coaches who are there full-time. It's different to the stuff that the clubs and county associations are getting involved in. This will be for the very, very best. The cream of the country's best young footballers. The young coaches around the country will strive to get there. They will have to be promoted to get there. None of this long ball shit. These players will learn everything that I want them to learn so that we have an endless stream of future international footballers."

"It sounds like Russia and East Germany churning out Olympic athletes."

"Yes, but without the drugs. We don't need drugs."

"We want generation after generation of top class players, technically brilliant. But here's the thing. It will be a leading sports medicine centre too. To research and investigate football injuries. If young players can avoid what happened to me, then that's excellent. An outstanding university but with the accent on football. And the best professional players will come there and show the youngsters how to be model professionals. Get the best out of a career that, let's face it, doesn't last very long. Even shorter for some of us, as players, which is the best bit of all, of course."

In the six months or so before the 1982 World Cup finals, Clough and Taylor experimented with various players but hadn't changed their minds about the nucleus of the first choice squad.
Some players showed flashes of interesting elements to their play, notably Arsenal's Graham Rix and West Ham's Alan Devonshire who could both play on the left.
In defence Terry Butcher, a tough centre half, was beginning to show promise but, ultimately, it was back to the originals.

In the various friendlies throughout the build up to the finals, the mood in the England camp had been professional but without an obvious enthusiasm for the task in hand.
It had troubled both Clough and Taylor but neither of them had been able to figure out the problem.
The team was winning, apart from that fiasco against Norway in Oslo, and though some of the wins were ugly, they were stills wins. Surely, that was what it was all about.

And so it was on to the finals in Spain where England were based in Bilbao. The group opponents were France, Czechoslovakia and, relative lightweights, Kuwait. It was a group that held no real fears for England.
Linda had booked a hotel in the Basque region that admirably suited the squad's needs so the players had plenty to do in the hours they spent away from the training ground. There was a professional atmosphere around the place that Clough and Taylor wanted but there was still the feeling that the players didn't seem to be having fun.

On the first night of their arrival, in a private bar of the hotel, for the England entourage only, Clough and Taylor sat

downing whiskies as they contemplated their starting line-up against France.
They pretty much knew what the starting team would be but hadn't told the players. Tim Cox came in.
Cox had produced a wonderfully persuasive document that Clough, even with all his nasty comments against the government of the day, had delivered to Margaret Thatcher in Downing Street some time before.
Clough had convinced Thatcher that if she wanted to keep her job as Prime Minister she had better think about funding the national football centre that Clough had proposed.
They offered Cox a drink and he readily joined them. Although, he would never be regarded as a member of an inner sanctum, like Jimmy Gordon, Taylor asked Cox whether the players were saying anything that they ought to be aware of.
"They absolutely think the world of you two guys," he said. He paused for a moment. "I'm not saying they like you, in fact some of them dislike you intensely, but what they do have for you is respect. They wouldn't be the European Champions without you. You have shown them what it is like to be winners and they like that bit. So, basically, it's down to respect. If you think something's bothering them and you want to find out, why don't you ask them?"

After the evening meal, Clough and Taylor called the squad into the hotel bar and ordered a round of drinks of whatever the players wanted. Some had nothing.
Clough spoke first. "Gentlemen, as reigning European Champions, you have every right to be regarded as one of the favourites to win this trophy. But you won't. There is

something wrong. And a team that is not pulling together is worth fuck all. I don't think we will win this thing. I am bloody certain that we have the ability, but the way things are, it won't happen. The team is the thing. You are the lucky bastards who can go on to the pitch and win for England but, more importantly than that, go and win for yourselves and your families."
There was a total hush in the room. Clough and Taylor looked around for a flicker of something that might betray a feeling or an idea of what was holding the team back.
Eventually, Larry Lloyd put his hand up and asked to speak. Permission was simultaneously granted by both Clough and Taylor. Lloyd stood up.
"I think I might be speaking on behalf of the rest of the squad, and if I'm out of line," he said, looking round the room, "then say so, but there is something that is, shall we say, and has been, a topic of conversation among us for a long time now."
"Go on, "said Taylor.
"Well, I know that, particularly with you Mr. Clough, I have never been your favourite person. I know I've done a decent job for you, and I am aware that I am about to lose my place to young Terry there, and all the best to him, but I'm not stupid. In many ways I've had my best days, but one thing is for certain. You might not like me and I might not particularly like you, but everything I've won in football has been down to you two. Everything. I'd have won nothing without you.
We, and again I think I'm speaking for the rest of the squad, don't like to see the amount of booze you are putting away. We all like a drink but I, we, think what you are doing is dangerous. And it's a pity because, as managers, you are the tops. I was with Shankly and he was a genius but this is something else. I think we all would like to think you might

cut down a bit because we would like to win this tournament. It's the World cup for Christ's sake, and we'd like to win it for you as well as ourselves. And we'd like you to see us win it. See us properly, I mean." Lloyd sat down.
Clough said, "Is that it?"
Taylor said, "Well, bugger me. I never saw that coming."
"In that case, gentlemen," said Clough, "you have a bargain. I'll not have a drink, it's up to Peter whether he feels the same, until we are out of this tournament. But if that happens after the end of a winning final, then the champagne, and lots of it, is on me. Right?"
"I'll go along with that," said Taylor.
There was a generous and loud murmur of approval from around the room. Clough looked at Taylor and raised his eyes to the ceiling.

The opening game against France, coming two days after the end of the Falklands War, was spectacular.
The game was only twenty seven seconds old when Steve Coppell took a throw on the right, it was flicked on by Terry Butcher into the penalty area and there was Bryan Robson steaming in to hook the ball past the mesmerised French goalkeeper.
There was a whole, new, invigorated England performance. Robson was to score again, with one from Mariner, in for Woodcock, nursing a strain.
A solitary reply from the French was treated with some verbal bile from Clough but, generally, the feeling was that England had regained some of the enthusiasm that had been missing for several months.

The final two group games were won 2-0 against the Czechs and, a little disappointingly, 1-0 against a Kuwait team that defended stoically for ninety minutes.
Trevor Francis scored in both games with the other goal against the Czechs coming from an own goal.

Bryan Robson thought that, the way the results were going, the lads could go all the way. Algeria had beaten Germany 2-1, showing that the Germans weren't that good. Perhaps Robson's positive thoughts were because he was the hero of the hour.
Or maybe it was because Clough had moved him from the left of midfield to centre where he could exert more influence.
How to include Robson, Wilkins, Brooking and Hoddle was a problem. Clough and Taylor solved it by leaving out Hoddle. With Robson as the perpetual motion and Brooking's thoroughbred class, through balls ignited the fit again Francis up front. With Wilkins steadying the ship, the team looked balanced.
Hoddle, told he could come in at any minute, wanted to play Brazil in the final because he'd noticed how they built up slowly and he felt he could release the speedy Francis and Woodcock up front.
Taylor told both front men to try to go past defenders when they got the ball because he'd spotted that most of the defenders in this competition didn't like people running at them.

The competition moved on to a second group stage so that FIFA could introduce 24 teams instead of the usual 16 to the finals.

This was seen purely as a money-making exercise, but it meant that England had to overcome Germany and Spain in the next stage. However, both had been fairly recent, defeated foes. Two 1-0 victories left England to face France in the semi-final after they'd also progressed as runners-up to England in the initial group stage.

A dull 0-0 draw was looking on the cards. After their initial defeat in the group game, the French packed their midfield and stifled any of England's attacking threat.

England had easily coped with a muted French attack and, with only a minute to go, Robson threaded the ball through to Francis who accelerated past a lunging French defender to slide the ball under the advancing French keeper. A 1-0 win.

Back in England, the scenes around the country were crazy, especially so in London, where Trafalgar Square became the magnet for wild celebrations.

The packed crowd was chanting, cheering and jumping in the fountain at the news that England were through to the World Cup Final, the first time since 1966.

Not far from Trafalgar square, several members of various FA committees were watching the jubilant scenes on a television at the Football Association headquarters in Lancaster Gate. They sat smoking cigars and drinking whisky in comfortable chairs. Most of them had arrogant, smug looks on their faces.

"Well I'm blowed," one member said. "They've gone and done it."

Another member, drawing dramatically on his cigar said, "It's twelve years since we even qualified for the finals. Now we've reached the final itself. I for one am glad we appointed Mr.

Clough. Look at the scenes of joy and triumph. I'm only sad that Mr. Clough wouldn't allow us to go."

"You could have gone if you paid," pointed out a third committee member.

A fourth committee member chimed in, "What a great boost to the country after the turmoil and heartache of the last several years in the football wilderness. And the last couple of years for England, as a whole."

"If you mean the Falklands, don't forget the Welsh, Irish and Scots went down there too."

And yet another, anonymous committee member mused, "I can see a few gongs being awarded and maybe even a few knighthoods if we actually win the cup. I know I'm due one."

Sir Harold Thompson broke in. "That's not the point," he snarled. "Now, we'll never get rid of that bastard."

Brian Clough and Peter Taylor led England out for the World Cup Final against Italy in the stadium that had hosted their original group matches.

"It's like home from home," Taylor told his players as they walked on to the pitch.

As the teams broke to warm up after the official presentation to King Juan Carlos I of Spain and FIFA President Joao Havelange, the autocrat from Brazil, Clough called his players together.

They were expecting words of encouragement but all they got was, "Look lads, I've kept my word. And I'm gagging for a drink. So, for Christ's sake, win this. Don't forget, I'm buying."

Taylor added, "That Princess Sophia, the King's wife. She's a bit tasty, isn't she?"

It was a scintillating England display as they beat the Italians 4-0 in one of the most one sided finals ever.
Trevor Francis scored twice with Woodcock adding to the Italians' misery before Bryan Robson capped a majestic display with a stunning individual goal minutes before the final whistle.
England played slick, clinical football, and Francis put them ahead after only six minutes when Wilkins played the ball up to Woodcock who knocked into the path for the super quick striker to prod home.
Francis was to grab the headlines but England had heroes all over the pitch.
Even Shilton, hardly in the game due to the resolute defence in front of him, had to come off his line to smother an Italian attack shortly after England's opener.
After that, he became a spectator for most of the game.
Robson, it was, who was dictating the pace of the game and, after half an hour, his incisive pass to Coppell saw the speedy winger beat his man down the touchline to cross for Woodcock, coming in at the near post, to beat the defender to it and nudge the ball home.
A half time 2-0 score was more comfortable than it suggested. Clough and Taylor asked the players to continue doing the same as they had in the first half and victory would be theirs. Clough smiled at Taylor but nothing else was said.

After the break England's young lions roared forward once more and a further breakthrough came after sixty seven minutes.

A smart interchange of passes between Wilkins and Robson saw Wilkins float the ball out to Coppell. The little right winger, who was giving the Italian full back a torrid time, once again delivered a telling ball that Francis controlled instantly near the penalty spot before firing home.

The Italians played for their pride but their much-heralded engine room only had a brief ten minutes when they looked that they might get something back in the game.

Thereafter it was a stroll for England.

And, finally, after a quick, five man move, the ball ended up at Robson's feet. The Italian defence seemed to open up in front of him as he moved forward with determination.

Brushing past two desperate lunges, Robson pushed the ball in between the final two Italian defenders, ran round the outside of one, and chipped the ball over the advancing Italian keeper Dino Zoff.

For Zoff, captain of the Italians, bowing out of international football at the age of forty, it was a sad end to a glorious career.

Italian fans headed for home in their thousands, bewildered by their own team's inept performance but enthralled with England's total superiority on the day.

The England supporters stayed right where they were, jumping up and down hysterically, chanting the names of Clough and Taylor, happily wondering whether it was all a dream.

At the final whistle, the players ran instantly towards the management and hugged them almost violently.

Clough and Taylor allowed themselves to celebrate with the players on the pitch for a few minutes before making their way back to the changing rooms.

Keegan, who had played cleverly just behind Francis and Woodcock but in front of the midfield, led his team forward to collect their medals.

Shilton, Anderson, Butcher, Sansom, Coppell, Wilkins, Robson, Brooking, Keegan, Francis and Woodcock had achieved Clough and Taylor's, and the whole of English football fans' dream.

Back in the changing room, Clough and Taylor sprayed champagne around the dressing room, congratulating the players, slapping players playfully on the shoulders. It was a riotous and joyful occasion.

Clough, eventually, held both hands up and the players became quiet in an instant.

"Gentlemen, it feels good to be World Champions, doesn't it?" said Clough. "Remember this moment and cherish it. One day you'll be able to tell your grandkids you were a World Champion. We beat the French, the Germans, the Italians and whoever else it was. It doesn't get any better. Remember it. Now Peter and I are off for a drink. I hope you don't mind. I think we deserve it. We'll see you in the bar of the hotel as soon as you can before we go to the banquet. We won't get pissed, so I suggest you don't either."

Keegan stood up. "Mr. Clough, Mr. Taylor, on behalf of the lads I would like to thank you for your efforts in all that you have done to make this a very special occasion for all of us. It is beyond our wildest dreams, well, beyond mine anyway. I can't think of words to describe how grateful I am. However, I think it only right and proper that I resign from the team and the squad now. While I'm at the top. It can't get any better. It's been a privilege being captain of my country but now it's time to give somebody else a go."

"You are clever," said Clough.

"Shall I be clever as well?" asked Trevor Brooking.

"I think so," said Clough. "You've done your stuff."

Clough took the captain's armband from Keegan and threw it at Robson. "Here," he said. "Look after it."

Clough and Taylor left the room, and left the champagne to the delirious players who screamed and shouted and drank and fooled around. And so they should.

Clough and Taylor were met in the corridor outside by a lone reporter. It was Tim Cox.

"Brian, Peter," he said. "Now you have reached the pinnacle of success, will you be calling it a day?"

"Young man, have you enjoyed today?" asked Clough.

"It's been brilliant, hasn't it?' said Cox. "All those years with nothing."

"Don't you worry, young man. Sir Alf won it once. I want to prove I'm better than him. So I want to win it twice. Bless him. Now, there's an exclusive for you."

"And the finals are in Mexico," said Taylor. I've heard it's lovely weather there. I wonder what their wine is like."

"You're right, Peter," said Clough. "A bit of sun on our backs. Does you the world of good."

Brian Clough stood up in front of the assembled national press in the Briefing Room at the Football Association headquarters in Lancaster Gate. Behind him, on the white painted wall, was the three lions' emblem of the England team.

"I am happy to announce today that plans for a permanent training base for the England team have been approved and will be ninety five per cent funded by the government. Mrs.Thatcher has promised me a three hundred acre site, somewhere in the middle of England that will have a dozen pitches, in door and out, plus sports medicine and sports science facilities.

There will also be a hotel and conference centre, but essentially it will be the home of future England football teams, to train and learn and keep us where we are – the World Champions.

You know I am not one to blow my own trumpet but it was my idea. However, even I am surprised how quickly it has taken shape.

It will be an inspirational site, a place for coaches and players to work, learn and develop. It is a much-needed facility and, especially after my own experiences, it will be absolutely first class with regard to dealing with football injuries.

The Football Association has put a sizable amount of money into this but the main thing is that the government has seen how important sport and sport facilities are, not just to this country, but Scotland, Ireland and Wales too.

The aim is to make the centre a football focal point for coaches, players, administrators and officials alike.

It will be a place to inspire world-class performance. I think the government has realised that, as World Champions, we have to lead the way if we are to maintain our high standards.

Other countries will follow suit, so we must not rest on our laurels.

Peter Taylor and I have never done that. There are a couple of massive sportswear companies that are vying to sponsor the place and I will be screwing every penny I can out of them for the benefit of football in this country.

It's not going to be in competition with professional clubs, in fact, if they've got any sense, they can come and see what we have to offer. It will be, simply, a state of the art football excellence centre.

There has been some opposition that the location is going to be so far from London but that doesn't surprise me at all. People who are saying that are all based in London. I think I'm a reasonable chap and I will listen to the views of others. It's like I say to my players though. I'll sit down and listen to you for twenty minutes, and then we'll decide I was right. It's got to be easy to get to from anywhere in the country. Simple.

This is will mean England success for the long term. Long after Taylor and I have gone.

It will be world class but that doesn't mean it will have money wasted on it.

The future of England football looks very, very good with this announcement. And I'm telling you that as a football man. Professor Sir Harold Thompson, Chairman of the Football Association, might prefer to talk to you about that bloke who has won the Nobel prize in Chemistry for his development of whatever it was. But I wouldn't know about that. Gentlemen, I only know about football."

Over the course of the next two years, Clough and Taylor followed their usual practice of trying out different players and, though Keegan and Brooking had voluntarily retired themselves from international football, Coppell was forced to call it a day following a tackle that shattered his knee. Clough placed him on the coaching staff for England games.

The players that Clough and Taylor chose, easily qualified for the 1984 European Championships to be held in France. Perhaps perversely, Clough and Taylor now regarded it as a tournament to be endured, if still to be won, but a big notch down on the most prestigious competition, the World Cup. It was as if the England team expected to win, but without showing an ounce of the arrogance so naturally displayed by their manager.
In France, there were very few hooligan-related incidents but none involving England fans.
In fact, the whole competition was blessed with exceptionally fine weather and a high standard of football.
France, as the host nation, effortlessly made it through to the final, mostly due to the sublime skills of leading play maker, Michel Platini.
Clough and Taylor had assessed the other seven teams in the tournament and had apprised the England players accordingly. France were the favourites, not least because they were on home soil but they had some decent players. Taylor was doubled up with laughter when he found out that France's first choice keeper was called Bats but accepted he was out of the top drawer. Battiston and Le Roux made a formidable central defensive duo. The midfield was rightly regarded as one of the best in the world, boasting the gritty, defensive Fernandez to complement Tigana, Giresse and, of course, the inspirational Platini. Without a world class striker, the team was built to

allow Platini to get forward and provide the main threat. Taylor knew that England could deal with that.

Belgium had a solid team, experienced in tournament football. Taylor was again hysterical at their goalkeeper whose name was Pfaff but he admitted the lad was good. They also had an exceptional midfielder in Scifo and a world class striker in Ceulemans.
Yugoslavia had a crap goalkeeper according to Taylor, and a bunch of talented individuals but he couldn't pronounce their names.
The final team in that group was Spain who also had players with tournament experience. Taylor rated their goalkeeper, Arconada, and said they had a good defender in Camacho, decent midfielders in Maceda and Gordillo , and a couple of good lads up front in Santillana and Carrasco. No problem to England though, he was sure of that.

In Group B, England's group, West Germany were their usual strong bet. Schumacher, in goal, was one of the best but not as good as Shilton. Briegel was good in defence and Matthaus was very good in midfield but it was up front where they shone. Littbarski, Voller and Rummenigge would have to be watched. They could be beaten though.
Portugal were widely regarded as an emerging team but not by Taylor. He agreed they had a first class attack, in Diamantino and Jordao, but other than that he wasn't worried.
Romania, as a team, was largely unknown but Taylor had spotted a very talented striker called Hagi but collapsed when he recounted that the only other decent player they had was a midfielder called Boloni.

The opening game of the tournament saw France carve out a 1-0 win against Spain, Platini getting on the score sheet for the host nation.

In the next game, against Belgium, the French midfield maestro scored a hat-trick, then did the same in the third game, against Yugoslavia. Spain also went through to the semi-finals after beating Belgium and Yugoslavia.

Group B was less exciting in terms of the number of goals scored.

England beat Portugal and Romania, 1-0 with Woodcock scoring in both games and drew with West Germany 0-0.

So, host nation France met West Germany in the first semi-final which left England to meet Spain in the second semi-final.

France opened the scoring in an excellent match through Domergue but Rummenigge equalized fifteen minutes from the end to send the game into extra-time. The French nation was stunned when the Germans then took the lead though Voller but rallied when Domergue notched his second.

With a penalty shoot-out looming, Platini popped up to score his eighth goal of the tournament to give France a 3-2 victory and a place in the final.

The other semi-final saw Spain cancel out England's more ambitious approach but, ten minutes from the end England were awarded a penalty.

Francis was brought down in the box and Robson stepped up to plant the ball firmly in the corner.

The final was played to a capacity crowd at the Parc-des-Princes and the home crowd was delighted as they launched attack after attack at England's beleaguered defence.

Wilkins and Robson stood firm in front of a defence in which Butcher was outstanding.

The team had been inspired by Clough and Taylor to combat Platini's central threat by constantly having players too near to him for comfort so that he couldn't dictate proceedings.

In a viciously swift counter-attack, after Sansom had won the ball, Robson played the ball forward to Francis and a quick one-two with Woodcock left Francis with only the goalkeeper to beat.

The crowd gave a collective sigh of relief as Bats parried the ball, but it ran to Woodcock who poked the ball home.

After that, England shut up shop and ground out a thoroughly professional victory.

The crowd were incensed and made their feelings known against the English who had stolen the game like common thieves.

"Altogether a pleasant experience," said Clough, "coming, as it did, on French soil."

But it was not a tournament that Clough and Taylor were particularly bothered about anyway. They wanted the World Cup again because they wanted to beat dear old Alf Ramsey.

Clough and Taylor had long since begun planning for the 1986 tournament in Mexico.

They had arranged a summer trip to South America, a year in advance, because they had never been there before. Taylor had thoroughly researched wine from that continent and pronounced that the visit would be worthwhile.

After Larry Lloyd's speech some time before, Clough and Taylor had confined themselves to wine only and had forsaken the whisky that used to be their standard at any time of the day. Now, they found themselves, if they were in a hot climate, usually having beer or white wine during the day and never to excess.

At night they would have a glass of red with their evening meal in the hotel restaurant and share a bottle as they talked football afterwards. But it was significant that they had reigned in their behavior.

Clough insisted that he didn't feel any better for it but, nevertheless, continued the regime. After all, it was he who set the regulations and he understood that the players were only doing what was best for the team. He had to set an example.

In fact it turned out to be a good system to have fallen into. Some of the players liked a beer, notably the captain, Bryan Robson, who would often arrange a tour of local bars with Peter Shilton. Other, less regular, drinkers often came along to have a look round.

Finding themselves in Brazil on that leg of the trip, England were staying at the Copacabana Palace Hotel in Rio de Janeiro, along Avenida Atlantico facing the famous Copacabana beach. The hotel had been welcoming the rich and famous since it had opened in 1923 including such luminaries as Fred Astaire and Ginger Rogers. Now it had the England football team.

Robson and a few others wandered out of the hotel and turned left, and left again, more into the city than on the beach front. They hadn't walked very far when they came to a bar on the corner of Duvivier and Barata Ribeiro.

The bar was called 'Antonio's' where a game was being shown on a television perched precariously high on a shelf. While the players were sipping their beer, a patron of the bar turned round, looked judiciously at the group of gringos and screamed, "Peter Shilton!"

Their anonymity blown, the players laughed and joked with the bar's clientele even though they hadn't a clue what was being said.

It didn't seem to be anything less than complimentary so they readily accepted another beer from the owner.

Soon they were joined by a couple of scantily clad Brazilian girls who flashed their eyelashes provocatively.

Whether any of the players had become interested in the charms of the local beauties was irrelevant because, at that moment, Peter Taylor arrived.

"She's all right, John, isn't she?" he said to an exciting new member of the touring party, black Watford winger, John Barnes.

The young lad agreed and might have fancied his chances until Taylor pointed out that she wasn't a she at all.

The youngster couldn't believe that he could easily have become embroiled in what, at best, would have been a scandal. As usual, Taylor had had his ear to the ground and, on trips where he was unfamiliar with his surroundings, it was his habit to keep a close eye on his charges.

The next night Barnes scored one of the most breathtaking individual goals ever seen by an England player as they took on Brazil in the giant Maracana Stadium in Rio.

Barnes collected the ball on his chest, ten yards inside the Brazil half from a pass by centre forward Mark Hateley, and dribbled past half the Brazil team to score a wonder goal in true Brazilian style.

Brazil would claim they were without their star names of the 1982 World Cup, Zico, Socrates and Falcao, but this was still Brazil in the Maracana, a venue that had not witnessed a home defeat since the 1960s.

England had another black player on the right wing, Mark Chamberlain, lining up alongside the more established Peter Shilton, Ray Wilkins and Bryan Robson. It was exciting.

After the game, Barnes was asked to describe his goal. "The Brazilians never put a tackle in, but maybe they were shocked," he said. "They probably thought no Englishman could do this. I don't remember much about my goal. I can't remember doing any of it. None of it was planned, it was just instinct and reaction. I really didn't know what I was doing."

A second-half header by Hateley confirmed England's victory, but Barnes' goal was the story of the game.

Clough complimented Hateley's expertly timed jump to claim his goal. Neither Clough nor Taylor mentioned Barnes.

1985 had been a terribly sad year for football fans everywhere. A fire broke out at Valley Parade football stadium in May as Bradford City prepared to celebrate winning the Third Division. Fifty six people died.

Two weeks later thirty nine Juventus fans were killed when a wall collapsed at the European Cup Final against Liverpool in Brussels.

And then in September, Jock Stein, the first British manager to win the European Cup, with Celtic in 1967, died of a heart attack when on duty in Cardiff as the Scottish national team manager against Wales.

Wembley Stadium did feature in an uplifting event when it hosted Live Aid in July, but since it was a concert for the starving millions in Ethiopia, things were put in perspective.

Over the next few months and, as holders, not having to qualify for the World Cup finals in Mexico, Clough and Taylor tried out more players.

Out went Chamberlain, Mark Wright came in as a central defender, midfielders Peter Reid and Steve Hodge made their debuts, Chris Waddle, a skilful Geordie proved he could play on both flanks, and a couple that linked well up front, Gary Lineker and Peter Beardsley, had edged out Francis and Woodcock.

The old guard of Anderson, Sansom, Butcher, Wilkins, Robson and Hoddle were still there, and so too was keeper Shilton though his understudy now was Chris Woods rather than Ray Clemence.

And so it was that England began their defence of the World Cup in Monterrey against a Portugal side that hadn't sounded any alarm bells.

But it was all to start horribly wrong. If Clough and Taylor had once taken their eyes off the ball, then so had England's defence.

First Sansom allowed the speedy Diamantino to slip past him and cross from the goal line.

Butcher was in no man's land and Anderson was still lumbering back from a foray up field. Carlos Manuel slid in to score.

Clough and Taylor bellowed instructions and expletives from the dugout but to no avail. Disappointingly, and worryingly, England had lost their opening game.

Afterwards Clough blamed himself, believing that by playing Hateley up front alongside Lineker they would be able to exploit the central defensive pairing of the Portuguese. It was a plan that didn't work but that was one game out of three.

If that wasn't disaster enough, a second, worse one, was to befall England on the same ground three days later against a Morocco side that ordinarily should have been swept aside.

In the first half, captain Robson fell and dislocated a shoulder. His replacement, Hodge, though relatively inexperienced, was full of running but England were becoming frustrated. This was shown by Wilkins throwing the ball at the referee after what he thought was a poor decision.

The referee, to Wilkins' amazement, sent him off.

Momentarily Taylor was speechless though Clough more than made up for his partner's silence by condemning all his players, and especially Wilkins, as he trudged disconsolately off the field.

At half time, Taylor pointed out that it was still 0-0 and that they should protect that score. If they could do that, then they were still in the competition. The Moroccans played their part by not seeming to not realise they had a man advantage in the second half.

With Wilkins and Robson missing for the final group game against Poland at the Azteca Stadium in Mexico City, Reid and Hodge were brought in with Beardsley alongside Lineker at the expense of Hateley.

It was a change that was almost miraculous. Lineker, lightning fast, was able to capitalise on the service from the unselfish Beardsley by scoring twice in the first fourteen minutes and completed his hat-trick when the Polish keeper Mlynarczyk inexplicably dropped the ball at his feet.

So England, after a couple of frights, had squeaked through, and had five days to regroup before a return to the Azteca to face Paraguay.

Clough and Taylor arranged a team meeting in the team's private hotel bar in Santillo.

"Gentlemen," Clough started, "have a look at this." He held up a glass of orange juice. "This has nothing in it except orange. The way you played in those first two games was nothing less than scandalous. I can only think you were nervous and if that's the case then Peter and I haven't done our jobs properly. But, if you play again like that I am going to fill this glass up with vodka or whatever so that it blows the top of my head off. I've sent your captain home to get his shoulder fixed. There's no way he was going to recover and I didn't want you seeing him struggling around the place. Wilkins, you've been a good servant to your country but you did something I will not tolerate and that is to complain to a referee. You won't be playing for England again, at least not in our time as managers of the England team and that will be at the end of this tournament. So, Hodge, Reid and anybody else I might bring in, our stall is set out. We lie down and give up our crown as World Champions, or we fight to the death. It's up to you to decide how we go forward. Shilton is your captain now and I hope you do him and yourselves proud when we take on Paraguay. Anything you want to add, Peter?"

"I'll back everything Brian has said," Taylor went on. "But remember. You're not playing for us anymore, and we can't do anymore for you. It's down to you now. You're playing for yourselves. You'll be slaughtered if you lose to Paraguay. If that's putting pressure on you, then it's meant to. You've brought everything on yourselves. Sort it."

Early on against Paraguay, Shilton pulled off two smart saves after Butcher had blundered and Clough and Taylor in the dugout were screaming so violently that they were glowing red even through their suntanned faces.
Within seconds, though, England had raced up field and scored. Hoddle and Hodge combined to leave Lineker the simplest of chances.
Later, in the second half, while Lineker was off the field for treatment to a throat injury, sustained from a karate chop by his Paraguayan marker, Beardsley scored a second to give England breathing space. It was fitting that when Lineker returned to the field of play, and could breathe properly again, he scored his second and England's third. The game was won. So it was on to the quarter-final at the Azteca again to face the old foe Argentina.

A crowd of just short of 115,000 greeted the old sparring partners.

"The fans are on your side," said Taylor. "Believe me, there's a lot of good feeling about the English from the Mexicans. Anybody neutral is for you, rather than the Argies. And if they're not, then fuck 'em."

In the pre-match press conference Taylor had been asked how he would cope with Maradona and he had replied that he wouldn't, because he wasn't playing.

Clough, on the other hand, pointed out that England had eleven good players whereas Argentina had only one. If they couldn't beat one man then they didn't deserve to get to the semi-finals.

The first half was quiet with nobody, not even Maradona, making a mark.

That was all to change, however, five minutes into the second half.

Maradona lost the ball in the middle of the field, about thirty yards from the England goal. The ball fell to Valdano the tall Argentinian striker but he failed to control it. Inexplicably, Steve Hodge, lumped it back over his own head and into England's penalty box.

Shilton came out but Maradona, running in at speed, jumped up and punched the ball into the net.

The Tunisian referee and his linesman saw nothing wrong and signalled for a goal.

"Hand ball, ref," shrieked Clough.

"Fuck me, he's given a goal," shouted Taylor.

"Shilton, you are a bloody disgrace," screamed Clough. "He's a fucking midget."

The England players swarmed around the referee pleading for hand ball. It seemed that the referee and his linesman were the only two in the stadium who hadn't seen the hand ball.

"Wait," shouted Taylor. "He did see it. He's disallowed it. Fuck me, I thought he was going to give it."

"Chop his bloody hand off, ref. Bring him here. I'll do it. The cheating little bastard," raged Clough.

When everything had calmed down, Clough turned to Taylor and said, "The ref's an idiot."

Soon after, Maradona scored a brilliant individual goal, beating several England players on a mazy dribble into the England penalty area before sliding the ball past Shilton.

"Now that was good," said Clough.

"Magic," said Taylor.

"Bastard," said Clough.

Now one nil down, Clough brought on John Barnes who had been left out to allow a more conservative approach to the game.

His impact was immediate. Collecting the ball on the left touch line he tempted the Argentinian full back before slipping past him and putting over an immaculate cross. Lineker, running in at speed, headed past the keeper.

Two minutes from time, Barnes repeated the move and Lineker finished in a carbon copy.

The last frantic minute was spent deep in defence as England's midfield closed out Maradona, and they hung on until the referee blew for full-time.

"Fuck me, that was close," said Taylor.

"If I get hold of that cheating bastard Maradona, I'm going to tear his balls off," said Clough.

After the game Maradona was asked if the goal had been given would he have said anything and he replied that he wouldn't because it would have been scored by the hand of God. He actually said, 'un poco con la cabeza de Maradona y otro poco con la mano de Dios' or 'a little with the head of Maradona and a little with the hand of God.'

Clough had just come into the room and said that if that was the case then he was going to grab Maradona's balls and twist them until they came off in his hand.

"Everybody knows that I am God," said Clough, and he rushed towards Maradona, knocking reporters out of the way. "Let's see how he deals with the real hand of God."

Maradona, known for his speed and quickness of thought on the pitch, jumped up from his seat and ran as fast as his legs could carry him out of a door on the other side of the room.

Clough continued. "You know me, gentlemen, I'm the first to defend referees but that was ridiculous. Everybody saw that. Still, I blame Shilton. How can a bloke over six feet tall let a little midget outjump him? Maybe I'll calm down later. That was close. Jesus, I need a drink. But I won't. We're still in the competition and so we march on."

"I think we'll take the lads to the coast for few days in the sun, said Taylor. "Relax, have a few orange juices and then come back and beat the Belgians."

A few days later, a calmer Clough and Taylor watched contentedly as their England team stifled whatever threat the Belgian team threw at them. The England team was always in control.

Once again the elusive Barnes on the left was the provider for Lineker. Beardsley had made an opening with his customary two-footed shuffle and sent Barnes down the line. The left winger's accurate cross was met, typically, by the onrushing striker to clinically slot the ball home. A deserved 1-0 win. England had a World Cup Final to negotiate again, this time against tournament favourites Brazil.

It was to be Clough and Taylor's last game in charge of England and, although the players knew it, it had been kept a secret at their request.

Well over 100,000 thousand football fans gathered in the Azteca Stadium in Mexico City for the 1986 World Cup Final between England and Brazil.
Brian Clough and Peter Taylor led England out and made their way to the dugout as the players lined up.
Maradona might have already won the Golden Ball as the best player of the tournament but England's Gary Lineker was well ahead in the race to win the Golden Boot as the leading scorer in the tournament.
It was a match that was to live on in the memory of football fans across the world for the sheer majesty of the play that day. The two teams were committed to attack and England had to be sharp in defence from the outset to cope with the bewildering skills of the South Americans.
But it was a defence that was to first weather a storm, and then completely calm it.
The way Brazil started off was how young players around the world could only dream of playing, with each Brazilian player intent to show all the tricks they had learned as they grew up in that football mad country.
"It was one of the greatest games I have ever witnessed," said Tim Cox, covering the game for the Daily Herald. "The genius of the players, particularly the Brazilians, shone through. Entertainment defines football and Brazil had the supreme talent in Zico, Careca, Junior and Falcao and other, lesser, football magicians. They showed the world countless examples of the Brazilians' uniquely creative brilliance."
In those early stages it was enough for Butcher to try to live up to his name and muscle the brilliance out of the opponents. Except he, and the other defenders around him, couldn't get near the ball.

Most of the crowd was happy to see the less physical players on top, but the one thing the Brazilians couldn't do, faced with such a stoical defence, was score. When they did manage to get through, there was Shilton, playing the game of his life to thwart every effort on goal.

At one point, Fenwick who had been chosen to partner Butcher in the middle of the defence, created some welcome respite from the incessant attack when he ran into his central defence partner and they knocked each other out.

"Shit. They're out cold," said Clough.

"I think Butcher's dead," said Taylor.

"Run on with a sponge," Clough told Fred Street.

"What sponge?" said Street.

The crowd marvelled at the Brazilian play but that soon turned to abject astonishment when England broke away and scored.

A thunderous shot from Zico was struck so violently that it rebounded off Shilton's bar very nearly to the half way line. There, Beardsley was able to collect it in space, unchallenged, and release Lineker on goal. As he slid the ball past the advancing Carlos , there was an audible gasp from the crowd that, on another day, might have qualified as a Guinness World Record 'Ugh'.

"It only takes a second to score," said Clough.

"Aye, but that will have riled them," said Taylor.

Shilton's crossbar was still humming as the Brazilians kicked off.

England were defending like heroes and, not used to the blistering heat like their South American counterparts, kept pretending to faint so that Fred Street could run on with some water bottles. It was a tactic that was clearly saving lives.

On and on the Brazilians pressed, not knowing when to give up, and not knowing when to defend either.

Another desperate clearance, this time by Sansom, found Lineker goal hanging again. It looked as if he had enough time to sit down and read a newspaper, in the style of Len Shackleton, but he hadn't and didn't.

Carlos' face wore a frown as the speedy striker bore down on him and, although Lineker's studs scuffed the rock hard surface, there was enough power in the shot to completely deceive the Corinthians keeper.

Twice Carlos had touched the ball and both times was to return it to the centre circle so that his team could kick off again. He might have wished he was back in Sao Paulo but, if he had've been, he would have been lynched by now.

Then England had a narrow escape. Muller, way out on the right, suddenly swung in an inviting cross that went beyond Fenwick and Butcher and tempted Shilton to come off his line. The keeper ended up in no-man's-land as Careca, bursting through the middle, did the same as Lineker minutes before and stubbed his toe on the hard surface.

The Brazilian immediately started to stumble and the ball hit him on the top of the head and looped over the onrushing Shilton.

Careca, valiantly trying to maintain his balance by whirling his arms round violently, sped past Shilton as the ball reached its zenith and began to descend.

As Careca's attempt to remain upright failed, his chin hit the goal line and the ball dropped on the back of his head and bounced backwards.

Anderson, alert to the danger, and seeing Shilton still stumbling around the penalty spot, hoofed the ball up field where Lineker was waiting like the natural predator he is.

The crowd could see that Carlos was displeased but the ever inventive keeper tried a tactic to distract the advancing Lineker. He began waving his arms vigorously, as if he was trying to warn an oncoming train that a car had stalled on a crossing.

It worked for a split second as Lineker's mishit shot hit the keeper in the midriff, but the ball rebounded, smacked Lineker on the shin and trickled over the line.

There was that collective 'Ugh' again as both teams made their way back to the half way line.

England weathered several more storms before the referee blew for half time allowing both teams to take stock.

In England's dressing room, the players looked shocked and most of them were gasping for air.

"Well done lads," said Clough. "Counter attack is the best way to deal with these slippery characters. I've always believed in counter attack."

"Don't let them off the hook in the second half," said Taylor. "Keep drawing them in and hit them on the break."

It was a plan that was working brilliantly and the aficionados in the crowd were enthralled by the different tactical styles that had thrown Europe against South America.

Clough would often point out that coaches often make the game too complex but here was a battle of wits to delight the watching coaches from around the world.

The second half started as the first with England pinned on the edge of their own penalty area and, after ten minutes of incessant pressure, it was inevitable that they should cave in.

Whether it was a penalty or not was debatable. Brazilian striker Casagrande, whose name translates as 'Big House', collected the ball and burst dangerously into the penalty area where Anderson was bent over being sick.

Casagrande crashed into the stricken full back and threw himself theatrically to the ground. The referee blew for a penalty and, as Clough has always said, the referee is always right.

Still, Shilton could be seen vociferously complaining to the match official. Clough was livid at this flagrant breach of his disciplinary code until he found out afterwards that Shilton was pointing out to the ref that there was still quite a lot of Anderson's vomit on the ball.

Casagrande took the penalty himself and blasted the ball low into the corner but, to many people in the crowd, Shilton's dive in the opposite direction was suspect.
Brian Clough considered the situation for a moment and meant to say, "That's put a cat among the pigeons" but instead said, "Fuck it."
Then England had the stroke of luck that was long overdue. Careca, who had badly grazed his chin in that earlier goalmouth incident, started to feel queasy. It turned out that there was a chemical in the line paint that caused severe stomach cramps when it got into the bloodstream, and it was this that had laid the striker low.
While he was being stretchered off, England took advantage of their numerical supremacy. Anderson, with a second wind after getting rid of all that ballast, surged up the right and put over a splendid, teasing cross. Carlos was momentarily blinded by the sun, just long enough for the ball to sail over his head and into the top corner.
At 4-1, England looked safe, but you can't keep these Brazilians down. A lot of them, as street urchins, had had to scrap for a living and now they dug deep.
Urged on by former captain Socrates, on for Careca who had been rushed to hospital, the Brazilians upped the pace.
His relentless probing was fitting in that he was a qualified doctor and it soon paid off. He had diagnosed a weak link – the England defence.
The normally sturdy back line was wilting in the intense heat and Socrates bade his countrymen to surge forward as one. This they did, leaving Lineker all on his own in the centre circle. "Welly it," screeched Taylor, as Clough held his head in his hands, a vein throbbing violently on his forehead.
Fenwick and Butcher both connected with the ball at the same time, narrowly avoiding serious injury, and the ball flew to Lineker.
He controlled the ball instantly and made off towards the Brazilian goal in which Carlos seemed to be ranting.

Lineker drew the keeper to him and, in an act of sublime selflessness, he laid the ball off to Beardsley who he had heard wheezing up alongside.

Beardsley had the easiest of tasks to tap the ball into the open goal for England's fifth but, instead, lashed it in off the underside of the bar.

The street fighting qualities of the Brazilians were beginning to irritate everybody in the English camp. Even at 5-1 up with only ten minutes left, they didn't feel safe.

Clough's throbbing forehead was causing Fred Street some concern, almost as much as it was causing Clough. The last thing Street wanted was a burst blood vessel to deal with. It wasn't his particular field of expertise and, anyway, somebody on the pitch might trip over.

With the minutes ticking away, the English fans in the crowd began to celebrate a famous victory but two penalties in two minutes stopped them in their tracks.

First Sansom deliberately tripped Muller in the area thinking that would waste some time. Edinho, the Brazilian captain stepped up to take the kick in order to get on the score sheet and whacked the ball home.

Taylor stabbed his watch so forcefully with his forefinger that the watch broke indicating there were only six minutes left. Straight up to the England end again and Sansom, staggering about like a man in a desert without water for days, trod on Muller who was nowhere near the ball.

A fight broke out between Edinho and Casagrande about who should take the penalty and while that was going on, Socrates put the ball down on the spot and whacked it into the back of the net.

There were now only a couple of minutes left as England kicked off, Beardsley nudging the ball to Lineker.

Ordinarily Lineker would have knocked the ball back to Reid or Hodge but both were doubled over, knackered, so Lineker, summoning whatever strength he could, belted the ball forward as far as he could to waste more valuable seconds. Unfortunately for Brazil, Carlos had wandered off his line to wave to his Mum and Dad in the crowd and the ball floated past him for Lineker's fourth and England's sixth. Socrates shouted out something philosophical to Carlos.

The final score was 6-3, the highest scoring final in the history of the World Cup. And so the greatest ever World Cup Final came to a close and with it the England careers of Brian Clough and Peter Taylor.

But what a fantastically successful managerial career it had been for the pair.

It started with keeping Hartlepools in the Football League and then taking them to eighth from top in their second season. From there it was all the way to the top – with the odd, minor blip on the way, of course.

Back in England, crowds around market squares and town halls screamed and chanted crazily for their victorious team and the architects of the success, Clough and Taylor.

In pubs and clubs up and down the country drinkers were celebrating the most fantastic day of their football lives.

Elgar's **Land of Hope and Glory** blared from innumerable musical outlets. England, World Champions again and everyone was determined to celebrate.

Including Clough and Taylor who knew it was time to end their virtual abstinence from the bottle.

"You know what me and di Stefano had in common?" Clough asked Taylor.

"You were both great players who scored great goals," said Taylor, with his tongue planted firmly into the side of his cheek, "but, of course, you were the better of the two."

"That's true enough," said Clough. "But that's not what I'm on about. He was a lover of Scotch, just like me. Except, I'm not going to bother with that stuff anymore. I quite like this wine lark you've got me on to. Let's have a glass to celebrate. Shiraz, I think."

And that was it. No pomp and circumstance. Clough and Taylor sipped their wine and mulled things over contentedly.

Outside Buckingham Palace, on the day of the investitures, a large, excited crowd had gathered to greet Clough and Taylor and the members of their families.

The ceremony, in their case the conferring of Knighthoods, was to take place in the Ballroom.

Built in 1854, it is the largest room in the palace, about a third the size of a football pitch.

During investitures, the Queen stands on the throne dais beneath a giant, domed velvet canopy. Architect John Nash, who had supervised the alterations, had envisaged that all the large, double-mirrored doors stood open, reflecting the numerous crystal chandeliers, causing a deliberate optical illusion of space and light.

The Clough and Taylor families, and other guests, made their way into the Ballroom where they were seated by four Gentlemen Ushers to await the recipients of the awards.

Clough and Taylor, resplendent in their formal attire, were led to an adjoining room as a military band, one of the Bands of the Household Division, played an assortment of tunes in the musicians' gallery.

"Who'd have thought," Clough whispered to Taylor, "that we would end up here when we started out in Hartlepools?"

"Watch out," said Taylor, "here comes somebody important judging by the gear he's got on."

The Central Chancery of the Orders of Knighthood, part of the Lord Chamberlain's Office, is responsible for the organisation of each Investiture. This includes the briefing of recipients on the day, and those gathered to receive their awards became silent as one of the big smells from Buckingham Palace spoke. "The Queen will enter the Ballroom of Buckingham Palace attended by two Gurkha Orderly Officers, a tradition begun in 1876 by Queen Victoria. On duty, on the dais, are five members of The Queen's Body Guard of the Yeomen of the Guard, which was created in 1485 by Henry VII. They are the oldest military corps in the United Kingdom. The Queen will be escorted today by the Lord Chamberlain. After the National Anthem has been played, he will stand to the right of Her Majesty and announce the names of each recipient and the achievement for which he or she is being decorated. The Secretary of the Central Chancery of the Orders of Knighthood is responsible for ensuring that the correct awards are in order of presentation. The Queen will be given brief background details by her Equerry of each recipient as he or she approaches to receive their award. Those who are to be knighted will kneel on the Investiture stool, that you will see in front of Her Majesty, to receive the 'Accolade'. This is bestowed by The Queen using the sword that her father, George VI used when, as Duke of York, he was Colonel of the Scots Guards. The Queen then invests all recipients with the Insignia of their award. My colleague here will demonstrate how you approach Her Majesty and you must remember that you will not speak unless Her Majesty speaks to you. Your names will be called out alphabetically by surname."

The ceremony played out as various recipients of the Knights Bachelor were called forward. When it came to the Knighthood of Brian Clough, the usual Investiture procedures took a slight deviation.

The Lord Chamberlain called out 'Brian Howard Clough'. Clough stepped forward, looked down the line of recipients for his friend, found him and grabbed Peter Taylor by the hand.

To the shock and amazement of all assembled recipients, courtiers and guests, Clough and Taylor walked through to the Ballroom and The Queen together.

Her Majesty Queen Elizabeth the Second of the United Kingdom of Great Britain and Northern Ireland, Queen of Canada, Australia, New Zealand, Jamaica, Barbados, the Bahamas, Grenada, Papua New Guinea, the Solomon Islands, Tuvalu, Saint Lucia, Saint Vincent and the Grenadines, Antigua and Barbuda, Belize, Saint Kitts and Nevis, Head of the Commonwealth, Supreme Governor of the Church of England, Duke of Normandy, Duke of Lancaster, Lord of Mann and Paramount Chief of Fiji, and Freeman of Hartlepool, Derby and Nottingham among other places, leaned forward and said, "I wondered if you'd come alone, Mr. Clough. The shop front and the goods in the back, eh?"

"We come as a package, ma'am," said Clough, as he and his best friend and mentor knelt on the Investiture stool.

Clough and Taylor received the accolade, dubbed by the sword, but the two football geniuses remained kneeling for an inordinately long time, causing everyone to become restless. After a while, the Lord Chamberlain leaned forward and whispered, "Contrary to popular perception, Her Majesty does not announce 'Arise, Sir Brian Clough. Arise, Sir Peter Taylor'. This is a complete fiction."

Clough and Taylor stood up, looking miffed, as if a decision had gone against them.

As Her Majesty The Queen pinned the Insignias to the chests of the proud recipients she spoke again. "And thank you both so very much for all the joy you have brought to the people. I just wish you hadn't decided to retire. I have so much admired the way your teams have played football over the years. On the deck and not up there in the clouds."

The two football geniuses took a step back, bowed, and turned round.

Clough grabbed Taylor's hand and held it aloft, as if in victory, as they faced the proud members of their families.

"That's the first time anyone has ever thanked us," said Taylor.

"And that's even better than winning the World Cup," said Clough.

Other books by Rick Crowe

Just the Job
(ISBN 9781456589684)

Rick Crowe's Complaints
(ISBN 9781466215726)

Robin Hood's Diaries – Volume One
(ISBN 9781466315549)

Robin Hood's Diaries – Volume Two
(ISBN 9781467952491)

Printed in Great Britain
by Amazon.co.uk, Ltd.,
Marston Gate.